The laughter es
knew it was coming.

"Sure. Go ahead and laugh. It's a real hoot. Big hockey player brought to his knees by a tiny needle. Hysterical."

"I'm sorry."

"No problem. Anything to brighten your day." Nathan smiled, then rose from the chair. Her breath caught as she watched him stand, only inches from her.

"Don't stop." Nathan reached out and gently grabbed her chin with one hand, turning her face toward him. "You have a nice smile. You should do it more often."

"Mr. Conners, I—"

"Nathan, please."

"Nathan." Catherine stepped back, needing to put distance between them.

"And should I call you Catherine?" He focused on her with a charm that was nearly irresistible.

"Yes. I mean, no. I don't believe in doctors and patients getting personal with one another."

"Then I guess it's a good thing you're not my doctor, isn't it, Catherine?"

Dear Reader,

The first time one of my sons took a hit during a hockey game, I learned that it really is physically possible for your heart to lodge in your throat. There I was, on the other side of the boards, watching and wondering what to do: Run out on the ice, or wait? Thankfully I never had to decide; in less than a very long minute, he was back on his feet and speeding down the ice after the puck.

I had to make a hard admission that day: I could be just as overprotective as my mother was (okay, so she still is!). But how far is too far? It's a question that every parent asks themselves at one time or another, and there's not always an easy answer. Sometimes you struggle to let go while you struggle to hold on, and hope that the battle gets easier down the road.

And sometimes...well, sometimes you actually learn something from the least likely source!

Happy reading!

LBK

FINDING DR. RIGHT

LISA B. KAMPS

Silhouette®

SPECIAL EDITION®

Published by Silhouette Books

America's Publisher of Contemporary Romance

ISBN-13: 978-0-373-28072-8
ISBN-10: 0-373-28072-6

FINDING DR. RIGHT

This edition published by arrangement with Harlequin Books S.A.

Visit Silhouette Books at www.eHarlequin.com

Printed in U.S.A.

Books by Lisa B. Kamps

Silhouette Special Edition

Finding Dr. Right #1824

LISA B. KAMPS

developed a zest for life at an early age. As a young child she wanted to do many things, from being an astronaut to becoming a marine biologist. Feeling a strong calling, she chose to become a firefighter. She successfully served in a job dominated by men, becoming highly respected in her field. After a rewarding career with the Baltimore County Fire Department, she retired and found new happiness in retail management.

Throughout her entire life, Lisa has had the ability to express herself through writing. She has never looked back, and has never regretted any of the detours that life may have thrown at her, because she knows that she is able to become anything she wants through the power of writing.

Lisa lives in Maryland, where the most exciting role in her life is that of a mom, raising her two boys. Lisa would love for you to visit her Web site at www.LisaKamps.com.

For Gerrit and Connor, who keep me young and crazy, and for my parents, who supported me from the time I could hold a crayon in my hand. Mom, Dad—you guys always knew I could do it. Thank you!

And finally, for my pals from the last two years: I'll always remember the Alamo!

Chapter One

Nathan watched as the puddle grew. *Drip, drip, drip.* At first held together by surface tension, the sheer volume of blood forced it to spread across the stark white floor.

Blood. His blood.

A buzzing sounded in his ears. His breaths quickened, the edges of his vision fading to a swirling gray-black. He closed his eyes, trying to banish the sight from his mind, as his stomach clenched around his breakfast.

Not that. Anything but *that.*

He swallowed against the inevitable, finding a shred of self-control in the part of his mind that remained detached. His eyes opened again. How could there be so much of it?

He stared, mesmerized in the most morbid sense, as the pool grew. Dark crimson against the gleaming white. He imagined he could feel the heat of it, still warm as it hit the floor with a plop. And the smell. Was he only imagining it, or did the room suddenly become heavy with that sticky metallic odor?

His vision continued to swirl as the buzzing grew louder. He squeezed his eyes shut, tried to steady himself with a deep breath to keep from swaying.

"Mr. Conners?" The voice was thin, a wisp of reality reaching out to him from far away. He looked up and saw a hazy vision in white, the features indistinct against the brightness.

He swallowed, hard, and attempted to reach out. His hand turned to lead as it dropped heavily beside him. He opened his mouth to speak, thought he may have muttered something as the buzzing exploded in his head with an anticlimactic *pop* a second before he hit the floor with a thud.

Catherine Wilson muttered at the commotion coming from the closed room. She wasn't supposed to be here today, had come in only for a personal favor. Now she was stuck.

She jammed the pen into her pocket, clutched the clipboard tightly in one hand and took a deep breath. No sense in drawing it out any longer. It was her own fault she couldn't say no.

The bitter smell of ammonia stopped her midstride as she opened the door, and she wrinkled her nose in distaste while biting back a smile. A man was sitting on the floor, his legs drawn up to his chest, his head resting limply on his knees. Large hands curled protectively around his ankles and his shoulders heaved with his heavy breathing. Beside him, on the clean tile floor, was a small pool of blood.

Catherine observed the scene in the space of the few seconds it took her to close the door. Gwen was bent over the man, telling him to breathe deeply. She shook her head and glanced quickly at the chart.

"Mr. Conners?"

The man released his grip from his ankle and waved absently in the air, brushing her off. Catherine took another deep breath, reminding herself it wasn't his fault she was here today. "Mr. Conners? I need you to take a seat on the table, sir." Her voice was brisk, businesslike. It was the tone she reserved for the possible troublemakers, and Gwen looked up at her sharply. The man released a loud groan and shook his head, muttering something into his leg.

"Mr. Conners, I really do need you—"

"I said no." The voice was still muffled but louder, with as much force as Catherine's request. She stared at the figure on the floor, then looked questioningly at Gwen.

"Um, it seems that Mr. Conners had a slight… accident."

"Accident?" Catherine bit the inside of her cheek at the flash of amusement that sparkled in Gwen's eyes.

"Yes. He, um, fell off the table. When I was trying to draw some blood."

Catherine turned from the nurse to study the man on the floor, sympathy surging to the surface as she realized he must be embarrassed. She looked back at Gwen, her voice less brisk. "Did he hit his head at all?" The nurse shook her head.

Catherine placed the clipboard on the small table in the corner before leaning down closer to the man.

"Mr. Conners, are you feeling okay? Here, why don't we help you stand up." She motioned to the nurse and reached for one of the man's arms, surprised by the heat of his flesh. "Then we—"

"No."

Catherine was surprised at the quiet demand in the man's voice as he pulled his arm from her grasp. But not before she'd noticed the hard muscle beneath her fingers and sensed the leashed tension thrumming through him. She took a breath then motioned for Gwen to get assistance.

Catherine settled on the floor a few feet from him and leaned against the wall, her arms folded in front of her as she studied him. Thick black hair fell forward, hiding his face, and his muscular arms were wrapped around sturdy legs. His hands were large, as well, with long, tapered fingers.

Normally she would be hesitant to stay by herself with a potentially difficult patient, but some inner instinct told her that she needn't worry with him. Yes, he was a large, powerful man. His physical build alone was intimidating, but she felt no threat. If she felt anything, it was empathy for the keen embarrassment that pulsated around him. She could certainly identify with humiliating reactions at the worst possible time.

Catherine took a deep breath and spoke softly in an effort to alleviate some of his embarrassment. “Mr. Conners, you’d probably be more comfortable if you weren’t sitting on the floor. Why don’t you let me help—”

“Please. Just let me wait here until the doctor gets in.” The voice was low, a faint twinge of resignation entwined in the mellow undertones. Catherine raised her eyebrows in the man’s general direction and let out a hasty sigh, her sympathy decreasing several notches.

“Mr. Conners, maybe I should—”

The exam room door swung quickly inward, admitting Gwen and one of the men who passed for building security. “Dr. Wilson, did you need some help?” Catherine waved off the security officer’s help, wondering why Gwen had called him for help when a strangled exclamation erupted next to her.

“Doctor!”

She turned suddenly in the direction of the voice and breathed in so quickly she nearly coughed. The man was staring at her with the fierce glare of a predator, his look all the more dangerous because of his eyes. A deep golden color fringed in a wealth of dark lashes, they were a lion’s eyes.

Feral in their intensity, they traveled from the well-worn flats she had hastily thrown on this morning, along loose-fitting trousers and casual blouse, stopping finally to meet her gaze. Catherine swallowed tightly and reconsidered her earlier assessment of any threat the man presented. She'd been wrong to think he wasn't dangerous. *Very wrong.*

"Doctor?" This time the word was uttered as a questioning groan. Catherine had endured plenty of surprised patients in the past but this man seemed genuinely shocked to realize she was a doctor. She swallowed her irritation at his chauvinism, cleared her throat and leaned slightly forward, forcing a smile.

"I'm Dr. Wilson. I'm filling in for Dr. Porter today. I thought he had informed all his patients about that." She offered her hand, felt it grow warm as it was suddenly clasped in the grip of his larger one. Her face flushed as the man continued to stare at her, and she self-consciously cleared her throat as she tried to remove her hand from his.

Instead of releasing it, he held tighter and she realized he was trying to stand, pulling her up along with him. He was merely using her as leverage to stand. She tightened her own grip and stood with him, watching as he slowly rose.

And rose. *And rose.*

She leaned her head back to look up at him, then blinked. Her imagination had kicked in again. He was only a few inches taller than six feet, not towering over her by a foot as she first thought in that single second when he had straightened.

"Dr. Wilson, do you still need me?" The uncertain voice from behind made her realize she had been staring. She cleared her throat and turned quickly to face the security guard, thankful for his interruption. Catherine shook her head and dismissed him with a quick word of thanks, then faced her patient, motioning again to the exam table.

"I think you might be more comfortable sitting down, Mr. Conners." She busied herself with studying his chart, cursing the heat in her face as she tried hard not to notice the play of muscles in his bare legs as he hoisted himself onto the table.

"I'm sorry about earlier." His voice was deep, tinged with embarrassment. Catherine stepped next to the table and offered him a gentle smile, then placed a hand on his shoulder.

"No problem. Why don't you lie back while I have a look at your knee." His body relaxed under her touch as he laid back. She focused her attention away from his powerful thighs and on his left knee, gently probing around the kneecap, careful of pushing too hard around the recent incisions.

The flesh beneath her fingers was slightly swollen and warm to her touch. She studied the movement of the kneecap, slowly pushing it back and forth. The leg jerked slightly when she pushed in at the bottom of the kneecap.

"Did that hurt?" She turned to study his face for the telltale signs of a patient unwilling to admit pain. She didn't have to look too hard; it was there in his careless shrug, in his too-hard study of the hands folded across his waist.

"Not too bad."

Catherine nodded with a noncommittal murmur and continued her probing, this time pushing in slightly on the kneecap. Barely perceptible under her touch was a minor grating, resulting in another small jerk. She gave his leg a reassuring pat then retrieved his file from the countertop as he sat up.

"When was your surgery?"

"Two weeks ago."

"And you've started physical therapy?"

"Yes."

Catherine murmured and made a note in his file, the scratching of her pen loud in the silence.

"Is…there a problem?"

"Nothing to worry about." Catherine looked up from the notes she was scribbling on his chart and gave him a reassuring smile. "Your knee is still a little swollen and there's some roughness under the kneecap, but it's early still. Make an appointment to see Dr. Porter next week. In the meantime, keep up with the therapy but don't overdo it."

He looked at her with an unreadable expression and Catherine waited patiently for the usual questions. Instead, he shrugged once and offered her a hesitant smile. She smiled back and turned, only to be stopped by the ever-present Gwen.

"Catherine, I didn't get a chance to draw the blood sample Dr. Porter had requested." There was a touch of subtle humor in her words, which were immediately followed by a nearly inaudible groan from Mr. Conners. Catherine bit the inside of her cheek to keep herself from smiling at his pale face.

"I think we can probably get away without it this time, Gwen. If Brian really needs it, he'll get it next week."

Catherine closed the door behind her and allowed herself a small chuckle at the sound of Mr. Conners's huge sigh of relief.

Silence. Absolute silence.

Catherine leaned back in the oversize chair, propped her feet on the desk, and closed her eyes to enjoy the brief solitude. She had reports to dictate, files to review and a work schedule that needed to be revamped in order to fit in another dozen or so things that just had to be done. But for now all she wanted was to enjoy the solitude.

The harsh buzz of the intercom shattered the quiet and she bolted upright. Her foot slipped and she winced as her bare heel scraped the rounded edge of the desk. Muttering, she leaned over the desk and jabbed the intercom.

"Yes? What is it?"

"Dr. Wilson, Mr. Conners has asked to see you."

Taking a deep breath, Catherine counted to three then jabbed the button again. "Give me a few minutes—"

Before she could release her finger, the door to her office swung open and the man in question walked in.

"Never mind…" Her voice trailed off as she lifted her hand from the machine. Catherine immediately straightened in her chair, searching with bare feet for the shoes she had kicked off just a few minutes earlier. She managed to slip a foot into one just as he approached the desk.

"Mr. Conners. Is there something I can help you

with?" She motioned to the chair across from her desk, still searching for the other shoe. Her toe brushed against soft leather and she stretched her leg in an attempt to pull it closer. The curious glance from the man across from her didn't stop her as she leaned back in her chair and probed farther under the desk.

"It's Nathan."

"I beg your pardon?"

"My name. Please, call me Nathan." Heat rose to her face under his close scrutiny. "Dr. Wilson, is something wrong?"

"Wrong? No, your knee seems to be recovering—"

"I wasn't referring to my knee. You look…" His voice trailed off as he glanced down at the floor. A look of confusion crossed his face and she knew instantly that she had succeeded in pushing her missing shoe from under the desk.

She sat up and tried to look professional, even when he bent over to retrieve the lost shoe. He held the worn leather loafer in one large hand, raised his eyebrows, then passed it across the desk to her. Catherine's face heated as he flashed a sexy, crooked smile at her. Mentally cursing herself for blushing, she grabbed the shoe from him, snapped it onto her foot and folded her hands on the desk in front of her. Nothing out of the ordinary had just happened, she thought. *Then why do I feel like a clumsy schoolgirl?*

"Mr. Conners, you wanted to see me?"

"Please, Nathan."

"All right." Catherine nodded, mentally wrinkling

her brow in thought. Nathan Conners. Why was that name so familiar?

"I wanted to apologize for earlier. I…things have been on edge for me lately."

"Really, that isn't necessary. It's understandable."

"Yes, but I still wanted—"

"Nathan," she began, surprised at the waver in her voice when she said his name. She cleared her throat. "Nathan. Your apology is accepted. Was there anything else?"

"I did want to ask some questions about my recovery. You looked…please don't take this the wrong way, but you looked almost as if you were hiding something. Is there something wrong with the way my knee is healing?"

Catherine stilled and met his tawny gaze without flinching. Nathan Conners was more perceptive than she had realized.

Nathan Conners. Again she had the nagging feeling that she knew his name from somewhere else. She focused on the man across from her. Deep eyes, thick, dark hair that hung a bit below the collar of his short-sleeve Henley, a slightly crooked nose that looked like it had been broken once or twice before. Tall, very well-muscled—definitely in good health.

And young. Catherine judged him to be in his early to mid-twenties, and she suddenly felt old. She shrugged the feeling off and continued studying him. He had physique, health and age on his side, which would help him through any extended recovery period he would need—if he needed it. She hadn't studied his file as thoroughly as she would have liked, and she didn't know what kind of recovery time Brian expected of his patient.

"No, your knee seems to be healing well. There's still some swelling and I detected some roughness under the kneecap, but that's to be expected. Dr. Porter will be able to better answer any questions you may have the next time you see him."

"So there shouldn't be any problems?"

"No, I don't see why there should be." Catherine noticed the slight lines that creased his forehead as he frowned. He was overly worried, and she offered him a comforting smile meant to reassure him. His sigh of relief would have gone unnoticed if she hadn't been watching him closely.

"Good. I was starting to worry. It looked like you were ready to permanently confine me to a wheelchair for a minute there. I'm not sure I could handle being crippled."

Catherine's sympathy immediately vanished at his choice of words. She mentally chastised herself, cautioning against the overreaction blossoming in the pit of her stomach. She forced a tight smile but failed to keep the coldness from her voice.

"I really don't think you need to worry about that, Mr. Conners. Now if there's nothing else…"

Nathan didn't miss the slight narrowing of her eyes, or the sudden frost in their brown depths. Her shoulders stiffened, too, and he knew without a doubt that he'd just offended her. She was dismissing him. Plain and simple. And he was torn between leaving without saying another word or staying to apologize for whatever he'd said or done to cause this reaction in her. The abrupt buzzing of the intercom stopped him.

"Dr. Wilson, Matthew's here." A disconnected voice made the announcement. Nathan winced as the doctor's slender finger punched the intercom button. There was no doubt that she wished she were punching something entirely different—like *him.*

"Tell him I'll be out in a minute." Her frosty voice melted only a few degrees before she turned a cold look on him. "If you'll excuse me, I have other business to attend to."

He finally stood when she did. She was shorter than he was, but he suddenly felt small as she fixed him with that cold look.

No, not small, he corrected himself. He felt like a worm.

"Dr. Wilson, I obviously—"

"Good day, Mr. Conners."

Nathan studied her a second longer then turned to leave, knowing that whatever he'd said, he wasn't going to correct it just then. He walked out of the office, feeling the chill of her stare in the middle of his back. Not until he reached the end of the hall did he dare turn around, certain her attention was no longer focused on him.

With that one quick look behind him, he reconsidered his earlier self-assessment. He cursed under his breath as he watched the scene in the hallway.

Catherine was kneeling on the floor, her arms wrapped protectively around a little boy about nine years old. The boy motioned wildly, obviously embarrassed as he tried to shrug off her embrace. Absolutely nothing out of the ordinary with the scene, except for one thing: the boy's slight frame was nearly lost, engulfed by the bulky wheelchair that surrounded him. Nathan didn't need to look hard to see that the boy's right leg was missing, amputated just below the knee.

No, he wasn't a *worm,* he was worse. No wonder the doctor's warmth had suddenly vanished and she'd seemed ready to throw him from her office. A chill swept through him as he pulled his gaze away from the boy and saw Catherine looking straight at him.

Nathan pivoted around and jabbed the elevator button. The child's excited voice at the end of the hall drew closer, and he closed his eyes as a feeling of utter dread swept over him.

"C'mon, c'mon," he muttered impatiently, watching the digital readout above the elevator with a sense of helplessness.

"But, Mom, don't you know who he is?"

"Matty, I don't think—"

"C'mon, Mom!"

Nathan smiled to himself at the whine in the boy's voice as it got closer still. No matter what else may be wrong with him, he had the normal impatience of all kids his age.

"Hey, Mr. Conners! Mr. Conners! Can I have your autograph?" Nathan heard the excitement in his voice, knew that the boy in the wheelchair had nearly reached him. He took a deep breath, turned around and forced himself to look only at the boy.

"Sure, no problem, kid." Nathan automatically kneeled and winced as a sharp pain shot through his knee before he repositioned himself. He sensed the doctor's sudden reaching and waved her away before taking the paper and pen the young boy offered. He looked into the kid's brown eyes and felt a smile spread across his own face at the hero worship he saw in their depths. "So are you a big fan, Matthew?"

"Wow!" The kid reached up and tugged on Catherine's arm. "Hey, Mom, he knew my name! Wait till I tell everyone at school! I love hockey, Mr. Conners."

"Matty, that's enough."

Nathan winced at the ice in her voice but still refused to look at her. He scrawled a brief greeting on the paper, followed by his name, and handed it back to the boy.

"You can call me Nathan. So, how many hockey games have you been to, Matthew?"

The young boy shrugged. "Not a whole bunch. Mom says she doesn't like it. But I watch on TV. When it's not real late, I mean. Hey, Nathan, when are you going to start playing again?"

"I guess that'll be up to the doctors. So...I bet your dad's a fan, too, huh? How'd you like to go see a game? I could get tickets for you and your dad. Your mom, too, if you'd like."

"I don't have a dad."

"Oh." Nathan swallowed around the foot in his mouth as Catherine's icy glare drove deeper into him. "Um, well, how about just tickets for you and your mom then?"

"Wow! Could you? That would be neat!"

Nathan felt the urge to laugh at the boy's excitement and tried to recall the last time he had felt like that. The joy was short-lived, though, dampened by Dr. Wilson's quiet voice. "I don't think that's a good idea, Matty."

"Mom—"

"Matty, we shouldn't put Mr. Conners to that kind of trouble."

Nathan stood up, trying not to flinch against the pain in his knee. He turned and finally faced Dr. Wilson, meeting her cold brown eyes with his own steady gaze in silent challenge. "Really, it's no problem. I'll send the tickets over by the end of the week. Will two be enough?"

Her lips pursed into a tight line as she met his stare and Nathan knew she wouldn't be able to say no. It would kill her, he was sure, but she wouldn't say no to her son. A bell dinged behind him, followed by the hiss of the elevator door opening. He took a step backward and placed his hand on the frame of the elevator to prevent it from closing as he waited for her answer, surprised he was anxious to hear it. There may have been no dad, but that didn't mean there wasn't someone else.

"Two. It's just me and Mom."

"Matty!" She pointed a look of openmouthed surprise at her son then turned back to face him, a tinge of red scattered across her cheeks. Nathan offered her a slow smile and an even slower wink as he released his hold on the elevator door.

"Two it is."

He was glad no one else was in the elevator to witness the cold look she gave him.

Chapter Two

"I realize that, yes." Catherine looked up at the knock on her door and waved Brian inside when he poked his sandy-haired head through the opening. "Yes, Mrs. Johnson, I'm aware of that. I really do need to go now. I'll call you later this week."

She placed the phone back in its cradle with a sigh, then offered Brian a half smile. "That woman is going to send me to an early grave."

"Was that Matty's principal?"

"The one and only." She motioned for Brian to sit. "She seems to think that Matty should at least attend gym class. I keep telling her that I don't think he's ready."

"Catherine, it's been ten months since his amputation. The cancer is gone. He should have started with his prosthesis months ago. I have to side with Mrs. Johnson this time."

Catherine met her partner's serious blue gaze and let out a weary sigh. She pushed a strand of hair back over her ear and began straightening the papers scattered on her desk.

"I think I know what's best for Matty. I don't need you ganging up on me, too. Not now."

"You're going to have to give him some freedom sooner or later. He's young and active. And healthy. Give him the chance to enjoy what he's been missing."

She slammed her hand on her desk. "Not now. Not yet—he's not ready."

"Are you sure he's the one who's not ready?"

The words hung in the air between them, suspended in the sudden tension that threatened to overwhelm Catherine. Slowly, she released her pent-up breath and focused on the papers in front of her. Brian was right!

If she was completely honest with herself, she'd admit that a large part of the problem with Matty was that *she* wasn't ready. His health problems and the resulting amputation had happened too recently. The pain of seeing him suffer was still a raw wound, one she had no intention of reopening. She swallowed around the thickness in her throat.

"His doctor suggested not letting him use the prosthesis now would cause more harm later." Her words came out as a whisper, not quite hiding the pain and anxiety that was a part of her everyday life.

She felt Brian's gaze on her and reluctantly looked up, putting on her brave face. One glance at his sympathetic expression told her she had failed miserably. She blinked her eyes against the tears that threatened.

"And?"

Catherine took another deep breath and shrugged. "As a doctor, I know he's right. But as Matty's mom…I'm afraid he's not ready yet. I'm afraid he'll hurt himself. I'm afraid of a million other things I have no control over. I can't go through that again."

She squeezed her eyes closed, willing the memories to disappear with the pain. All those months of uncertainty, of anguish. And fear. Her whole life had changed with Matty's diagnosis, and while he seemed to have made a full recovery, Catherine was still terrified, still not ready to reenter life.

"What does Matty want?" Brian's quiet voice broke the silence, pulling Catherine from her maudlin thoughts.

Unwilling to meet his clear gaze, Catherine kept her head bent. "I haven't talked to him about it."

"Oh, Catherine."

She finally looked up and saw the censure mixed with sympathy. He shifted in his chair and continued to fix her with that clear gaze, made all the more powerful when seen through his wire-rimmed glasses. The seconds ticked by, echoed by the old grandmother clock that stood in one corner of her office.

"All right, enough of the stare-down. I know I need to talk to him." Her voice was scratchy and she cleared her throat. "I will. I just need a little more time."

Brian nodded once, seemingly satisfied with her answer. "Fine. I'll give you a week."

"Brian—"

He held up one hand to interrupt her, a slow smile spreading across his face. "I don't want to hear it, Catherine. You know as well as I do that you'll keep putting off telling him, just like you're putting off living your life. You need the pressure of a deadline hanging over your head. Consider me your deadline. And speaking of living life..." He lifted a bulky package covered with the red and blue tape of a delivery service. "Are you ever going to open this? It's been sitting out there with your name on it for two days. The staff is dying, wondering what the ever-dependable Dr. Wilson is ignoring."

Catherine shrugged, feigning indifference. She had seen the package delivered, had even made the mistake of signing for it before she realized what it was. She had tossed it onto the outside desk as soon as she had seen the sender's name.

"Who says I'm ignoring anything?"

Brian tossed the package onto the desk, where it landed with a gentle smack in the middle of the papers she had just finished stacking. "Then open it."

"I don't need to open it." She pushed it to the side, only to have Brian push it back.

"Don't you want to see what's in it?"

"No, not really." She picked it up and threw it back at him. Brian wasn't ready for the sudden move and raised his hands in an attempt to ward off the flying missile, deflecting it to protect his face. The package landed at his feet.

"Hmm." Brian stared down at his feet, then looked back at her, his eyebrows raised in question. Catherine covered her mouth with her hand to hide her embarrassed smile.

"Brian, I am so sorry."

He waved away her muffled apology and bent down to retrieve the package. He held it out to her, daring her with his eyes to take it, promising dire consequences if she didn't. "If I didn't know you better, I'd almost swear you were afraid to open it."

The challenge was clear in his voice and Catherine knew she'd never hear the end of it if she refused. Suddenly irritated with herself, she yanked the package from his hand and violently ripped it open. A fluff of light blue material fell to her desk, followed by a crisp white envelope.

Brian released a low whistle as he pulled the material from her desk and held it up. The fluff turned out to be a jersey emblazoned with the logo of the *Baltimore Banners,* including Nathan's name and number. Her heart twisted when she realized it was Nathan's actual jersey, not a replica.

"Not bad. Matty'll get a kick out of this. Wish Nathan would have sent me one. These things are a hot commodity right now. Especially with the way the *Banners* are playing." Brian motioned to the envelope. "What's in there?"

"Probably tickets." She thrust the envelope into his

outstretched hand, ignoring the fact that her fingers trembled. "Here. You take them."

Brian looked at her questioningly then opened the envelope. He studied the contents then looked back at her, a glint in his eyes. Catherine involuntarily pushed away from the desk.

"If I didn't know you better, I'd almost swear that you did something to Nathan Conners when he was in here the other day."

"What? Why? What's in there?"

"Two tickets for very, very good seats. On the ice. And I mean, on the ice. You can't buy these seats anywhere—they're saved for special promotions and businesses."

Catherine's throat closed up. She hadn't expected him to follow through with his promise of tickets, had done her best creative thinking to come up with excuses to tell Matty so he wouldn't be disappointed when the time came. Now here they were. And not just the tickets, but a jersey, as well. Catherine knew Matty would melt with excitement when he saw them.

"I—I didn't think...why don't you take him, Brian? I can't really see myself at a hockey game."

"Since when? I mean, I know you don't follow the players or anything, but I've seen you watching with Matty. I think you should go. It'll be a fun night out for both of you, which is something *you* definitely need."

"No, I can't. I didn't think he'd send the tickets." Catherine fought the heat that spread across her face as Brian studied her. He neatly folded the jersey and placed the tickets on top, then crossed his arms and stared at her.

"Do you want to tell me what's going on?"

"Nothing is going on. I just don't like the idea of some kid jock sending these things to Matty because he feels guilty." Catherine inwardly winced at her tone of voice, wondering why she sounded so bitter and cold, knowing she had no reason to feel that way.

"Wait a minute." Brian leaned across the desk and grabbed one of her hands. "Number one, Nathan is twenty-nine, only a year younger than you. Hardly a kid. Number two, I can't see him doing anything out of guilt. Number three, why would he feel guilty in the first place?"

Catherine pulled her hand free and gently played with the folds of the jersey in front of her. "Because he made some crack about being confined to a wheelchair then happened to see me with Matthew a few minutes later. Matty knew who he was right away and had to drag me over to get his autograph. That's the only reason he sent this stuff."

She squirmed under Brian's gaze, realized she was still fingering the jersey and quickly sat back. To her own ears, the reply sounded stiff and immature, a complete overreaction, but she didn't know how to phrase it any differently. There was something about the whole situation—the way he had acted with Matty, the jersey, the tickets…it was too good to be true. She didn't believe in good fortune, not anymore.

"As far as the wheelchair comment, I don't know what to say. But I do know that he wouldn't go to all this trouble just out of guilt. Listen, Catherine, I don't know Nathan that well, but he is a nice guy. I think you should just take the tickets and go. Matty would enjoy it, and so would you."

Forget about what happened. How could Catherine explain how that single, haphazard comment had biased her against everything else? The careless way he had let it pass renewed the pain she had felt when they had first told her Matty's leg would need to be amputated. She pushed a strand of hair away from her face and sighed, knowing she would never be able to make Brian understand how much that single comment had hurt her.

"Fine. I'll think about it."

"Good." There was a brief pause as Brian studied the tickets then thrust them into her hand. "I hope you made up your mind to go, because the note in here says a limo will be picking you and Matty up in two hours."

"What?"

"They're for tonight's game so you'd better move. Matty would really be disappointed if he found out he had a chance to go and missed it because you couldn't move fast enough."

Catherine's mouth opened and closed but she couldn't form any words. Brian picked up the jersey then gently led her to the office door, chuckling the entire time.

"Let me know how you enjoy your hockey game, Dr. Wilson."

* * *

The excited screams nearly drowned out the voice and music that blared over the arena loudspeaker. Catherine looked down at Matty, a smile tugging at the corners of her mouth as he laughed and cheered with the other 19,000 fans that had come to their feet when the *Banners* scored a few seconds into the third period, widening their lead with a score of 4 to 1.

Catherine leaned back in her seat, the magazine in her hand forgotten as she finally allowed herself to relax and enjoy the game. She would never admit it to him but she was glad Brian had all but demanded that she attend tonight. The look of excitement on Matty's face when he put on the jersey and saw the tickets had been enough to bring tears to her eyes. Seeing the sparkle in his eyes when the limo picked them up had removed all but the smallest doubts that she was doing the right thing.

"Wow! Did you see that, Mom?" Matty finally pulled his attention away from the ice long enough to look over at her. She smiled and reached out a hand to ruffle his short hair, not surprised when he pulled away, his ears pink with embarrassment.

"Yes, I certainly did." Catherine curled her hand in her lap, resisting the urge to reach out again and pull Matty to her, knowing he would only become more embarrassed. It was so hard not to smother him, so hard to realize that he was growing up in spite of everything he had been through.

A loud thud directly in front of them caused her to

jump, forcing her gaze from Matty to the glass. Brian had been right about the seats: they were in the very front row, separated from the players on the ice only by the protective glass.

"Nice hit!"

The voice came from her left, loud enough to be heard over the cries of the crowd. Catherine's heart gave a funny little lurch before pumping wildly when she saw Nathan Conners standing in the aisle next to Matty, a tray full of drinks and snacks cradled in his large hands. He was still facing the ice and she had time to notice his profile, full of sharp angles that screamed strength and raw power. Her heart gave another lurch when he finally turned and looked down at her, meeting her gaze with a crooked smile before she could look away.

"Hey, Matthew. Mind if I join you? I brought some snacks."

Catherine's fists clenched around the magazine as Matty eagerly pointed to the empty seat beside her. She swallowed any comment she might have made, wondering why the hockey player seemed to rub her the wrong way and knowing she couldn't spoil this night for Matty. Reluctantly burying her pride and anxiety, she rose and moved over one seat before Nathan could maneuver his long legs around the wheelchair.

He sat between them and immediately turned to her, his crooked smile even wider as he offered her a soda. She looked at the paper cup then shook her head, refusing even as she realized how thirsty she was. Nathan looked at her a second longer, his smile losing some of its wattage before he shrugged and turned his attention to Matty.

"So what do you think of the game? Are the seats okay?"

"They're awesome! Thanks, Mr. Conners. And thanks for this, too. It's cool." Matty fingered the jersey that hung on him.

"*Nathan.* Remember I said you could call me Nathan."

Catherine watched as the two quickly became engaged in animated conversation and she suddenly felt like the proverbial fifth wheel, a ridiculous notion that didn't sit well with her. The feeling grew in direct proportion with Matty's excitement, and she again forced herself to stay quiet. No matter what she thought, Matty seemed to truly like the obtuse man and there was no way she would ruin this for him.

She leaned back and pretended to read the crumpled magazine while studying Nathan from the corner of her eye. Once again she found herself eyeing his legs, long and obviously muscular even in the black dress slacks he wore. He leaned toward Matty, listening attentively. She couldn't hear the words because of the noise from the crowd, but she saw that crooked smile grow and had no trouble hearing the deep chuckle that rumbled from his broad chest. The sound sent a flash of warmth through her, which only irritated her more.

The shrill horn that signaled another score interrupted their conversation, and Nathan let out a cheer for his teammates as music echoed in the arena.

Catherine noticed that he remained seated with Matthew when the crowd surged to its feet, and she couldn't stop the sudden warming in her heart at the gesture.

Oh, stop it! She shouldn't let herself feel anything warm toward this complete stranger who had suddenly pushed himself into their lives. The thought sped through her mind even as she tried to force it away. Who said anything about him pushing his way into their lives? *Not even close.* He just happened to be a patient of Brian's who suffered from a pang of guilt and gave up a set of tickets to ease his conscience. Nothing less, certainly nothing more. After tonight, they would never see him again.

Nathan laughed at something Matty said, and Catherine wondered why she felt a tinge of regret at her last thought.

Stop it! she chided herself again and squirmed in the seat, trying to get comfortable and pretend she wasn't bothered. The man on her right was also squirming and it took a few minutes before she realized he was deliberately pushing against her to get her attention. She turned to him, knowing there was a frown on her face and not caring. She hoped it would make him sit still.

"Lady, can you ask Nathan to sign this?"

Catherine looked down at the souvenir *Banners* pennant and black marker the man had thrust into her hand and rolled her eyes. She leaned over and nudged Nathan in the shoulder, pushing him harder than was necessary. He turned to her, those tawny eyes widened in shock as he rubbed at the spot she had touched.

"Here. He wants you to sign this." She motioned to the man beside her and nearly threw the flag in Nathan's lap, then sighed loudly as he took it and leaned across her to speak to the man. He was so close that she could smell the aftershave he wore, a light scent of something outdoorsy mingled with the clean aroma of soap.

Catherine held her breath. She refused to be drawn in even as her eyes swept over his features, from his strong jaw to the soft hair that swept just below the collar of his sports coat, to the rounded curve of his ear. She wondered suddenly if the spot on his neck below his ear was as sensitive as it looked. He was close enough that all she had to do was lean slightly forward before her lips—

She sat bolt upright, mortified at the thoughts running through her mind. "This is ridiculous!"

Nathan turned his head to look at her, so close that his mouth nearly brushed against her cheek. Catherine stood, not caring that she came close to knocking Nathan out of his seat, not caring that the man to her right was staring at her as if she had lost her mind. She pushed her way across Nathan, getting tangled in his feet and nearly tripping until he put a hand on her elbow to steady her. She ripped her arm out of his grasp and leaned over Matty, wanting to leave right that minute but knowing her irrational reaction would only hurt him.

"I'm getting something to drink. Do you want anything?"

"No, I'm fine." Matty looked up at her with round eyes and she had the uncanny feeling that he saw more than she wanted him to see. "Are you okay, Mom? Your face is all red."

Catherine ignored Nathan's soft chuckle as she leaned over and brushed a kiss over Matty's forehead, assuring him that she was fine before climbing the steps to the main concourse.

Nathan turned in his seat and followed her progress up the stairs, smiling to himself as he watched the angry sway of her hips. She looked different from when he had first seen her at the office. Her dark blond hair fell in soft curls around her shoulders, a stark contrast to the deep green sweater that she wore. She turned and looked back, and he saw the flash of fire in her brown eyes even from that distance.

He chuckled to himself then finished scrawling his autograph and handed the flag back to the man. He turned to Matthew. "I don't think your mom likes me too much."

"Nah. She likes you. Mom likes everyone."

"Oh, yeah?"

"Of course. That's her job."

Nathan studied the boy, surprised at his enthusiasm. The bulky wheelchair seemed out of place in an area so full of activity but Matthew didn't seem to notice. He sat up straight, a soda in one hand as he watched the action on the ice in front of him. The jersey Nathan had sent with the tickets was too big for him, hanging on the boy's slight frame. The way all boys wore sports jerseys, Nathan thought. His gaze traveled down, resting on the wad of denim that was neatly folded and pinned just below the knee.

"It doesn't hurt."

Nathan looked up and saw Matthew's eyes on him, felt a rush of embarrassment when he realized he had been caught staring. He cleared his throat and offered him an awkward smile. "Sorry."

Matthew shrugged and took a noisy slurp of the soda. "That's okay. Lots of people stare. I'm used to it. You can ask if you want, it doesn't upset me."

"Ask you what?"

"How it happened. Everybody does. They had to cut it off because of the tumor."

"Tumor?"

"Some kind of cancer. But it's all gone now. That's why they cut it off."

Nathan felt the color drain from his face and he took a long swallow of soda to hide his embarrassment. Good Lord, what the poor kid must have gone through. It was a wonder Dr. Wilson really hadn't thrown him out of her office the other day—through the window. At least it explained why the temperature had dropped so dramatically when he showed up tonight.

"How long ago did it happen?"

"Ten months ago. I'm going to get a pro—prost…a fake leg soon. Mom doesn't think I'm ready yet, but the doctors do."

"How come she doesn't think you're ready?"

Matthew turned to face him, a look of pure annoyance scrunching his features so comically that Nathan couldn't help but laugh. It was the look boys of all ages used whenever they didn't get their own way. "She doesn't even know I know I can get one—she thinks I'm going to get hurt."

"Hmm. I think I can see why she'd think that. I get the idea you're all rough and tumble."

"Mom says I'm hell on wheels right now."

Nathan's eyes widened, momentarily stunned at the no-nonsense tone of the boy's voice. He noticed the flush creeping up from Matthew's collar and knew the words had been said for effect only. "She does, huh?"

"Uh-huh. She says it's probably a good thing she knows lots of doctors because I'm going to give her a heart attack." Matthew pulled his attention from the game and studied Nathan with such an intense scrutiny that he had the sudden desire to squirm in his seat. "Do you like her?"

Nathan squarely met the boy's serious gaze with one of his own, feeling like his intentions were suddenly being questioned. "Yeah, Matthew, I do."

"Good. I'm glad." Matthew's face lit up with a huge smile and Nathan let out the breath he had been holding, feeling very much as if he had just passed some required test. The relief rolled over him unexpectedly and he was unable to suppress the stupid grin he knew was on his face.

The light feeling dimmed momentarily when a short blast of the siren sounded, this time signaling a score for the opposing team. Nathan bit back a curse and focused his attention on the JumboTron to watch the replay, surprised he had missed it.

A groan escaped him when he saw that the rookie playing his spot had failed to clear the puck from in front of the net, letting the other team score. One hand reached down and absently rubbed his knee, willing it to heal faster so he could get back to playing. He couldn't afford to spend too much more time off the ice. If he did, there was a chance he'd miss making it to the finals. The way the *Banners* were playing, there was no doubt they'd be in the running for the Cup this year.

"Nathan?"

"What?" He flinched at the sharpness of his own voice and made an effort to soften it with a smile at Matthew.

"Don't worry, you'll play again. I know you will." The certainty in the child's voice touched a hidden spot deep inside him, a spot he didn't want to examine too closely. Swallowing hard, he leaned over and ruffled the kid's hair then pulled back guiltily when Dr. Wilson came to a stop behind the wheelchair. There was no mistaking the glint of warning in her eyes as she stared down at him.

The shrill sound of the buzzer echoed off the ice and pierced the noise of the crowd, silencing the excuse that had formed on his lips as effectively as it signaled the end of the game. The cheering crowd moved to its feet and slowly turned into a throng of beasts just two steps shy of a stampede, doing their best to scramble out of the arena. Nathan was struck by the uncomfortable silence that engulfed the three of them, setting them apart from the hordes. Embarrassment raced through him when he realized they were waiting for the crowd to thin before moving Matty's wheelchair.

He glanced at his watch. "Hey, Matty, how'd you like to go meet everyone?"

"I don't think—"

"Oh, too cool!" Matthew's squeal of excitement drowned out the doctor's objection. "Please, Mom, can I?" He turned in his wheelchair and looked up at her with wide brown eyes full of pleading, and Nathan knew that whatever objections she had been about to voice just died a swift death. Hell, even he wouldn't have been able to resist that look. He noticed the doctor's pursed lips and met her narrowed eyes as she reluctantly nodded her consent. Without a doubt, Matty knew *exactly* what buttons to push with his mom. Nathan decided he'd have to talk to the kid and find out what he was doing wrong. There was no doubt he was pushing the good doctor's buttons, too.

It was just a shame they were all the wrong ones.

Chapter Three

Sweat poured from Nathan's face; he reached up and absently wiped the stinging from his eye. Focus. He needed to focus. He struggled against the weight, feeling the pull in his knee. *Focus!* He repeated the word with a mental shout, over and over until the refrain obliterated the tearing pain he felt.

One more. Just one more.

He leaned back and gripped the padded handles harder, pulling, lifting, until a flash of heat tore through his knee. The sound of steel hitting steel rang out like a shot and echoed through the empty gym, taunting him with his failure.

"Damn!" Nathan wiped a towel across his face before resting his elbows on his knees. Just that little bit of pressure caused more pain and he winced before shifting positions.

"Damn!" The curse echoed around him. This was definitely not going the way he had planned. He was into his fourth week of physical therapy. He *should* be able to lift more weight by now. They had told him not to push it, but what did they know? If he waited as long as they suggested, he'd be old and gray before he went back to playing. That was a chance he couldn't take.

Nathan ran his hands through his damp hair then stood, ignoring the throbbing in his leg that threatened to topple him to the floor before he got his balance. He limped halfway to the locker room, thinking of nothing but a long, hot shower followed by several ice packs when the gym door opened behind him.

"What the hell do you think you're doing?" The voice was unnaturally loud, the anger and accusation bouncing off the walls. Nathan stopped with a sigh and slowly turned.

Sonny LeBlanc stormed across the floor, his meaty fists clenched by his sides when he stopped a foot away. Nathan fought the urge to flinch and make up excuses like a child. Sonny had that effect on everyone. At a stocky six feet tall, Sonny looked more like a former drill sergeant than a hockey coach. His dark eyes were harsh slits and the squareness of his face was made more austere by the buzz cut of his salt-and-pepper hair. The straight-edged scar that ran down the left side of his cheek glowed red under the bright overhead lights, an incongruous slash in an otherwise smooth face.

Sonny had the misfortune of running into a skate

blade during one of his final games years earlier. Now one of the best coaches in the league, he had the reputation of remaining outwardly impassive—except for the scar. No matter how poker-faced the man stayed, the scar always betrayed him, glowing like a brand during times of anger and duress.

Right now, the brightness of the scar would light the gym if the power failed. Not a good sign for Nathan. He took a deep breath and let it out, waiting for the inevitable explosion.

"How stupid are you, Conners? How stupid do you think I am? What are you trying to do, blow every chance you have of coming back? I oughtta suspend you just for being dumb! I'd've thought you knew better! Well? What the hell are you doing?"

"Therapy." Nathan's tight voice seemed liked a whisper after Sonny's outburst.

"Bull! I just got off the phone with that doctor of yours and he said you ain't supposed to be doing any of this crap until you're cleared." Sonny's finger came up and jabbed Nathan in the chest for emphasis. "And you're not cleared! Now get in there and wash up and don't let me catch you back here! I'm not going to have you blow your chance because of some bullheaded notion swimming around that thick skull of yours!"

Nathan clenched his jaw and stared at Sonny's broad back as he left, feeling like an ultimatum had been laid at his feet. So now they were trying to keep him from working on his own, were they? Well, he'd just go see about that. He had too much at stake to let it rest in someone else's lap.

* * *

"I need to see Dr. Porter," Nathan repeated for the third time, leaning closer to the desk so he hovered over the receptionist. He felt a second of gratitude when she flinched.

"Mr. Conners, I'm sorry, but I already explained he left for the day. I can make an appoint—"

"No! I want to see him. Now."

"There is nothing I can do. I'm sorry."

Nathan glared at the small woman staring back at him and called himself every kind of fool. He would get nowhere by browbeating the poor lady, but he couldn't just turn around and walk away. He had come here full of steam, eager for a face-off. He couldn't give up so easily, not when there was so much at stake. "What about Dr. Wilson? Is she in?"

The receptionist eyed him warily then flipped through one of the many appointment books in front of her. He was grabbing at straws, he knew, but he was desperate.

"Yes, she's still here."

"Fine, then I'll see her."

"Mr. Conners, you can't just walk in…she has patients."

Nathan shot a quick look around the empty waiting room then turned back to the receptionist. "I need to see her!"

"Mr. Conners, I said—"

"What is going on out here?" Nathan turned at the sound of the cool voice, swallowed hard at the look of steel in the dark eyes that impaled him.

"I'm sorry, Dr. Wilson, but Mr. Conners insists on seeing someone…."

"In my office!" She turned smartly on her heels and walked down the short hallway, stopping at the open door of her office and shooting him a look of impatient anger. Nathan clenched his jaw and followed, preparing for the battle he had initiated. He flinched when she slammed the door behind them. The apology that hovered on the edge of his lips died before he could utter it.

"Who do you think you are, storming in here and shouting like that?" Clenched fists rested on her slim hips as she stared at him, the fury evident in her flushed face and heavy breathing. Nathan fought back his own anger, knowing he had instigated her temper with his loud demands. It would be easier to ignore her if his gaze would stop traveling the length of her body, noticing how different she looked from the other night. She was dressed more conservatively in dark trousers and an oversize lab coat that hid the blouse she was wearing.

"Well?"

Nathan pulled his gaze back to her face, noticed the flush that had spread across her cheeks and realized he had missed the last part of her angry tirade. He shifted from one foot to the other and tried not to wince at the sudden flare in his knee. "What?"

"I wanted to know who you thought…never mind." She pushed a loose strand of hair behind her ear and walked back to her desk, passing close enough to Nathan that he could smell the faint hint of her perfume. Something flowery, he thought. "I assume you have some reason for barging in here like Attila the Hun on steroids?"

"Uh, yeah." Nathan straightened, determined to think of the woman in front of him as a doctor only. The sudden thought that she could possibly be his chance to go back to the ice sobered him. "I want you to look at my knee. I've been in therapy for four weeks, and I want to be cleared to go back. At least to practice."

"Absolutely not."

"Excuse me?"

"I said no." She lowered herself to her chair and bent over some paperwork, the tip of her pen making scratching noises in the silence. Nathan stared at her in bewilderment before realizing she had, once again, dismissed him.

"Why not?" They were the first words that tumbled from his mouth, far from the angry demand he wanted to make.

Catherine's impatient sigh brought him up short. She leaned across her desk and pointed at him with a stern finger. "Number one, you are not my patient. If Bri—Dr. Porter wants you released, that's up to him, though he'd be a fool if he did. And number two, you're not ready. Period."

"How do you know what I am and am not ready for?"

"You can't even stand there with all your weight on that leg, can you? No, you can't, and don't lie and say you can. I'm a doctor, and it'll take more than minor acting to fool me!" Her voice was chilly and she slowly stood, her hand shaking as she pointed at him with that long finger. Nathan knew something else was wrong. There was a split second when he thought to question her, to discover the reason for her misplaced anger, before her earlier words actually sunk in.

He took a hasty step toward her desk and curbed the urge to collapse against it, choosing instead to lean his fists on the glossy surface for support. "What do you mean, he'd be a fool to?" Nathan struggled to keep the fear and anxiety from his voice. "You don't think I'll play again, do you?"

She stared at him, a flash of sympathy in the depths of her eyes. She didn't have to answer him—her look said it all. Her sympathy struck anger inside him. Anger and irrational fear. Nathan stepped back, stunned. He wanted to lash out at her unspoken statement, to scream his denial. The words that finally tumbled from his mouth shocked them both.

"Please don't make the mistake of trying to protect me the way you are your son. That would cost me my entire career!"

Catherine's face drained of all color as she flinched. Too late, Nathan realized that his words had hurt her more effectively than if she had been slapped. The anger inside him suddenly disappeared, replaced with deep humiliation. He struggled to find a way to break the growing silence. An apology seemed so trite, but it was the only thing he could offer. The empty words fell from his mouth in a hoarse whisper.

Catherine stumbled backward into her chair, her

face void of any expression. Knowing that staying would only make things worse, Nathan turned to leave.

"No, wait." He halted at her shaky voice, then slowly turned back, expecting some heavy object to come hurtling through the air at him. "What did you mean by that?"

"Nothing. I'm sorry. I shouldn't have said it."

"But you did. What did you mean?" She stared at him, her brown eyes dark with anticipation as she pointed to the empty chair. "Please?"

Nathan hesitated only a second before walking back to the desk and easing his weight into the chair, stretching his left leg in front of him and giving it a quick rub. "Matthew said something about you not letting him get a prosthesis because you were afraid he'd be hurt."

"He told you that?" It was phrased as a question but Nathan heard the bewildered shock that laced the words. "But he doesn't even know you!"

"Sometimes it's easier for a kid to talk to someone he doesn't know. I got the idea that there weren't many people willing to talk to him about his amputation." He watched her expression, saw the tiny flinch in her shoulders and slight pursing of her lips at the word *amputation*.

"No. I, uh, that is, I thought it would be best…"

"Listen, Matthew's a bright kid. It was his leg that suffered, not his brain. Don't treat him like an invalid."

"Did he tell you what happened?"

"He just said it was some kind of cancer."

Catherine pulled her attention away from the pen she had been studying and finally looked at the man sitting across from her. Those strange eyes were focused on her and she had the uncanny sensation that he was seeing more than she wanted him to see. If it was her choice, she would be sharing nothing of her personal life with him; it seemed Matty had different ideas. She released her breath on a long sigh and leaned back in the chair.

"Matty was diagnosed with Ewing's sarcoma a year and a half ago. It's a bone disease that affects children, usually boys. It was decided that amputation and chemotherapy would increase his chance of survival. Matty responded very well to everything, and so far there's no sign that the cancer has spread. But there's always that fear." Catherine choked out the last words, the ball of fright still tight in her stomach. She watched Nathan's expression, looking for either the horror or the pity that people seemed to have after hearing the story.

Instead, she saw understanding in the clear eyes that held her gaze and swore she almost heard some kind of *click.* She looked away, swallowing against the sudden realization that Nathan Conners had somehow, suddenly, become a part of their lives. It wasn't a realization she was eager to embrace.

"I take back what I said earlier. Your son's a lot more than just a bright kid."

Catherine wasn't sure what to make of that comment so she said nothing. Instead, she tried to figure out exactly what had changed between them in the past five minutes. More importantly, why it had changed. She missed the last part of what he was saying and looked back at him, asking him to repeat it.

"I said, there's a sports clinic for kids with disabilities. I think Matthew would enjoy it." He pulled a card from his wallet and passed it across to her. She set it to the side with nothing more than a passing glance.

"We'll see." Catherine fidgeted in the silence that hung between them, feeling like she should say or do something. She cleared her throat and pointed to his knee. "Um, did you want me to look at that for you?"

"I thought you said there was nothing you could do."

"I can't clear you, if that's what you're expecting, but I can look at it. I can tell it's swollen. Draining may help, and maybe a shot of—Mr. Conners, are you okay?" Catherine jumped from her chair and quickly circled the desk, alarmed at the sudden change in him. His face was pale and sweaty. She didn't have to be a doctor to realize he was close to passing out and she placed a hand on his shoulder to ease him slightly over.

"Put your head between your legs. That's it. Nice deep breaths. No, not so fast. You'll hyperventilate. Nice and deep. There you go." Satisfied that he wasn't going to topple over in the next five seconds, Catherine released her hold on him and leaned over to push the intercom on her desk.

"I'm okay." His deep voice was muffled as he continued to bend forward, his head between his knees.

"No, you're about two seconds away from passing out."

Nathan took another deep breath and slowly sat up. She was relieved to see that some of his color had returned and that his face was no longer covered with sweat. "It's needles."

"I beg your pardon?"

"Needles. I hate them. Always have."

Catherine remained still, eyeing him warily, wondering if he was playing some kind of joke on her. She noticed both sincerity and embarrassment in his eyes. The laughter escaped her before she knew it was coming, before she had a chance to push it back. The look of mortification in his eyes only made her laugh harder and she clamped her hand over her mouth.

"Sure. Go ahead and laugh. It's a real hoot. Big hockey player brought to his knees by a tiny needle. Hysterical." His deep voice was light and laced with irony, making Catherine laugh even more.

"I'm sorry." Another deep breath. "I just didn't think… I mean…" One more breath. "I'm sorry."

"No problem. Anything to brighten your day." Nathan smiled then rose from the chair, his large frame unfolding with a feline grace in spite of the obvious discomfort in his knee. Her breath caught as she watched him stand, only inches from her.

"Don't stop." Nathan reached out and gently grabbed her chin with one hand, turning her face toward him. "You have a nice smile. You should do it more often."

"Mr. Conners, I—"

"Nathan, please."

"Nathan." Catherine stepped back, needing to put distance between them. She heaved a sigh of relief when he released her from his gentle hold.

"And should I call you Catherine?" His crooked smile and tawny eyes were focused on her with a charm that was nearly irresistible. She took a nervous step back and silently cursed when the edge of the desk bit into the back of her thighs.

"Yes. I mean, no. No. I don't believe in doctors and patients getting personal with one another."

"Then I guess it's a good thing you're not my doctor, isn't it, Catherine?" His smile never faltered as he turned and walked to the door, stopping to look back at her with an unreadable expression on his face. "I was serious about that clinic for Matthew. And I think it would be good if he went to more games, too. I'll send over some more tickets. Catherine."

She stared after him, astounded at the onslaught of charm she had just been subjected to, wondering which was worse: that she had allowed the flirting banter, or that she had enjoyed it.

Don't do it.

A voice of conscience piped up and screamed at her before she could get any idiotic notions in her head. She could not—would not—let Nathan Conners into her life. Or Matty's. It would only invite disappointment for both of them. Matty would become attached, then be hurt when he left. And he *would* leave. It was unthinkable that any steady dependability would come from someone who wasn't family.

Catherine sat behind the desk and absently shuffled the files in front of her. She couldn't allow anyone else into their lives. She had to think of Matty's feelings, nothing else. She grabbed the card Nathan had given her and threw it into the wastebasket beside her desk, hoping she could remove the other influences he had left behind just as easily.

"You don't need to be so tense, Catherine."

"I can't help it." She unclasped her hands and wiped them down the front of her jeans before facing Brian. "What if he gets hurt?"

Brian chuckled then swung his arm in a wide arc, encompassing the large room with machines of all shapes and sizes, with an attendant at each one. "Here? You're sounding unreasonable. This is the safest place for him and you know it."

"I *don't* know," she whispered. They were standing off to one side, watching as Matty practiced with his new prosthesis. Two weeks had passed since he first got it, and even his therapist was amazed at how well he was doing. Catherine kept her gaze on Matty, watching for the slightest indication that he might fall or that he was tiring. Then she would firmly suggest to everyone that the prosthesis could wait until later.

"He's not going to give up, you know."

Catherine pasted a smile on her face and waved to Matty, then faced Brian. He was watching her with a hooded expression, his eyes serious behind the wire-rimmed glasses. "I don't want him hurt. He's been through too much already."

"So you'd take away his new freedom? I thought I knew you better than that."

The accusation hung between them, made worse by Brian's quiet voice. In all the years she had known him, he had always been reliable, always supporting her and Matty. It wasn't like him to sound so critical.

"You need to let him go, Catherine."

"He's nine years old. I don't *need* to do anything but protect him." The words came out in a hiss and caught the attention of another parent standing several feet away. "I'm sorry. I just don't want him hurt. Is that so terrible?"

"No, it's not. As long as you don't go overboard."

"But what's overboard? Are you saying it would be better if I just let him go, let him do what he wants?"

"That's not what I'm saying, Catherine, and you know it. And you also know how far is too far for him. Don't let the voice of reason get lost in your need to protect him."

"Voice of reason." Catherine forced a half laugh, her attention focused on Matty. He was back in the wheelchair, removing the prosthesis with the therapist's help. "He told me the other day he wants to play hockey. Hockey, for crying out loud! Like I don't know where that idea came from."

Brian crossed his arms in front of him and shrugged, almost too nonchalantly. "Who knows? Maybe one day he will."

"What? You didn't just say that. I'm imagining things." Catherine studied her friend, saw the barely noticeable blotch of red creeping up from his shirt collar. A muscle twitched in his jaw. "What is it, Brian? What aren't you telling me?"

His mouth opened and closed silently. He pursed his lips together and shrugged again, still refusing to face her. She folded her own arms in front of her and stepped into his line of vision, ready to demand an answer.

"Hey, Mom! Did you see that?" Matty's excited voice came from behind and she turned to face him, forcing a bright smile. She gave the therapist a passing glance then bent down so she could be on eye level with Matty.

"I sure did. You're getting better each day."

"He's done remarkably well, Dr. Wilson. At the rate he's progressing, it won't be long before he's sprinting with that new leg of his." Catherine straightened and leveled a serious look at Matty's therapist, Paul. She wanted to tell him, to scream at him, that there was no way she would allow her son to risk getting hurt by doing something as foolish as sprinting with a prosthesis. Or running. Or even walking fast. But there was no way she could say any of that, not now and certainly not here, so she just smiled tightly and said nothing.

Matty waved goodbye to Paul then looked from her to Brian and back again, a look of excitement on his face. Catherine felt the bottom of her stomach drop in anticipation.

"Did you tell her yet, Uncle Bri?"

"Um, not yet."

Catherine looked from one to the other, at the excitement dancing in Matty's eyes and the frown creasing Brian's forehead. Her stomach did another funny little dip. "Tell me what?"

"Uncle Brian got me into this neat camp for kids like me. It's got sports and all kinds of stuff, and there's even going to be some pro guys there. Isn't that cool, Mom?"

Catherine clenched her jaw against the sudden fear and fury that ripped through her and turned to Brian, ignoring Matty as he pulled on her hand. "What is he talking about?"

"I heard about this sports camp run by the players of some local teams and thought it would be good for Matty. I made arrangements to have him enrolled."

"How dare you go behind my back and do something like this! And who told you about it?" She didn't know why she was asking; she already knew the answer.

"Mom?" Matty pulled on her hand. "I can do it, right?"

"Matty, I…I don't think so." She tried to soften her voice, to lessen the blow to Matty, but disappointment still flashed in his eyes. He yanked his hand from hers and looked away, sending a sharp stab of pain through her. She faced Brian, her anger clear. "Who told you about it, Brian? Who?"

"Nathan Conners."

"He went to you? After I already told him no, he went to you!" She shook her head, wanting to say more, knowing she couldn't. She stepped behind Matty's wheelchair and grabbed the handles, squeezing until she thought they would bend. "I think you know what both of you can do."

"He came to me because he thought you were being unreasonable. I happened to agree with him."

"Mom, I can do it, can't I? You're going to let me do it, right?" Catherine's throat constricted at the pain in Matty's voice and she had to swallow before answering.

"Matty, sweetie. You're not ready. I don't want you hurt."

"But, Mom—"

"Matty, I said no, not right now."

"Catherine, don't you think—"

She shrugged Brian's hand from her shoulder. "I think you need to mind your own business. I think you need to tell your patients to mind their own business."

"Catherine…"

"I have nothing more to say to you." She leaned into the heavy chair and pushed. Brian's betrayal bit into her, hurting her in a way she hadn't expected.

"Mom, why can't I?"

"Because I said. I don't want to hear another word."

Catherine squeezed her eyes against the tears, blinking back all but one that rolled down her cheek. She wiped her face on her sweater. The last thing she needed was for the waterworks to start, not here and especially not now.

Matty was doing enough crying for them both.

Chapter Four

Catherine rolled the tension from her shoulders, closed her eyes and let her head fall against the back of the sofa. The faint scent of candles surrounded her and she breathed in the mix of vanilla and rose, searching for some inner relaxation.

Three days had passed since she had told Matty in no uncertain terms that he would *not* be participating in any sports clinic. Three days since he had talked to her, not even a murmur of anger or argument. It had been a long three days.

Catherine sighed and opened her eyes, stared down at the nearly forgotten glass of Chardonnay in her hands before taking a sip, not caring that it was no longer chilled. She had finally caved in, unwilling to face the anger and hurt that stared back at her whenever she looked at Matty. She had called Brian that morning, told him to pick up Matty and take him to the camp.

An excited Matty had called a few hours ago, telling her that he and Brian were going to a hockey game. Before she could protest, Brian got on the phone and explained that the tickets were a gift and not to worry, Matty could spend the night.

Dead silence floated back from the phone before Catherine had a chance to question or argue.

So here she sat, alone and lonely, brooding over a glass of warm white wine. Wishing she had never laid eyes on Nathan Conners but unable to banish his image from her mind.

She sighed again then tossed back the last of the wine in her glass, wincing at the warm bitterness. It was just past eight o'clock and already she felt lost. She didn't want to consider why, didn't want to face the truth that any normalcy in her life had stopped with Matty's illness. Now that he was on the quick road to recovery, doing normal things for kids his age, it was time for her to do the same. And she was afraid.

Catherine muttered a curse then pushed herself from the sofa and walked to the kitchen, blinking at the bright overhead light. She took several steps then stopped, looking around as if seeing the room for the first time.

Clean white surfaces, gleaming steel appliances, shiny green-and-white tile floor. A small pine table surrounded by four ladderback chairs sat in front of a bay window framed in cheery yellow gingham curtains, two place mats arranged at either end with green napkins neatly rolled and waiting in the center of each. The cheeriness of the room escaped her, and the only thing she noticed was its cleanliness. Neat, clean and orderly.

Efficient. And boring.

"I'm losing it." Her voice echoed back to her, making her feel worse. She placed the empty glass on the counter then opened the refrigerator and pulled out a pint container of orange juice and drank from it. Matty would have been surprised, considering how often she admonished him for the same thing.

She rinsed the empty carton and tossed it into the recycling bin. More efficiency.

It was a Saturday night and she was home alone. Her nine-year-old son was out having a good time while she stood in her kitchen. Alone. Thinking about how efficient everything was.

Definitely boring.

She glanced at her watch again and saw that only a few minutes had gone by. There was no reason she should be home by herself. Never mind the fact that she had nothing to do and nobody to do it with. Matty and Brian were at the hockey game. She could meet up with them, apologize for being so touchy the last few days and see if they wanted to go do something. Maybe go to the Inner Harbor, walk around and get some ice cream.

The keys were in her hand and she was out the door before she realized they might not want her company.

She shoved the thought to the back of her mind, leaving it behind as she pulled the minivan out of the driveway.

The soles of Catherine's tennis shoes squeaked on the polished tile floor, the sound echoing strangely in the hollow silence. She stopped and pushed a strand of hair behind her ear, sighing. Except for a few stray voices that floated up to her from the lower seats, the arena was deserted.

She looked around, swallowing an insane desire to cry. How could she have missed the entire game? She exhaled a long breath and began the dizzying descent to the arena floor, her gaze lowered to concentrate on the unusually spaced concrete steps.

If not for the delays with the light rail, she would have had time to at least find Matty and Brian and see part of the third period. Instead, she arrived at the arena and learned that the game had ended twenty minutes earlier, with the *Banners* winning 3 to 2. The victory did little to boost her spirits as she tried to convince the security guard to let her in so she could see if Matty and Brian were still there.

The fact that she had to finally say they were guests of Nathan Conners was a fresh wound to her pride. She waited while the guard made a phone call, then grimaced at his slick smile and flash of innuendo. It made her feel like a groupie. She briefly wondered how many players were accustomed to groupies, how many times security had called down to Nathan Conners.

Catherine refused to look too deeply into where *that* thought was leading, telling herself instead that it was just one more reason to keep Matty away from the hockey player.

She reached the bottom of the steps, rubbing her hands against the chill running down her arms as she looked around, hoping to see a familiar face near the players' box. Row after row of empty chairs stared back at her.

"Catherine?" The voice came from behind, startling her even as the flesh on her arms prickled with heat. She turned and swallowed against the sudden lump in her throat as Nathan descended the last few steps. "I didn't expect to see you here."

Her mouth worked silently as she stared up at him. His dark hair was slicked back, still damp from the shower he had obviously just taken, the ends hanging below the collar of his polo shirt. The faint scent of fresh soap mingled with his aftershave and teased her nose as her mind tried to connect the circuits in charge of her conversational skills.

"Neither did I." The words tumbled from her mouth, causing Nathan to smile wider as she mentally winced. "I mean, I didn't plan on being here. I, uh, I thought Matty might be here."

"No, I haven't seen him." Nathan stepped closer to her and she scooted backward. A flash of amusement lit his eyes and he motioned for her to sit. Catherine lowered herself into an aisle seat as he sat across from her. Her gaze ran down his long legs in a quick sweep, coming to rest at the spot where his bare ankles showed between the frayed hem of his faded jeans and the top of his Birkenstocks. "Should I have?"

"Pardon?" Catherine yanked her gaze away from his bare ankles and met his stare, embarrassment heating her face.

"I said, is there a reason I should have seen him?"

"Uh, I thought, that is, Brian took him to the sports clinic today and they called to say they had tickets for tonight. I just thought..." Catherine let her voice trail off, feeling the first twinge of worry scratch along her spine like nails on a blackboard. There was no reason to worry, she told herself. Matty was with Brian. They were fine.

"They probably got the tickets from the clinic. I wouldn't worry too much. I wish I had known they were here, though."

"You didn't see them at the camp?" Catherine's pulse pounded louder in her ear as anxiety crept in. They had to have been at the camp—Matty had called saying how much fun he'd had.

"No. I'm not usually there."

"But I thought—" Catherine jerked in surprise at the vibration that thrummed near her hip then let out a loud sigh. Cursing the pager that kept startling her, she unclipped it from the waistband of her pants and squinted at the number flashing across the LED screen. A sigh of relief escaped her when she recognized Brian's home number.

"Good news, I take it."

Catherine flashed a wry smile at Nathan, suddenly feeling foolish. She reached into her purse and rummaged for the cell phone. "It's Brian. Probably wondering where I am."

"I see." A flicker of something lit his eyes for a moment then disappeared. He stood and motioned behind him with a quick point of his thumb and grinned, drawing her attention to a small group of fans who were hanging back from them. "I'll let you have some privacy for that call."

Catherine stared after his broad back as he walked away, feeling like she had just missed something. She watched as two young girls sauntered toward Nathan, smiling and flirting with serious intent in their eyes. A knot of impatience swelled in Catherine's stomach as she realized that the "girls" were in their early twenties. The laughing group suddenly made her feel old. She couldn't remember ever being—or acting—that young.

"Knock it off," she whispered, stabbing at the buttons of the cell phone. Brian's voice greeted her on the third ring.

"I'm at the arena. I thought I'd meet you guys here but I guess not, huh?" Catherine said when he asked where she was.

"Sorry. We would have waited if we had known. But Matty's fine. He's sleeping now." There was a long pause as Catherine tried to think of something to say to ease the tension that had hovered between them the last few days.

"Listen, Brian, about the other day. I acted like a jerk."

"You sure did."

Catherine felt her lips turn up in a small smile at the sound of humor in his voice. "Don't rub it in."

"Not now, anyway. I'll save it for later. So tell me why you're still there. Are you with Nathan?"

She glanced sideways at the smiling crowd, feeling like an interloper as they laughed at something Nathan said. She pushed a strand of hair behind her ear and looked away. "Hardly. In fact, I'm getting ready to go home now."

Catherine began the climb up the steps, careful to keep her distance from the crowd while keeping one eye on her footing as she made plans to have Matty dropped off tomorrow. She was dropping the phone back in her purse when she heard her name being called. The urge to stop and turn was overwhelming, but the memory of the young girls kept her feet moving. She didn't need to make herself feel any older by seeing them up close.

The light rail was her headache for the evening. Now, in addition to humiliating herself with her hasty retreat from Nathan, she had missed the train back home. The wait for the next one wouldn't have been so bad, except for one thing.

Nathan Conners had beat the train to the stop and was staring up at her from the driver's seat of a flashy BMW convertible, its top down in spite of the chilly February air. His high-wattage smile was turned on her full-force as he tried to convince her to let him drive her home. Catherine glanced at her watch, then down the tracks, hoping the train would be early.

"No, thank you," she repeated through clenched teeth.

"C'mon, Doc. One ride. It's the least I can do."

Murmurs of encouragement grew from the crowd waiting at the stop with her. She gritted her teeth together, wondering what she should do. With a sigh, Catherine hitched the straps of her purse higher on her shoulder and grabbed for the door handle of the car, nearly yanking it off in frustration. Nathan was all smiles as he jammed the car in gear and sped away. Catherine braced her hand against the dash and reached for the seat belt, feeling only slightly safer when she had it securely fastened.

"So is it always playtime for you?" Catherine raised her voice to be heard above the cold wind racing past them as Nathan maneuvered the small car along the dark city streets. He flashed her his crooked smile and shrugged.

"You looked like you could use a laugh."

"At my own expense, right?" Catherine winced at the sharpness of her words, wondering why she always seemed to be so bitter around him. Brian was right. Nathan really did seem like a nice guy. So why did she always act this way around him?

"What?" Nathan turned to look at her, surprised at the brightness of her eyes and the flush he could see in the passing streetlights. His foot hit the brake and he pulled the car to a stop on a deserted side street as Catherine braced herself with an outstretched hand. He threw the car into First gear and cut the engine, then turned in his seat and stared at her. "I wasn't making fun of you, Catherine, I was trying to make you smile. I didn't realize you took everything so personally. I'm sorry."

He watched as a muscle worked in her jaw, noticed the way her chin came up a fraction of an inch and the way her lips pursed together, though in anger, hurt or stubbornness he couldn't tell. Probably all three. "No, I'm the one who's sorry. I didn't mean to snap at you. I'm not very good company right now. Maybe you should just take me back to the light rail stop."

Nathan sighed and ran his hands through his hair. This was not working out as he had planned. Seeing Catherine at the arena had been an unexpected but definitely welcome surprise. He had wanted to ask her to go for a cup of coffee or a drink or something, but backed away when she had mentioned calling Dr. Porter. Then she left the arena so fast he wasn't able to catch up to her. It had been pure luck seeing her at the light rail stop. Only now, instead of laughing or smiling, she was sitting next to him looking like she had lost her best friend. And suddenly he wanted her to smile, just for him.

He sighed again and reached for the key in the ignition, wondering what he should do. The engine turned over with a small purr as he faced her. "Where's your car? I'll drop you off there so you won't have to take the light rail."

"Um, the Timonium stop."

Nathan nodded then made a U-turn in the middle of the street, tires squealing as he gave the car too much gas. He reached down and adjusted the stereo until a classic rock tune blared from the speakers. His foot pressed harder on the accelerator in response to the music. From the corner of his eye he saw Catherine's white-knuckle grip on the edge of her seat, and he eased up on the gas.

He turned the stereo down, then shot her a cautious glance. "Instead of taking you home, we could go out somewhere, get something to drink and maybe have some fun. Unless you have something against having fun, that is." Nathan had meant the last comment jokingly and was surprised when her expression turned even gloomier. She bit down on her lower lip then hesitantly looked over at him, her dark eyes wide and sad.

"Why do you think I have something against having fun?"

"What?" Nathan stared at her, surprised to hear her voice waver when she repeated the question. A horn blared behind them and he muttered to himself before turning onto a side street. There were no empty spots here to pull into, so he double-parked before turning his full attention on her.

"I don't, you know." Her voice was small and soft, nearly lost in the underlying noise that made up Baltimore's nights. She cleared her throat and sat up straighter, and Nathan had the distinct impression that she was trying not to squirm. "I think our ideas of fun are probably just different, I guess."

"Oh, yeah? So, what's your idea of fun?" Nathan asked. She shrugged one small shoulder, refusing to look at him. He took a deep breath and looked around, then smiled. Without a word he put the car in gear and drove off.

"Where are we going?"

"To have some fun."

The smell of beer and Old Bay rushed from the open door and mixed with the damp smell of the harbor, creating an aroma that was both bitter and appealing. Catherine wrinkled her nose and pushed a hand against her rumbling stomach as Nathan led her through the crowded bar to a back table that was barely large enough to seat one person. He pulled the chair out for her then commandeered another for himself, sitting too close for comfort.

"Do you like steamed shrimp?" Nathan's voice was a warm whisper against her ear, causing a shiver to work its way through her. She tried to pull away, to put some distance between them, but there was no room to move. She swallowed against the lump in her throat and nodded, then sighed when Nathan stood and walked to the bar. It was hard not to notice the stares he attracted, including her own.

Catherine pulled her gaze away and looked around the smoky room, taking in the anonymous faces of the crowd and wondering again why she was there. Nathan had said nothing about their destination, only smiled when she asked. It had been a bit of a surprise when he wheeled the sports car down the cobblestone streets of Fells Point and led her into the waterfront bar famous for its steamed shrimp. She had heard about it before, of course, but this was her first time there. It made her think about other things she had missed out on.

What was with her tonight, she wondered. Every thought working its way into her mind was dismal, morose and depressing. If she wasn't careful, she'd turn into an old biddy with no life. Not like she had much of one as it was…

Catherine rubbed her hands along her arms and tried to warm herself against the inner chill that threatened to take over. Too much of her time lately had been devoted to Matty. No, she corrected, not her time. Her life. She would never trade those moments for anything, but with Matty discovering a life outside their world, it made her wonder what was left for her.

"You okay?"

Catherine jerked around, surprised to see Nathan sitting next to her, surprised that she had been so deep in thought that she hadn't noticed his return to the table. She nodded and offered him what she hoped was a passable smile then accepted the mug of beer he held out for her.

"Our shrimp will be ready in a few minutes." He motioned to the mug in her hand. "I wasn't sure what you wanted to drink. Is beer okay? I can get you something else—"

"No, this is fine." She took a small sip to prove her point then sat the mug in front of her, running a finger around the smooth edge of the glass.

"Are you sure you're okay? You look…preoccupied."

"Just thinking." Catherine shrugged, not wanting to look at him but watching him from the corner of her eye as if some force drew her attention to him. He was sitting so close to her she could feel the heat of his legs next to hers, the occasional brush of his foot against her own. Tall, well-built and confident, his presence was nearly overwhelming. People in the bar stopped to look at him, noticed him when he did nothing more exciting than sit there. Catherine shifted in the wooden chair, wondering if people actually recognized him or if they merely reacted to the energy that surrounded him.

"Maybe this wasn't such a good idea. We can leave—"

Catherine reached out and closed her hand over his arm to stop him from standing and shook her head, trying to ignore the vibrant heat that sent a jolt tingling through her where her flesh met his. She heard the words coming from her mouth, unable to stop them. "No, please. I want to stay."

Nathan glanced at the pale, shaking hand on his arm, then into Catherine's brown eyes and saw the wariness swimming in their dark depths. He took a deep breath to protect himself from the vulnerability that trembled through her and tried to offer her a carefree smile. The expression felt stiff on his face, must have looked stiff, too, because she suddenly removed her hand and looked away, a tinge of pink fanning her cheeks.

"I'm sorry. You're right. Maybe we should leave." She grabbed her purse and pushed her chair back, rising so quickly she stumbled. Nathan reached out and grabbed her, wanting only to steady her. His hand closed around her arm but instead of helping her, the contact stole whatever was left of her balance and she tumbled straight into his lap. The breath rushed out of Nathan in a hiss as her purse connected solidly with his left knee; a thousand needles of pain shot through his leg.

"Oh, God. Oh, God. I am so sorry. I didn't mean… Oh, God!" Catherine tried to scramble from his lap and elbowed him in the stomach, stepping on his foot in her hurry. He reached out, wrapped his arm around her waist and pulled her back to his lap, mostly to stop her from inflicting any more damage.

"Catherine, stop. It's okay. I'm okay. Just…don't hit me again. Please." He felt her body stiffen against him at the laughter in his voice, then realized she was shaking. He tried to shift her weight so he could see her face, thinking that she was finally laughing. A jolt clenched his stomach when he saw that she was doing her best not to cry.

"Oh, damn," he muttered. He looked around, realized there was no one who could explain why this woman was suddenly crying and felt completely helpless. She wiped at the single tear rolling down her face, refusing to look at him as he awkwardly patted her shoulder. He searched his mind for something to say, something to do, and came up blank. "Catherine?"

"I'm sorry. I'm fine. I'm sorry." She jumped from his lap and took a few steps away from him, then suddenly turned and raced out the door before he could stop her. He stared at the spot where she had been then shook his head in confusion.

Nathan motioned to the bartender to cancel the shrimp order then walked out the door, wondering what he had done to upset Catherine so much. He looked around, finally seeing her standing against the wrought-iron railing set up along the water's edge. She stood just outside the ring of light that fell from the street lamp but he could see that she was no longer crying. Her back stiffened at his approach but she refused to turn around.

"Are you all right?"

Silence.

"Um, did I do something to upset you?"

More silence. Nathan shoved his hands into the pockets of his jeans and shifted awkwardly, not knowing what to say or do. He stared out over the still water, watching the lights across the harbor twinkle on the black surface.

"I'm sorry if I did something to upset you."

"No, I'm the one who should be sorry. It's nothing you did." The whispered words were choked with emotion as she glanced at him then quickly looked away. "I guess I'm not used to…I mean, it's been awhile since I've gone anywhere and…"

Catherine's voice trailed off awkwardly and Nathan leaned closer to get a better look. Her eyes were dark hollows in a pale face. The shadows of the night washed across her skin and accented the delicate planes of her cheeks. She looked helpless and lost and scared, and Nathan wanted nothing more than to reach out and hold her, to reassure her that everything was going to be okay.

Instead of holding her like he wanted, he yanked one hand from his pocket and reached out to awkwardly pat her on her shoulder. She stiffened under his touch and he let his hand drop to his side, cursing himself for only making things worse. What did he know about comforting women? He had grown up in a family of three boys without a mother's influence, where talk of sports dominated every conversation. Any emotion deeper than that died a swift death, simply because nobody knew how to deal with it.

"I'm sorry," she repeated, louder this time. Her shoulders shook with a deep breath as she continued to stare out over the water. "It's just been a bad day. Actually, more like a bad week. I didn't mean to ruin your evening."

"That's okay. I didn't have anything better to do." Nathan winced at his poor choice of words and scrambled to find something else to say. "I mean, I did kind of force you to come along. I thought, well, I shouldn't have forced you."

Silence settled between them, awkward against the backdrop of the sounds surrounding them. Laughter from couples and small groups walking along the street, muffled sounds of music drifting into the night from the doorways of the different pubs, the steady *thump-thump-thump* of car tires along the cobblestone street. Nathan took a deep breath and wished for a way to draw Catherine out of the silence and into the life that ebbed and flowed around them. Forcing her had proved to be a mistake. Short of bodily dragging her, he could think of nothing else.

"Maybe we should just leave now." Her quiet voice pulled his attention back to her. She was watching him with those dark eyes, her hair a protective veil that fell across her face. He stared at her for a minute, trying to read her thoughts, but he couldn't see through the wall that surrounded her. He took a deep breath and pulled the keys from his pocket, trying to smile and failing.

"Sure, no problem." He motioned for her to lead the way and watched as she stepped from the curb, following her with his eyes and wishing there was some way to reach her. She stopped next to his car and turned, looking lost again. Nathan squared his shoulders and walked toward her.

Tonight could have gone a lot better. She wasn't as untouchable as he first thought, and he wanted to find some way to breach her protective barrier and get to know her better.

He just needed to figure out the best way to do it.

Chapter Five

"So how was your date with Nathan the other night?"

"It was not a date." Catherine didn't even bother to look at Brian. His snort of laughter told her he knew better but she ignored him anyway.

"Okay, so it wasn't a date. But how did it go?"

"It didn't."

"What do you mean, 'it didn't'? He took you out, right?"

Catherine sighed, knowing he wouldn't give up until she told him the whole embarrassing truth. She leaned back in her chair, took a deep breath and let the words fall in a rush. "We went out. Not a date. I hit his knee, fell on him, cried on him, he dropped me off at my car. End of night, end of story."

"What?"

Catherine leaned forward and pointed a stern finger at Brian, not caring for the way her hand shook. "Please, not a single word. It was the most humiliating night of my life, and I don't need you making it worse!" Not that it could be any worse, she thought. The memory of the quiet ride back to her car still made her shudder. She had no idea how to act around Nathan and it was worse than humiliating. It made her realize how out of touch with life she really was.

"But what happened?"

"How would I know? It was stupid. I was stupid. The whole thing was stupid. Stupid, stupid, stupid!" Catherine's voice choked on the last words and she slammed her hand on the desk, still not believing the entire fiasco. She forced a shaky laugh. "The night started out with me in the dumps and got worse from there. Seems to be my credo lately."

"Oh, Catherine." Brian's voice was laced with sympathetic humor and she knew he was only trying to help. It wasn't his fault that nothing seemed to go her way. It wasn't even her fault. It just was. She should just get used to it and move on.

"Yes, well, there you have it." She draped the stethoscope around her neck, more out of habit since she had no more scheduled patients. Her fingers toyed with one earpiece, rubbing the smooth plastic until all sensation of touch dulled.

"And here I was, hoping you guys would hit it off."

Catherine looked up at him, startled at the wistfulness in his voice. He was sitting across from her, lounging in the chair with his usual relaxed pose, an indefinable expression on his smooth face. It wasn't like her not to be able to see what he was thinking. The feeling rattled her. "He probably thinks I'm a nutcase by now. You were right, he seems like a nice guy. Too bad I don't know how to act anymore." She forced a laugh, determined to find some humor somewhere. "Besides, you only wanted some free game tickets."

"Touché." Brian waved one hand in the air, a smile finally breaking free on his face. Catherine breathed a sigh of relief, secretly glad that he was back to being himself. There were too many other changes, too many uncertainties, in her life right now. She didn't need her anchor to reality changing with them.

"So do you plan on releasing him?"

"Who, Nathan?" Brian took his glasses off, rubbed a spot with the edge of his sleeve and settled them back on his nose. "Of course I'm going to release him. Probably by the end of the week, depending on how his next visit goes."

"Oh."

"'Oh' what?" Brian's attitude was suddenly cautious. He straightened in the chair, fixing her with a steady gaze that made Catherine silently curse herself for opening her mouth. What on earth had possessed her to even bring it up? She blew a breath between pursed lips and decided to forge ahead.

"Are you sure his knee is ready?" She looked away from Brian before she continued. "I mean, it's obvious he's still having problems even though he tries to hide it. And he's going to continue having problems, no matter what you do. Playing is only going to worsen the condition. Have you told him that?"

"For someone who just said you liked him, you really seem to have it in for him." The quiet accusation in his voice pierced her dead center and she rocked back in the chair, shocked and deflated. Brian leaned forward and held up his fingers in response. "One, his knee has healed considerably since you've seen him. Two, he's capable of making his own decisions. Three, he knows his knee will never be the same but he's not willing to give up."

Catherine opened her mouth to speak then closed it again with a snap. She wasn't sure what to say, so she focused on the one thing that struck her hardest.

"Why do you think I have it in for him?"

"Oh, Catherine, come on." He pushed himself out of the chair and paced around the small room. "Today's the first time I've heard you say anything nice about him. You yourself said you didn't like the guy when you first met him!"

"That is not true."

"Isn't it?" Brian stopped, leaning across the desk until he was only inches away from her. "Catherine, you said you didn't like him because he made some comment you didn't agree with. He gets you and Matty tickets to a game and you damn near don't go. *Wouldn't* have gone if I hadn't forced you. And who would have been hurt by that? Matty, that's who!" Brian pushed away from the desk and resumed his pacing.

"You finally come to your senses and allow Matty to use his prosthesis, then nearly start a war when he wants to join a sports camp. You jump all over me when you find out I helped encourage him, and then blame *my* patient for interfering!"

"I most certainly did not—"

"That's baloney and you know it. And you wonder why I think you have it in for Nathan Conners? For crying out loud, Catherine, I'd think you would be thanking him for encouraging Matty, but instead you seem to resent him…." Brian's voice trailed off as a look of realization lit his eyes. He turned and faced her, a mixed expression on his face. Catherine looked away, knowing what was coming next, not wanting to hear it.

"You resent him!"

"That's ridiculous."

"It's the truth. Matty is finally doing what he wants to do, things that don't always include you anymore, and you think it's Nathan's fault!"

Catherine pointedly studied her hands, not daring to answer. She wanted to deny it, to jump from her chair and scream and yell, to tell Brian that he had never been more wrong, but she couldn't move.

Because he was partly right. Maybe completely right.

Her whole life had been spent taking care of others, the last few years devoted especially to Matty. That was what she did, possibly the only thing she did well, and the thought of not having that scared her. Seeing Matty become so independent scared her. Realizing that Matty was growing up and didn't need her anymore terrified her.

"Oh, Catherine." The sympathy in his voice bordered on pity, and the tears she tried to hold back flowed. She reached up and wiped at them, angry at herself for letting them fall, angry for letting herself reach that point in the first place.

Brian leaned close and took her in his arms and for once she didn't pull away, couldn't pretend that she didn't need to lean on anyone. She buried her face in his shoulder and let him hold her as the tears fell, her body shaking from the force of the sobs. Time dragged by until the flood finally slowed to a trickle, then stopped. Catherine wiped her face, offering him a weak smile that was immediately followed by a hiccup. Brian chuckled and gave her a tissue, which she used to blow her nose.

"Oh, boy." Her voice trembled, shaky and hoarse from crying. Brian patted her on the shoulder then sat back on her desk, heedless of the papers that rustled under him.

"That's why you're not supposed to keep things bottled up."

Catherine hiccuped again and covered her mouth, hiding her smile. "Some mother I make. When did I turn into such a mess?"

"Catherine, you're a great mother. Don't let yourself think otherwise. As for the mess…" Brian hesitated then shrugged. "You need to let yourself lean on others once in a while. There's nothing wrong with that, and it doesn't mean you're weak."

She saw seriousness in his pale eyes then leaned her head back and sighed. He was right, as usual. But it was so hard for her, never feeling like she could depend on anyone, always feeling like she had to do everything herself.

"I don't know, Bri. Everything is changing so fast. Matty is changing. I feel like he doesn't need me anymore."

"Catherine, Matty will always need you. You're his mother, and boys need their moms, no matter how old they get. But for now, let him spread his wings a bit. He's enjoying it. You should be, too." Brian stood, rubbed his hands down the sides of his slacks then clasped them together. "Speaking of which, when are you heading out to pick him up?"

Catherine glanced at her watch, surprised at how much time had gone by. "In a few minutes. He's supposed to get out in an hour but I wanted to swing by early and see how he was doing. Or is that too much of a mom thing to do?"

"No, it's not too much of a 'mom thing.'" Brian laughed. "I think Matty enjoys the chance to show off. You want some company? I kind of enjoy watching all the showing off myself."

Catherine grabbed the purse from under her desk and stood, smiling at the glitter of anticipation in Brian's eyes. "You're worse than a kid, do you know that? What is it with men and sports? All of you act like little kids!"

"Hey, be sympathetic. It's a genetic defect."

"A defect, hmm? That would explain a lot. Okay, Mr. Sports Nut, lead the way." Catherine followed him from the office, already feeling better than she had in a long time.

* * *

She tried to hang on to her good mood, but it evaporated at the sight that greeted her when she walked to the far side of the large remodeled warehouse. She wrapped her hands around the metal post and squeezed, fighting back the panic and anger and fear. Her jaw clenched with so much force that her back teeth actually hurt. "Catherine, don't." Brian's whisper reached her through a haze of conflicting emotions. She shrugged his hand from her shoulder and gripped the post tighter as she watched.

She should be happy. She *was* happy. And terrified and angry. Catherine told herself to focus on the positive feelings as she watched Matty skating in circles with none other than Nathan Conners. Skating! She couldn't believe it.

Both of them were laughing, so caught up in the moment that neither had seen her yet. Catherine's breath caught when Matty lost his balance and nearly fell. Nathan was beside him in a flash, one arm wrapped protectively around her son's slim shoulders until the danger passed. They laughed again, harder this time. The clear ring of Matty's joy echoed around her.

Matty was skating. The implications of that simple act overwhelmed her. She would have denied it if someone had told her he would be doing something so physical so soon. But there he was, not only doing it, but doing it well. Catherine took a deep breath and reached up with one hand to rub the painful squeeze in her chest, not knowing if it was from anger, fear or happiness. Maybe all three.

"Help me, Brian." She turned to her friend and pleaded, not knowing exactly what she was asking for. He offered her a small smile and wrapped one arm around her, giving her a friendly hug.

"Let him go, Catherine. He's fine. Just look at him!"

Catherine nodded and did exactly that, still not sure she should believe what she was seeing. Her throat tightened and she closed her eyes, opened them again and shook her head.

Her son was skating.

Her hand loosened its grip on the metal railing as she slowly relaxed and continued watching. Matty and Nathan continued their slow circles around the small rink, talking to each other and laughing. Catherine noticed how Nathan kept a casual distance, not crowding her son but staying close enough to offer a quick hand if it was needed. The expression on Matty's face was a combination of joy and concentration.

And pure hero worship.

Catherine saw that look and her stomach clenched painfully. She hadn't realized how attached Matty had become to him, but there was no denying it. *Too* attached if the look on his face was any indication. A dozen thoughts and worries swirled through her mind, begging for attention. Was it a healthy attachment? Did Nathan see it as clearly as she did? Most importantly, how hurt would Matty be when the attachment was severed? Because Catherine was sure it wouldn't last. Either deliberately or by some careless act, she was certain the hockey player would fail her son. She didn't want to imagine Matty's pain when that happened.

There was no time to decide what to do. Matty had spotted them and was skating over, waving and smiling. Catherine kept her eyes on her son, not trusting herself to look at Nathan but sensing his hesitation before he followed Matty.

"Hey, Mom! Did you see that? Whadya think? Pretty cool, huh?" Matty slid to a stop and leaned against the rail, fumbling for balance before standing upright. Catherine blinked away the film covering her eyes and leaned over to kiss him on the cheek, mentally wincing when he pulled away in embarrassment. She sighed and reached out to ruffle his hair instead.

"Yup, pretty cool. So when did you learn how to do that?"

"Today! Nathan's been teaching me."

"Oh, he has?" Catherine tried to keep her voice steady as she finally looked over and met Nathan's stare. Her mouth suddenly dried and all coherent thought left her when he focused that eerily intense gaze on her. She shifted and looked away, pretending she was unaffected, trying to make her voice sound casual and relaxed. "Maybe next time it would be nice if somebody asked me first, okay?"

"I kept a close eye on him. Nothing would have happened," Nathan said, only the slightest bit defensive.

"It would still be nice to be asked first." Catherine's voice was harsher than she intended. A sudden silence stretched over them and even Matty looked up at her in confusion. Brian quickly came to the rescue, offering to help Matty out of his skates. Catherine watched the two walk away then faced Nathan, an apology hovering on her lips.

Nathan spoke first, his deep voice lowered so that she had to lean slightly forward to hear him. "That was uncalled-for." The anger underlying the words surprised her, because she didn't think he would care.

"I'm sorry, I just don't want Matty hurt. Physically or emotionally."

"And you think I plan on doing either?"

Catherine quietly studied the man in front of her, saw the bewilderment and concern etched on the angular planes of his face. She took a deep breath and shifted from one foot to the other. "No, not deliberately. I just don't want him hurt."

"Catherine, you and I haven't exactly gotten along, but do you honestly think I would do anything to hurt your son?" He searched her face for several seconds then let out an exasperated sigh. "You really do! I cannot believe this!"

"Nathan, I…I need to go."

"Catherine, wait."

"I need to go," she repeated, more forceful this time as she turned around, feeling his stare in the middle of her back as she walked away.

"Pick it up! You're skating like an old lady!"

The bellow echoed off the ice and straight down Nathan's spine. He gritted his teeth, dug the toe of his blade into the ice and pushed off, the stick held like a weapon in his gloved hands. A speck of black flew into his vision and he reached out, sending the puck flying off his stick with a grunt. He paused, sweat pouring down his back as he watched the puck speed past Alec Kolchak and into the net.

"That's more like it! Now keep going!"

Nathan muttered under his breath. Ian Donovan stopped next to him, nudging his arm before skating off again. Nathan watched the younger player, his movements fluid beneath the heavy gear. Good-natured joking had been going on since the start of practice a few hours ago, but Nathan was no longer in the mood for it. In fact, he hadn't been in the mood from the start.

Sweat drenched him from head to toe, the equipment that he had worn with ease suddenly weighed as much as armor and his left leg had turned to jelly after twenty minutes on the ice. His knee throbbed painfully as he pushed off and skated to center ice, and he again questioned his wisdom in convincing the doctor to release him.

"Damn." He rubbed his face against his shoulder to wipe away the sweat and looked up in time to see another player come barreling toward him. Nathan crouched instinctively and reached out with his stick, stealing the puck with natural grace before racing off to the net. He pulled back and shot, missing by a few inches as he skated past the pipes.

A crushing weight hit him from behind, propelling him into the glass with a jaw-shuddering thud. The whistle blew, signaling the end of practice. Nathan glared at Donovan, resisting the urge to bodycheck him only because Kolchak came out of the net and skated between them with a warning look.

"Not cool, Donovan." Alec's soft voice carried only far enough for the three of them to hear. The rookie player looked at each of them with a smirk on his face, saying nothing before skating away. "The kid has no brains."

"No, but he's got the talent."

Alec reached up and tilted the mask back on his head, revealing wet brown hair and a flushed face. "Maybe, maybe not. He's too hotheaded for his own good, either way. And he doesn't like that you're back, either."

"Yeah, well. The way I feel, I may not be back for long. I don't think I've ever felt this old."

Alec's laughter was loud and instant, and he slapped Nathan on the back with a gloved hand as they skated to the edge of the ice. "You and me both. So, you expecting company?"

"Company? No."

"Well, I think you've got some." He pointed to a row of seats off to the side of the practice rink, close enough to watch the players but far enough away to be unnoticed. Nathan turned to look then groaned.

"What the hell is she doing here?" He didn't even try to keep the frustration from his voice, earning him a wry look from his friend.

"New fan club, maybe?"

"Humph. Firing squad would be more like it."

Alec patted him on the shoulder then stepped off

the ice, a smile firmly in place. "Seems like we all have one of them these days. At least yours isn't a reporter. Go see what she wants."

"Just like you always see what AJ wants when she shows up?"

Alec threw him a look that would have sent a weaker person to his knees, then walked away, leaving Nathan alone at the side of the ice. He watched the goalie's retreating back, then turned in Catherine's direction, away from the die-hard fans who showed up for practices. Muttering under his breath because he would probably regret it, he skated to the other side of the rink. He stopped and leaned on his stick, staring up at her in silence.

She looked different today, dressed in jeans and a baggy sweater that hid all of her figure. Her blond hair fell across her shoulders in thick waves, and a shyness hovered over her. As Nathan watched, she reached up and pushed a strand of hair behind her ear then straightened in her seat. With that one move, the shyness evaporated, replaced by an all-business attitude. Nathan sighed and called himself an idiot. It didn't matter that she seemed to have a softer side; all she let him see was the barrier that closed her off from the human race.

He continued to stare at her in silence, refusing to initiate any conversation. There was a brief moment of satisfaction when she squirmed under his gaze, but even that was short-lived when she remained silent. Nathan shook his head and turned to leave, not willing to guess at what she wanted.

"Wait!"

He almost didn't but the hint of desperation in her voice stopped him. With a sigh he turned and leaned on the wall, fixing her with a blank stare. Part of him was gratified to see she had at least stood, but he refused to speak until she came closer. He wouldn't give in on that.

Catherine looked at him then away, her eyes darting around the rink as if searching for help. Nathan watched her struggle before she finally walked down the steps and met him at the wall, stopping a safe distance away.

"I…I saw that Brian cleared you."

Nathan raised his eyebrows and continued to stare, saying nothing, knowing she hadn't come down here to say that. She squirmed and looked away, then straightened into a stiff pose before facing him again.

"I can tell you're favoring your knee. You should put ice on it and keep it up."

"Why thank you, Dr. Wilson. I was just about to do that." She flinched at the coolness of his tone but he didn't care. He was hot, he was tired and his knee throbbed so much that all he wanted to do was go soak it and wrap it in ice, just like she suggested. "Any other advice you care to give me? Free of charge, I assume, since this is your visit."

"I…no."

"Fine." Nathan turned and started to skate away, wondering what it was about this particular woman that got under his skin. Yes, she was attractive. Yes, there was something about her that drew him. He didn't know what, but he had the distinct feeling that it would be lethal if he ever discovered it.

"Well, goodbye to you, too, Mr. Conners."

Nathan froze, stunned at the sarcasm in her voice. The tension that had been building in him collected into a single dangerous outburst. The blood drained from her face when he turned and climbed over the wall, his gait awkward as his skate blades clanked against the rubber floor.

"That's it. That is it!" He closed the distance between them as she backed against the wall of the penalty box. He tossed his stick and gloves down then tore the helmet from his head, throwing that down, as well. "What is with you, lady? What have I done to you to make you drive me nuts like this?"

"I...I..." Catherine's voice trailed off as he leaned closer, placing a hand against the glass on either side of her, trapping her between the wall and his body. He saw the slight trembling of her body and the heated flush tingeing her cheeks, watched her tongue dart out and lick her lips. The tightening in his body was instant and powerful. His voice dropped dangerously low as he focused his gaze on her mouth.

"Do you have any idea what you do to me?"

She shook her head, staring up at him with those wide eyes and parted lips, and Nathan lost all patience, all restraint. He reached up with one hand and slipped it behind her neck, pulling her closer as he lowered his face to hers and claimed her lips with one swift move. She stiffened under his touch and her hands pushed at his chest, once, before she leaned against him.

Nathan sensed her surrender, felt her lips open at his invitation and he wrapped his other arm around her. As he pulled her more tightly against him, his tongue swept the sweet fire of her mouth. He groaned against the desire flaring inside him and silently cursed the heavy gear that prevented him from completely feeling the curves of her soft body against his.

Catherine leaned into him, caught up in the tide that swept over her. His grip on her neck was strong yet gentle, the sweep of his thumb under her ear almost as exciting as the warmth of his mouth on hers. She fisted her hand into the damp cloth of his practice jersey, falling more deeply into the kiss, all sense of reason gone. A hushed rumble surrounded her, growing louder, and she wondered briefly what was causing the noise. A loud yell penetrated her foggy senses and she jumped, breaking the contact with Nathan and looking around guiltily.

Heat flooded her face as she realized the rumble was the hoots and catcalls coming from the group of fans witnessing their steamy embrace. The loud yell had been bellowed by an older man built like a tree trunk. A ragged scar that slashed across his face glowed red as he stared at the two of them. Catherine pushed against Nathan, suddenly mortified.

"Conners! Are you joining us?" The reedy voice quivered with impatience and humor, and Catherine hung her head in embarrassment. She had just let herself be kissed, thoroughly kissed, in public. In front of strangers!

No, she amended, she hadn't *let* him—she had been a willing participant. Too willing.

"In a minute!" Catherine winced at the frustration in Nathan's voice, still refusing to look at him until he forced her chin up with one long finger. "Do you have to leave? I mean, will you stay here until we're done? It won't be long."

"I should go."

"Catherine, just please stay here. I won't be long."

"I…" She looked into his eyes and felt her resolve melt under the heat of his liquid gaze. "All right."

"Good." He leaned down and kissed her again, hard and quick, before walking away. Catherine watched as he left, amazed at the power and grace in his moves, and wondered what she had just gotten herself into.

Chapter Six

How hopeless could one person be? The thought went through Catherine's mind as she checked her watch again. She was still sitting in the deserted rink, waiting for Nathan to come out.

The memory of his kiss was sharp. A flash of heat warmed her as she recalled the taste of him, the comforting feel of being wrapped in his arms. She shifted in the seat, trying to let her impatience crowd out the memory.

She had swallowed some of her abundant pride and come to the practice to apologize for the way she had acted the other day. There had been no reason for her to treat Nathan that way, not when all he did was help Matty. Catherine had struck out at him in fear, and she owed him an apology. Her coming here had absolutely nothing to do with the unwelcome attraction she felt for Nathan. Just like it had nothing to do with the way Matty had suddenly come to life since his involvement in the sports camp. It had been the result of a polite streak, that was all.

She pushed her hair out of her face and sighed. Who was she kidding? Nathan Conners brought out a part of her she was afraid to acknowledge—a vulnerable desire to be wanted, to be taken care of. Her sensible side screamed out repeated warnings, telling her to not even think along those lines. The idea that she *wanted* someone to lean on in the first place was sobering enough. For that someone to be Nathan Conners was insane.

"Crazy," she muttered. Sitting here waiting for him was crazy. Having warm, fuzzy thoughts about him was stupid. She grabbed her purse, determined to leave before he came out, and stood up only to see him walking toward her. A lump formed in her throat as she watched him, his square jaw and high cheekbones and long legs closing the distance between them. His hair was slicked back off his forehead, damp from the shower.

He flashed her his crooked smile and her eyes caught sight of his chipped tooth, bringing back the memory of their kiss. She looked away, embarrassed at the warmth that surged through her. "Stupid. Stupid, stupid."

"What?"

She could feel Nathan's eyes on her as he got closer and she shook her head, looking up in time to see him leaning forward, his lips dangerously close to hers. She ducked her head and took a hasty step back. His lips barely brushed her cheek, soft and warm, and she swallowed nervously.

Silence dropped between them. Catherine cleared her throat and shifted her weight from one foot to the other, not sure how to act or what to say.

"I—"

"You—"

They started to talk at the same time then stopped, studying each other. Catherine pulled her gaze away from his crooked smile and cleared her throat again as he spoke.

"You look nervous about something."

"Me? Oh." Catherine searched for something intelligent to say, the liquid heat of his gaze making it difficult to think. She nodded, shook her head, nodded again and felt like the world's biggest idiot when he chuckled. She tried to act indignant, to come up with a cute remark and failed miserably. Nathan stepped closer and studied her with his lion's eyes.

"Am I making you nervous?"

"Yes!" The admission flew from her mouth before she could stop it, causing Nathan to laugh harder.

"Why do I make you nervous?"

Because you make me think stupid thoughts. Because you make me feel things I have no right to feel. The answers swarmed through her mind and she mercilessly stomped them. Nothing would make her admit those weaknesses out loud, especially not to him. She shook her head and searched for a way to change the subject.

"I wanted to apologize for the way I've treated you. Last week, and the other day at the camp. I…this last year with Matty has been…difficult, and I…I just wanted to say I was sorry for taking it out on you." There. The apology was out, she'd said what she had come here to say. Plus some things she hadn't meant to. She stepped around him, but his hand snaked out and wrapped around her arm, stopping her midstride.

"Was that it?" His voice was soft, husky. She turned her head and made the mistake of looking into his eyes, saw his heated stare as he watched her. "You just came to apologize?"

Catherine pulled her arm from his grasp and wrapped her arms around her middle, wishing that her stomach would unknot itself. She nervously swallowed and nodded. Her voice came out as a squeak. "Why else would I come here?"

Nathan ran a hand through his hair and shifted his weight, studying her with eyes that seemed to see right through her. She swallowed again, knowing that she should move away. Her reflexes were too slow, though, and she didn't see him move, only felt his arms come around her as his mouth swiftly descended on hers, warm and insistent. She softened under his kiss, then gasped as he pulled away and stared down at her.

"What about that?"

"I…that is…" Catherine fumbled for something to say, still reeling from the onslaught of emotions the brief kiss had unleashed on her. She gripped her purse tighter, thinking that would somehow help her hold on reality. "What about it?"

Of all the reactions she had expected, amusement was not one of them. His rich laughter caught her by surprise, wrapped around her like a warm cloak of comfort. Her face heated and she stepped away, once again caught off guard and unsure how to act. Only around him was she like this, so uncertain, and the confusion made her feel worse. It had to be unhealthy to feel so lost, which was just one more reason to stay away from him.

"I think we need to talk."

"About what? There's nothing—"

"Sure there is. C'mon." He reached out and folded his hand around hers, gently pulling her toward the exit. She tried to dig her feet in and stop, but the worn sneakers offered no traction and she only succeeded in stumbling.

"Nathan, what are—"

"Shh." He ignored her protests, leading her outside where the cold air swept over them. An instant chill descended over Catherine, made her even more aware of the heat that radiated from his hold on her. The chill increased when he stopped at the curb, only this time it had nothing to do with the temperature.

Nathan dropped her hand and fumbled with the motorcycle that was parked in front of them. He turned around and held out a helmet, obviously expecting her to take it. She looked from his outstretched hands to the motorcycle then at him.

"You're insane!"

"No, I'm not. C'mon, put on the helmet." He

lifted the helmet higher, urging her to take it. She stepped backward.

"It's February! It's forty degrees out, freezing, and you're driving a motorcycle!"

Nathan shrugged, indifferent, and stepped closer. "I'm from northern Minnesota. This is considered warm. Now here, put this on." He placed the helmet on her head and adjusted the chin strap before she realized what he was doing. She shook her head and reached up to take it off, but was stopped when he gently took both of her hands in his. He lowered his head so his eyes were level with hers and stared at her, searching. His gaze was warm, serious, and Catherine fought her sudden nervousness.

She could handle him when he was joking or when he was cocky. At least, she told herself she could. But the look he was giving her now, the fire in his gaze that seared through her, this was new to her. It filled her with trepidation and fear, and something else she didn't want to examine. All her survival instincts screamed to get away from him but she was helpless to move, locked in his gaze like a frightened animal. She wondered how much time she had left before he robbed her of what little common sense she still possessed.

"Come with me, Catherine." His husky voice hypnotized her and she felt herself nodding, agreeing to the quiet demand. He smiled and stepped away, breaking the spell so abruptly that Catherine wondered if she'd imagined the whole thing.

Nathan stepped off the curb and straddled the bike,

bringing it to life with a powerful kick before motioning for her to get on. She stared at him for a split second, wondering if she had any choice left at all, then climbed on and wrapped her arms around him.

Catherine released her death grip from Nathan's waist and tried to flex her hands, wincing at the cold numbness that had seeped into her joints. "I c-c-can't feel my f-f-fingers."

"Let me see." Nathan climbed off the bike and removed his helmet in a single graceful move then reached out and took her hands in his. He rubbed them lightly then pulled them to his mouth, blowing softly. A wave of heat washed over Catherine and she yanked her hands away, shoving them into her coat pockets.

"N-never mind. They're fine." She tried to climb off the motorcycle, stumbling as her foot caught on the kickstand. Strong hands reached out and steadied her, helping her regain her balance and making her feel as graceful as a three-legged elephant. She shrugged off his help and straightened, pointedly ignoring his expression of wry amusement as she looked around.

They had been driving aimlessly for little more than an hour, finally stopping on a side road that wound through the reservoir. The sound of water rushing over a man-made waterfall echoed around them, its noise loud against the silence of the surrounding woods. In a few months, when the weather warmed and the trees began to bud, the area would be filled with people eagerly welcoming spring. But it was deserted now, desolate with the bare trees and patches of brown grass. Catherine noticed the No Trespassing signs and wondered why Nathan had stopped here.

"Let's go for a walk." He didn't look at her, didn't stop to see if she would follow, just started walking. A shiver stole over Catherine at the sound of crunching grass under her feet; she wrapped her arms around herself, trying to shake the emptiness that wanted to grip her. Nathan stopped and looked down at her with an unreadable expression.

"What?"

"Are you okay?"

No. I'm lonely and scared, and I don't know why. She pushed the thought away and forced a smile. "Me? I'm fine. Why?"

He continued to watch her then shrugged and turned away. She started to follow again, then stopped when she noticed he was climbing out onto the dam.

"Where are you going?"

"There's something I want you to see," he called over his shoulder.

"But you can't go out there!"

Nathan stopped and turned around, his hands on his hips in a pose of pure masculine frustration. "Why can't I?"

"Because you're not supposed to, that's why. See that sign?" Catherine pointed to the sign clearly posted at the railing, warning trespassers away from the dam. She had no trouble hearing his sigh as he walked back to her.

"And do you always follow the rules? Never mind,

I already know the answer." He held his hand out, clearly expecting her to take it. "Forget about the rules, Catherine."

The tone in his quiet voice carried so many meanings, all of them terrifying. She saw the quiet reassurance in his eyes and looked down at his outstretched hand and wanted to reach out and grab it, feel his long fingers intertwine with hers. She wanted to forget the rules, to forget fear and responsibility and duty. For once she wanted to live, to do something just because. She pulled her right hand from her pocket and willed it to reach out, but let it drop at the last second.

"I can't."

Nathan studied her with a sadness that disappeared so quickly she thought she imagined it. Silence hung between them. Catherine lowered her head, afraid to meet his direct gaze, not willing to acknowledge the sudden guilt she felt.

"You asked for it."

"Wh—" Catherine shrieked as Nathan rushed toward her, scooping her in his arms and lifting her in one fluid movement. They were halfway across the dam before she realized what happened. A surprised yelp escaped her when she looked and saw nothing but water more than fifty feet below her. She wrapped her arms around his neck and buried her face in his shoulder.

A deep rumble shook his chest, and she realized he was laughing. She squeezed her eyes shut and tightened her grip, unable to see any humor in the fact that one misstep could cause them to topple over the edge of the dam to an icy death below.

"You can let go now. We're across."

Catherine realized they had stopped moving and she slowly peeled one eye open, surprised to see they had reached the other side safely. A sigh of relief escaped her and she loosened her grip, expecting Nathan to lower her to her feet. She looked up and felt the breath catch in her throat at the intensity of the gaze he fixed on her. Her eyes darted to the soft fullness of his lips and she wondered briefly if he would kiss her again. She looked away in embarrassment when the corners of his mouth twitched in amusement.

"I wasn't going to drop you." The laughter in his voice made her face grow warmer and she mumbled something unintelligible, not sure herself of what she said. He released his hold on her legs and lowered her feet to the ground, letting her body slide down his, so close and slow she could tell that she wasn't the only one affected by their nearness.

"Nathan, I—"

"Shh." He wrapped his hand around hers and tugged, pulling her behind him with a mischievous wink that sent tingles straight to her nerve endings. "I want to show you something."

Catherine bit down on her lower lip. There were so many questions she wanted to suddenly ask him, but she was afraid. Afraid of the questions, afraid of the answers he might give her, afraid that she even wanted to ask them. She lowered her eyes to concentrate on her steps and felt her face heat when she realized she was staring at a prime piece of his anatomy. Her embarrassment fled, replaced by guilt when her gaze dropped and she noticed he was favoring his left leg. Probably from carrying her. She stopped midstride and pulled her hand from his.

"You're limping!"

Nathan turned and fixed her with a look of impatience that would have made her laugh if she hadn't felt so guilty. He closed the distance between them, took her hand again and started walking. "It was a rough first practice."

"But you shouldn't be—"

"Quiet. Now come on." He tugged but she refused to move.

"But your knee..."

"Catherine." She was startled by how fast he spun around to face her, by how close he was and by the laughter in his eyes. "Do I need to find a way to keep you quiet?"

The meaning hidden in his words was not lost on her and her jaw snapped shut. His laughter was deep and rich, infectious, and she fought against her own answering smile. Nathan rested a single finger against his lips, motioning for silence, then turned and led her along a barely noticeable path.

Minutes crawled by, broken only by the sound of dried leaves and breaking twigs under their feet, the occasional scurry of a small animal darting just out of their view. And by the tormented taunts of her mind. Catherine questioned, not for the first time, what she was doing with him. Why she had followed him so trustingly. Why her common sense seemed to desert her when he was around. She swallowed a sigh, afraid to make even the smallest noise, and watched the sleek power of his body as he walked, his hand still firmly wrapped around hers.

If she had been smart, if she had possessed any common sense at all, she would have turned and run from her office the first minute she had seen him. She recalled the sense of danger she had felt at that first meeting nearly two months ago.

It seemed impossible that only two months had passed. So much had happened, so much had changed in that short time that Catherine's mind swam. Matty had become a different boy, laughing more than ever before, adapting to his prosthesis with greater ease than she would have thought. She had changed, so subtly that even she would have trouble describing how. And all of it was because of Nathan. By pure chance he had entered their lives and Catherine wasn't sure how she felt about it or him.

Or maybe she did, and that was another reason for the anxiety that seemed to grip her at the most unexpected times.

She looked up at Nathan and realized they had stopped; he was watching her with that intense gaze that saw too much. She flinched under his scrutiny and ducked her head, afraid he might see the thoughts swirling through her mind.

"Look around, Catherine." It was a quiet demand, one she was helpless to ignore. She raised her head, determined not to look at him, and took in their surroundings. A soft exclamation of surprise left her on a hushed breath. He had stopped at the edge of a stream, its clear waters gurgling over smooth rocks polished with years of caressing. Across the stream was a huge fortress of twigs, leaves and a mixture of nature's castoffs. As she watched, a furry animal lifted his head and fixed them with an impatient glare before diving under the water's surface, its flat tail kicking up water in indignation.

"A beaver!" The giggle that escaped her was unexpected and she covered her mouth with her hand, surprised the youthful noise had come from her. She looked at Nathan, saw the wide smile that curved his lips and felt her face flame in answer. Electric awareness hung between them, so thick and alive that Catherine swore she could hear the beating of his heart. She swallowed, expecting him to lean forward and kiss her. Disappointment flooded through her when he released her hand and stepped away, breaking the spell.

"I thought you might enjoy seeing it. Not what you would call a fancy date, but..." His voice trailed off as he walked to the edge of the stream. He lowered his lean body onto a flat rock, stretching his left leg in front of him. Catherine's stomach did a funny lurch at the word *date* but she was determined not to make anything of it.

Nathan patted the rock beside him, motioning for her to sit. She hesitated, questioning the wisdom of getting too close to him, then decided it was already too late to worry about that, at least for now. She sat down, making sure there were a few extra inches between them. "So why did we come here?"

"I just get the feeling that you've forgotten how simple life can be. That it's not all worries and responsibilities."

She stiffened at his words, even as she told herself the comment hadn't been intended to hurt. But the pain that sliced through her was real, sharp and accusing, made worse because it was true. She wanted to run, to hide from the painful truth. Nathan must have sensed her intent because he reached out and took hold of her chin, gently urging her to turn and face him.

"Catherine, look at me." He lifted her chin, forcing her to look in his eyes. "That's not always a bad thing. As long as you aren't deliberately trying to run away and hide."

"Sometimes I think I am." The admission tumbled from her, stinging like a scab picked from a fresh wound. She sighed and pulled her face from his gentle hold, not wanting to look at him, afraid she would see pity staring back at her from the depths of his golden eyes. "You must think I'm a mess."

"You don't want to know what I think right now."

"That bad, huh?" Catherine hunched her shoulders, wanting to hide her head like a turtle. She spun toward him at the sound of his chuckle, not understanding the reason for his amusement.

"Hardly." The look he gave her was hot and intense. His meaning was clear and her mouth dropped open in a soundless *O*. She shifted, too aware of him, too wary to trust herself. Her eyes darted around, finally resting on his knee, and she retreated behind the front she was most comfortable with.

"How's your knee?"

"It's fine."

Catherine fixed him with a pointed glare, not believing for a minute that it was fine. She shifted position and leaned closer, resting her hands on either side of his knee. His leg jerked under her touch, the muscles of his thigh tight under the faded jeans. "Does that hurt?"

"No, but—"

"Relax. I'm just going to rub it." She gently pushed down with her fingers, rocking them back and forth in an effort to ease the obvious soreness. His leg became more tense and she released a sigh of frustration. "You need to relax. Getting tense like that isn't going to help."

"Catherine—"

She looked up at the sound of his choked voice and couldn't understand the reason for his sudden discomfort. "If you don't relax, it's just going to get stiff."

His strangled laughter was immediate, the flash in his eyes too clear and Catherine suddenly realized they were talking about two different things. She pulled her hands from his leg with lightning speed and jammed them in her pockets, her jaw clenched against the keen embarrassment that swamped her.

"Catherine, look at me."

"Um, I think maybe we should go now." She pulled her legs under her to stand but was stopped by a hand on her shoulder.

"Catherine." His voice was husky, drawing her.

Against her will her head turned, just enough to see the fire in his eyes as he leaned closer. She swallowed, afraid of what she saw in his gaze, afraid of her body's uncontrollable response to the man next to her.

Nathan pivoted on the rock, trapping her between his legs. He freed her hands from her pockets and held them in his, one callused thumb rubbing the pulse that throbbed in her wrist.

"I want to kiss you, Catherine." He reached up and ran a hand along her jawline, caressing softly, running his thumb along her lower lip. "Will you let me?"

The deep huskiness of his voice wrapped around her like a web, weaving its magic so completely she was helpless to do anything but nod. One corner of his mouth twitched in a quick smile as he leaned closer, closer until his lips barely touched hers, rubbed against them in a soft kiss. A flame of desire and need erupted inside her and she leaned forward, eager for his touch, nearly crying out when his mouth claimed hers.

Catherine pulled her hand from his, placed it against the warmth of his neck and drew him closer. Her fingers tangled in the edges of his hair, feeling the softness of each strand against his neck. The tip of his tongue darted out, swept across her lips in an insistent demand that she open to him, a demand she eagerly met. A soft moan escaped her as Nathan pulled her closer.

A rush of cold air drifted under the edge of her sweater, replaced by a fiery touch as his hand swept across her stomach and up her back, kneading her flesh, pulling her to him as he leaned back, farther still until she was lying across him. She moaned in frustration when he pulled his lips from hers, sighed when the tip of his tongue trailed a hot path along her neck and around her ear. Dizziness washed over her as one sense after another crashed under the onslaught of his touch.

Her hands wandered over his chest and she felt the heat of his body through his shirt, the slight trembling of the hard muscles and the thudding beat of his heart under her palm. She wanted to touch him, feel the warmth of his flesh against hers, see if his body was as magnificently sculpted as it felt. She fumbled with the edge of his shirt, urging it free of his jeans, muttering in frustration when it became snagged. Her hand lowered farther, brushed up against the thick length of his erection and she froze, realizing what she was doing. Realizing how much of her control she had lost.

Nathan murmured her name softly against her ear, reclaimed her lips in a kiss meant to make her forget where they were, who he was. Who she was. Catherine tensed. She was afraid to give up so much of herself yet hesitant to pull away from the feelings and desires that cascaded through her. Feelings and desires that were foreign in their intensity.

Nathan must have sensed her silent battle because he gentled the kiss and slowly, reluctantly, pulled his lips from hers. His arms tightened around her when she would have pulled away. A long finger pushed the hair from her face as his eyes searched hers, seeing too much, saying too much.

"I knew I shouldn't have waited so long to kiss you." His hoarse voice was light and teasing, one corner of his mouth turned up in a slight smile. Her face heated but she didn't look away, was too mesmerized by the sight of his smile to give in to her embarrassment. Nathan shifted on the rock and eased her head onto his chest, holding her with one arm while his hand made lazy circles on her back. Catherine closed her eyes, wishing for nothing more than the ability to purr.

Minutes may have passed by, or merely seconds, as she lay curled on his chest. She had no way of knowing and wouldn't have cared except for the damp chill seeping through her leg. She shifted and felt the rough scratch of the rock under her hand, realizing that while she may be comfortable, Nathan had nothing to cushion him. She pushed herself up, suddenly guilty that she had been thinking only of herself.

"You shouldn't be lying on a cold rock."

Nathan offered her a lazy smile then slowly sat up and leaned forward to steal a quick kiss. "I was comfortable."

Catherine gave him a look that plainly said she didn't believe him, but she didn't say anything. Nathan took her hand and helped her to her feet, and she didn't protest when he kept it in his firm grip.

"Do you have plans for tomorrow night?"

Catherine closed her eyes and mentally pictured her calendar. A Friday night…no, she had absolutely no plans at all. Just like every night. But the question was whether or not she wanted Nathan to know that. She opened her eyes and saw him watching her, and knew that for better or worse, she wanted to spend more time with him. "No, no plans."

"Will you have dinner with me? I promise it won't be as primitive as today."

"Okay." She nodded her head in agreement and offered him a small smile. Part of her wanted to say that she enjoyed coming to this primitive place with him, but she wasn't ready to be that bold. It had been a big enough struggle to agree to dinner.

So she nodded again and let him lead her back through the woods, her mind already thinking ahead to the next night and wondering if she was ready, knowing she wasn't and worrying about how she would handle it.

Chapter Seven

Catherine placed her hands on her hips and surveyed the damage in her room. It looked as if her entire wardrobe had been hurled from her closet in a fit of desperation, which wasn't far from the truth. Mismatched clothes were strewn across the bed and over the polished hardwood floors, covering the glossy planks in every shade of the color spectrum. She blew a strand of hair out of her eye and faced the full-length mirror with a grimace. The disaster in the reflection was nearly as bad as the disaster surrounding her.

For two hours she had gone through her closet, trying on outfit after outfit, discarding all of them. Too professional. Too matronly. Too outdated. Just plain wrong. Even the simple black dress she now wore didn't look right. Too plain, too simple. She turned a bit in the mirror and frowned at the way the material clung to her. Probably too tight. Any other time the dress would have been more than suitable, but not tonight. Tonight she had been hoping for something a little more daring, something that would make her stand out without people pointing.

There was only one thing to do. She had to cancel the date. A flutter coiled in her stomach but she ignored it. She just wouldn't be able to go, and that was that.

Catherine was twisting herself around in an awkward attempt to undo the back zipper when there was a knock on her bedroom door. She glanced at her watch in panic then let out a breath of relief when she realized it was too early for Nathan to be there yet. The relief grew when Matty poked his head into her room.

"Hey, Mom, Uncle Bri is here. Wow! You look pretty cool."

Catherine smiled as he opened the door the rest of the way, her heart melting at how beautiful he made her feel. She wished it was just as easy to impress his adult counterparts.

"Thanks, Matty, but this isn't going to work. I think I should call Nathan and reschedule."

"What's this about rescheduling?" Brian's voice came from the hallway. "Are you going to chicken—whoa, Catherine!" He let loose an appreciative whistle and her face heated instantly. She ignored both her blush and his compliment.

"This isn't going to work," she repeated. If she was forced to admit the truth, though, she would have to say the dress was fine. She was the one who was a mess. "I can't do this."

"Sure you can," Brian said, coming up behind her and smiling. "You look fine. You have nothing to worry about."

"You're my friend, Brian. You're supposed to say that."

"When have I ever lied to you?"

Catherine met his eyes in the mirror then sighed. He was right. As usual. She just had a bad case of nerves, plain and simple. She frowned at herself and turned a little to each side, trying to see herself as others did. As Nathan did.

A little taller than average. Not too thin, not too curvy. Plain blond hair and plain brown eyes. There was absolutely nothing to make her stand out in a crowd, so why on earth would Nathan even be interested? It was a mercy date. It had to be.

"Oh, God, I can't do this." Catherine turned away and headed for the closet, intent on changing into more relaxing clothes and calling the whole thing off. She hadn't been out on a date in several years; she could certainly wait a few more.

"Catherine, you can. You can and you will." Brian led her to the middle of the room. "What else were you going to wear?"

"What else? Nothing. This was it!" Another wave of panic swept over her when Brian stood back and eyed her critically. He motioned for Matty to come closer and leaned down to whisper something in his ear. The two exchanged glances then laughed. Catherine took a step back, not liking their conspiracy one bit.

"What shoes were you going to wear?"

"Shoes?"

"Yes, shoes. Or were you planning on going barefoot?"

"No. I, uh..." Catherine shrugged and pointed to a pair of low-heeled black pumps. "Those."

Brian and Matty exchanged glances again, both of them shaking their heads. Brian walked to her closet and began rummaging around the bottom while Matty reached for her jewelry box. Catherine watched them, hands on her hips as annoyance began to replace anxiety. "What do you two think you're doing?"

"We're helping, Mom. Here." Matty wheeled over to her and held up a handful of jewelry. She looked down at his offering in confusion, wondering what was wrong with the pearl necklace she had on. She shook her head, ready to tell him no, but shrugged at the last minute and took the jewelry from his hand. What difference would it really make, anyway?

She unclasped the strand of pearls and replaced it with the long gold chain. The diamond heart pendant hung low in the scooped neckline of the dress, creating a softer look. She put on the simple hoop earrings and raised her eyebrows in Matty's direction, smiling at his look of approval.

"That's a lot better, Mom. You don't look so old anymore."

"I beg your pardon? Young man, what kind of thing—"

"I was just kidding!" Catherine let out a sigh, secretly glad for Matty's mischievousness. It took some of the edge off her worry. Until she saw the shoes Brian held out for her.

"Absolutely not!"

"Come on, Catherine. These are the perfect finishing touch." He held the shoes out for her and she backed away.

"I'll break my neck!" She eyed the four-inch heels with distaste.

"Oh, you will not. Here, try them on." He pushed her until she was sitting on the bed and forced the shoes into her hands. She frowned at them, recalling the feeling of wicked impulse that had seized her when she bought them several months earlier. She was able to walk on them, that she knew. But they were so unlike anything else she usually wore, she doubted if she would feel comfortable in them. Sleek black, with four-inch stiletto heels, the only way to describe them was *sinfully wicked.*

Why not? A tiny voice surfaced at the back of her mind, growing louder, daring her. Her brow furrowed as she continued to stare at the shoes, turning them over in her hands. Why not? This was supposed to be a date, a night of fun. Why shouldn't she be different? Why shouldn't she try something new?

The thought stayed with her, encouraging her, cheering her as she put on first one shoe then the other and stood up. Her ankles wobbled at the unaccustomed height then steadied, deciding at the last minute to support her weight. She said a silent prayer of thanks when she was able to walk across the room without falling. To show off, she did a little pivot.

"Much better."

"Yeah, Mom. Nathan's going to drool for sure."

Catherine stared at her son, slack-jawed with shock, but was stopped from saying anything when Brian tugged on his arm, not bothering to hide his smile. "Come on, Matty. Let's go out into the living room while your mom composes herself."

She watched the two of them leave before turning back to the mirror. She wasn't sure if she would ever be composed, but a few last-minute touches and she would be ready.

She hoped.

Nathan stared at the tidy rancher from the driver's seat of his car, telling himself that sitting there wasn't going to get the date started any sooner. He took a deep breath and glanced in the rearview mirror, running a hand through his hair before opening the door. He almost closed it when he remembered the flowers on the front seat, then hesitated, wondering if he should give them to her or just throw them away. The idea was so old-fashioned that he felt silly about it.

He muttered to himself and leaned in to grab the bouquet, grudgingly admitting that he had enjoyed buying them for Catherine. He thought she would appreciate the gesture. And hoped they would bring a smile to her face. *That* was the thought that had been with him when he picked them out.

It was that same thought that worried him as he rang the doorbell. Worried. Worried about the way his mind kept drifting to Catherine and what little time they had spent together. About why he couldn't stop thinking about her. About the time he wanted to spend with her in the future.

And about the way his palms were slick with sweat as he waited on the porch. He blew a breath between clenched teeth and ran his hand down his pants leg just as the door opened. The breath hitched in his throat and the sweat he had just wiped off instantly reappeared when he saw Catherine. He stood there awkwardly, unable to stop the idiotic grin on his face.

Her thick hair was pulled back into an exotic knot. A few wisps hung in loose curls around her ears, drawing his attention to the smooth column of her neck. His eyes drifted lower to the scoop neckline of her dress and rested on the pendant that hung just above the cleavage that peaked out, daring, teasing him. He swallowed and pulled his eyes away from that soft flesh, let them drift lower, taking in the way the black material clung to her, accenting her curves and tiny waist until it stopped above her knees. Nathan suddenly realized that he had never seen her legs before and he silently cursed Catherine for her conservatism. She had beautiful legs, long and well-defined, the sleek muscles set off by the amazing high heels she wore.

He felt an instant tightening in his groin and

shifted. The sight of those legs, the sight of Catherine, should *not* affect him that way. He cleared his throat and drew his eyes up to meet hers. The grin on his face grew wider.

"You're beautiful." He cursed the huskiness in his voice and tried to cover it by thrusting the flowers at her. She took the bouquet with a trembling hand, refusing to meet his eyes.

"Th-thank you." The simple words held so much uncertainty that Nathan nearly laughed, enjoying the honesty of her reactions. Catherine was so unaffected, so real, so refreshing a change from what he was used to, that he had trouble concealing his enjoyment at her every word and move.

The urge to kiss her at that moment was so overwhelming that he didn't bother to fight it, just took her hand in his and pulled her closer until his lips claimed hers. The heat between them was instant and consuming. Nathan swallowed a groan of disappointment when she pulled away. He looked at her in confusion then noticed that they had an audience.

"Hey, Nathan!" The excitement in Matty's voice and the smile on his face said there was no doubting the kid had witnessed the lip-lock he just gave Catherine. He straightened, suddenly embarrassed, and waved halfheartedly at Matty. He swallowed back another groan when he saw Brian Porter turn the corner of the hallway and stop behind Catherine.

"Doc." Nathan nodded his head in greeting, surprised to see his doctor at his date's house but knowing he shouldn't be. They were partners. They were obviously close friends, to the point that Matty referred to him as "Uncle Brian." So why the sudden flash of jealousy? Nathan pushed the unwelcome emotion to the back of his mind, refusing to acknowledge it.

"I, um, I'll put these in some water," Catherine said to no one in particular, blushing as she walked down the hallway. Nathan stood there, awkward, feeling like he was under close scrutiny. He nodded again, knew he looked like an idiot, and suddenly noticed that both Matty and Dr. Porter were staring at him with equally idiotic expressions on their own faces.

"So what do you think?" This came from Matthew. Nathan opened his mouth to respond then shut it again, realizing he had no idea what the kid was talking about.

"Think about what?"

"Catherine. She was a little nervous about tonight," Dr. Porter explained. Nathan shifted his weight from one foot to the other, secretly glad he wasn't the only one who had been—still was—nervous. "She wasn't sure if she looked all right."

Nathan wasn't sure how to respond to that, so he kept quiet. Catherine was beautiful, looked perfect, but he didn't think admitting that would be a healthy move. They looked like a pair with something up their sleeves.

"I'm spending the night at Uncle Brian's tonight."

"Matthew!"

"Excuse me?"

Nathan and Dr. Porter both stared at Matty, then

looked at each other with mixed expressions, sizing each other up.

"I think Matty means that there's no reason for you to hurry through your date since there won't be a babysitter waiting here. But you will be home early in the morning, isn't that right, Matthew?"

"But, Uncle Bri, you said we were—"

"Matthew..." The warning in the doctor's voice was clear, even if it did go over Matty's head. He caught Dr. Porter's eye and nodded, letting him know that he heard the message and understood. He wasn't happy knowing that his every move would be monitored, but that wasn't a problem he wanted to deal with at the moment. He wasn't even sure if it *was* a problem at all.

Silence descended as they continued to watch each other, Nathan obviously the most uncomfortable. He shifted his weight again and was about to make a feeble attempt at small talk when Catherine finally reappeared in the hallway. She looked at Nathan, a nervous smile on her face.

"I guess we can leave now."

"Sure." Nathan inwardly grimaced at how stupid he sounded. He watched as Catherine bent down to kiss Matty goodbye and offer a few last-minute instructions and motherly warnings. She turned and gave more last-minute advice to Brian, who waved her off with a small laugh.

"Catherine, don't worry. We'll be fine. Now go." Brian ushered them to the door then leaned over and gave Catherine a friendly peck on the cheek. Another irrational flash of jealousy shot through Nathan at the innocent gesture. He bit back the unwelcome sensation, not liking the feeling.

That didn't stop him from reaching out and taking Catherine's hand in his, as much a show of possession as a desire to just touch her, be near her. Warmth tingled the ends of his fingers when her hand clasped his in return. He cursed silently when they reached the car and he had to release his hold on her to open the passenger door.

His eyes lingered on her as she looked up and smiled at him. They drifted down to her legs as she lowered herself in the passenger seat and modestly tucked the hem of her dress securely around her thighs, allowing him just the briefest glance of soft flesh encased in sheer black silk. He swallowed against the instant tightening in his groin and shut her door, wondering how he was ever going to make it through the night.

The engine purred quietly as he backed the car out of the driveway and through the residential streets of Catherine's suburban neighborhood. The silence was broken by the soft background music coming from the stereo. Nathan swallowed, wishing his hands weren't so sweaty against the steering wheel, wishing for something intelligent to say.

"Do you like Italian? I thought we could eat dinner in Little Italy. If that's okay."

"Hmm? Oh, yes. That's fine."

"We could go somewhere else if you want."

"No, that's fine. I haven't been there in a while."

Nathan nodded for lack of anything better to do and returned his attention to the traffic that was growing heavier as they approached the city line. His eyes kept darting over to Catherine. He took in the way she held herself so erect, so formal. He realized she was more than just nervous and knew that the hands she kept folded in her lap would be ice-cold if he reached over and took one in his. The idea suddenly seemed like a good one and he did just that, ignoring her little leap of surprise. Just as he thought, her hand was like ice.

"Are you cold? Do you want me to turn up the heat?"

"No. I'm just…it's fine." Catherine ducked her head then turned her attention out the window, refusing to meet his eyes as he caressed the back of her hand with his thumb.

"Well, you know what they say. Cold hands, warm heart."

Catherine's head whipped around and she stared at him with an expression just this side of horrified. He bit back a sigh and released her hand to downshift, hoping she wouldn't take her hand back, not surprised when she did exactly that.

"That was supposed to be a joke, you know."

"I—I know." Again she focused her attention out the window, refusing to look at him as they pulled off the expressway. They drove the few short blocks to Little Italy in silence, Nathan at a complete loss for something to say. He imagined he heard a soft sigh of relief when he parked the car and turned off the engine, realized it probably wasn't his imagination when Catherine's hand darted for the door handle in her hurry to escape. He reached over and hit the electric lock, hoping it would at least make her hesitate.

"Catherine, do I really make you that nervous, or do you just really not like me?" Nathan wasn't sure what made her stop and whip her head around in surprise—his question or the flatness in his voice. Her dark eyes widened then narrowed in a frown and she shook her head, looking everywhere but at him. It was a habit he was quickly losing patience with.

He draped his arm across the back of her seat and leaned forward, deliberately crowding her, knowing the only way she could get away was out the door. "Well?"

She finally turned toward him, her face only inches from his. Her tongue darted out and licked her lips. "I'm just…you make me nervous."

"Good. That makes two of us." Nathan saw her eyes widen in surprise but wasn't sure if it was because of his admission or because she realized he was about to kiss her just seconds before he claimed her lips. She tensed under his touch then slowly relaxed, opening her mouth under his gentle insistence. Her tongue darted out and hesitantly met his, slowly at first then more daring as her hand came up and rested on his chest.

Nathan cupped her face in his hands and deepened the kiss, breaking away to drag his mouth along her jaw and down her throat, tasting the sweetness of her skin on his tongue, hearing her ragged breathing and knowing it echoed his own. He pulled his mouth back to hers, wanting to go lower but not daring to, knowing he wouldn't want to stop, already didn't want to stop.

His hand drifted to the middle of her back and pulled her even closer, wanting to feel every inch of her body against his. He shifted without breaking the kiss and dragged his free hand across her knee, feeling the silk of her nylons as he caressed her leg, traveling higher until his fingers edged under the hem of her dress, higher until the silk gave way to lace, which gave way to hot flesh under his hand. His mind grappled with the realization his touch already knew and he froze, afraid he would lose control in more ways than just the physical.

"Oh, God." The ragged moan escaped him on a hungry sigh as he dragged his hand from her leg, silently cursing the small confines of the sports car as he tried to get closer without hurting either of them. He felt an awkward weight on his chest, wondered if he was going to keel over right there before he realized Catherine was pushing at him with her hand. He pulled away and looked down at her, saw the passion and confusion in her eyes and knew it mirrored his own expression.

A charged silence surrounded them, pushing in and around, pulsating. Nathan reached out and traced her jawline with one trembling finger, wanting to say something but afraid of breaking the spell, afraid of saying the wrong thing. Catherine finally straightened in the seat, obviously uncomfortable. She took a deep breath and let it out on a shaky sigh.

"I knew you were dangerous." Her voice was husky, still laced with the passion he felt in her mere seconds ago. The words were so unexpected, so honest, that he laughed. She stared at him then smiled in turn, and Nathan was surprised at the sudden feeling of connection between them. He could tell she felt it, too, by the slight widening of her eyes and the look of confusion that was there and gone in the space of a heartbeat.

"I'm worse when I don't eat. What do you say we go stuff ourselves on some delicious food?" He offered her a wink and opened his car door then sprinted around to open hers. He was glad she finally felt comfortable enough to keep her hand on his arm as he led the way down the sidewalk to the restaurant.

Warm air and warmer spices wrapped around them in a sensory hug as Nathan opened the door. A middle-aged maître d' welcomed them with a hearty greeting, grabbed two menus from behind his podium and led them to a corner table slightly set apart from the crowd. He held Catherine's chair for her as she sat, told them that their waitress would be with them shortly, then left the two with wishes for a happy evening. Catherine focused her attention on the leather-bound menu in her hand, too aware of Nathan's gaze and the emotions he had unleashed inside her.

"Everything looks wonderful."

"I hope so. I've never been here, but a friend recommended it. He guaranteed great food and a low-key atmosphere."

Catherine looked up at the sarcasm in Nathan's voice but didn't have a chance to question it until after he placed their wine order. She blushed at the grin he flashed her when he caught her staring. A little jolt went through her when he reached across the table and took her hand in his.

"Still nervous?"

Catherine shrugged, ignoring the butterflies that took flight in her stomach at the sound of his voice, at the touch of his thumb as it caressed her hand. "Maybe. A little. Yes."

"Why?"

"I don't know." Catherine looked away, unable to meet his gaze as he studied her. She searched for a way to change the subject and latched on to his earlier comment. "What did you mean by low-key atmosphere?"

"People who come here are supposed to be more interested in the food than in the patrons."

"I don't understand."

Nathan sighed and leaned closer like he was ready to tell some deep, dark secret. Catherine discovered she was holding her breath, waiting to see what the gleam in his eye meant.

"It means that on the off-chance somebody sees me and actually knows who the hell I am, they'll have enough common courtesy to leave us alone while we're eating."

"People really do that?"

"Do what? Recognize me or come up to me?" The dry sarcasm in his voice hit Catherine and she bit her lip as embarrassment washed over her. She floundered for a way to apologize gracefully before she realized he was joking. He released her hand and took a sip of the water, then winked at her.

"Baltimore's not a huge hockey town but there are some die-hard fans who would follow the players around no matter where they went. It'll get worse the closer we get to the finals. All the nuts come out of the woodwork then, even if they don't know a puck from a slab of coal."

Catherine nodded, pretending she understood when she didn't. She took a sip of her own water then looked up at a sudden movement behind Nathan. A young girl in her early twenties stared at them, her blue eyes narrowed. Catherine leaned forward. "I don't think you're going to be low-key tonight. Some girl is coming over here."

"What?" Nathan looked then cursed under his breath.

Catherine sat up straighter, uncomfortable at the sudden tension that radiated from Nathan. There was no time to ask what was wrong as the girl stopped at their table and faced Nathan with one fist planted solidly on her arched hip.

"Well if it isn't Nathan Conners. Imagine seeing you here."

Nathan seemed to be fighting the urge to squirm and bolt. He pursed his lips, muttering a single word between clenched teeth.

"Amber."

Chapter Eight

Amber.

The name swirled through Catherine's mind. A sister. A girlfriend. An ex-girlfriend. A wife. The last thought slammed into Catherine and she realized how little she really knew about Nathan. Surely he wasn't married; he couldn't be. Could he?

She mentally shook her head. Of course not. Brian would have told her. If he knew. But what if he didn't know?

Catherine blinked, vaguely aware of hearing her name being called, vaguely aware of feeling two sets of eyes staring at her. She blinked again, pushing all thoughts to the back of her mind and forcing her attention to the man in front of her.

Nathan's attention was focused on her, his concern

clear in the depths of his eyes. His hand closed around hers and she felt the heat of his touch warming her. She offered him a weak smile.

"Sorry. I didn't hear what you were saying."

Nathan gave her a quizzical look that said he obviously didn't believe her then slowly released her hand and sat back a little in his chair. She sensed the tension in him as he rolled his shoulders and pointedly ignored the girl. Catherine was aware of their visitor staring, first at her, then at Nathan. The girl faced her straight on, her clear blue eyes narrowed slightly as she openly studied Catherine, then thrust her hand out in introduction.

"Nathan obviously won't introduce us, so I may as well. I'm Amber. Amber Johnson. Or AJ. And you are?"

Catherine stared up at her, caught off guard by the girl's forthright manner. She offered her own hand in return. "Cath—"

"Hey, AJ, why don't you go bug someone else?" Nathan's flat voice cut her off and she stared at him, wondering why his attitude seemed to have hardened. Nathan merely shrugged.

"AJ likes to think of herself as a reporter, only the sleaze rag she works for will never be called a paper. Which makes her nothing more than a gossip hound."

The girl shrugged nonchalantly and brushed a loose strand of black hair from her eyes. "Hey, it pays the bills."

Catherine watched Amber's movements closely, saw a flash of something that may have been hurt or anger in her eyes and realized that the show of carelessness was merely an act. Her heart softened toward the young woman as memories of trying to fit in and failing came back to her. She again offered her hand, not surprised to find that Amber's was cold and trembling.

"I'm Catherine Wilson. Nice to meet you."

"Same here." The two women pointedly ignored Nathan's groan. Amber released her hand, obviously choosing to pretend Nathan wasn't sitting there. "Nathan's just upset because we ran a piece that said this year might be his last on the ice."

Catherine sat up a little straighter and watched for Nathan's reaction. He slowly fingered the handle of a knife, rolling it over and over on the linen tablecloth. Her breath caught in her throat when he met her gaze. He was making a point of ignoring them, but Amber's comment clearly upset him.

"I think that may have been a bit premature, don't you?" Her voice was politely cool and devoid of any personal opinion.

"Oh, I didn't say I agreed with it. I didn't even write it. But ever since then, I've been blackballed." Amber pointedly stared at Nathan. "Now I can't get anyone on the team to even look at me, let alone talk to me."

"You mean you can't get Alec to talk to you."

"No, I can't get *anyone* to talk to me."

"What are you even doing here, anyway?" Nathan finally asked, fixing Amber with a deadly stare.

"I heard Alec sometimes came here. I thought if I

caught him off guard he'd give me something besides a headache."

"Alec. It figures." Nathan shook his head, a ghost of a smile playing around the edges of his mouth. "Well, AJ, you can leave now. I can guarantee that Alec will not be here tonight."

"I kinda figured that one out already." Amber made a face at Nathan that had Catherine biting back a grin. The young woman turned to her and smiled brightly. "It was nice meeting you, Catherine Wilson."

"She seemed nice enough," Catherine said when they were alone again. Nathan arched one disbelieving brow at her.

"You'll probably disagree later this week when you see something about you in that sleaze rag she writes for." Nathan took a sip of his drink and shook his head. "I'm going to kill Alec for this one."

"Alec who? And why?" Catherine asked. Nathan's laughter made her stop short and she realized suddenly that he had been talking about one of his teammates. "Sorry. Matty is the one who's up on all the players, not me. I'm lucky if I can keep track of the puck during the game."

"Oh, so you have actually watched a game. And here I thought you had to be dragged every time." Nathan took another sip and waved off her attempt at another apology. "In answer to your earlier question, Alec is Alec Kolchak. Our goalie. Soon-to-be dead goalie. He's the one who recommended this place to me."

"So you think he did that deliberately?"

"Oh, absolutely. There's no doubt in my mind that

he knew AJ would be here. Guess it was my turn to be the sacrificial lamb."

"I don't understand."

Nathan paused long enough to place their orders with the waiter then turned back to Catherine. "It's a game Alec likes to play. Whenever AJ pushes him too far, he throws one of us at her as interference, hoping she'll latch on to something and lose her interest in him. So far it hasn't worked."

"Oh." Catherine watched him through her lowered eyes and wondered what he wasn't telling her. His attention was focused again on the silverware, and she could sense his discomfort. There was still so much about him that she didn't know, and she sensed that parts of him went deeper than anyone would expect. That she wanted to discover those deeper parts frightened her.

"I wanted to thank you, too."

"For what?" Catherine looked up, a shiver creeping over her skin at the intensity of his gaze.

"For saying what you did about this year being my last." Nathan twirled the fork between his hands. "I know you think I shouldn't be playing."

"Oh. I…uh…"

"Catherine, it's okay. Don't worry about it." He took a deep breath and offered her a small smile. "There are times I wonder myself if I should still be playing."

"Nathan." Catherine stopped, knowing that he was opening a piece of himself up for her and not sure how to respond. She reached across the table and placed her hand on top of his. "Brian wouldn't have released you if you weren't ready."

He squeezed her hand then lifted it to his mouth, quickly kissing the tips of her fingers as he smiled at her. "Time will tell, I suppose." He let go of her hand as the waiter brought their food and placed it on the table. Catherine put her hand back in her lap and wondered if she had taken the easy way out by keeping her opinions to herself.

"Is there someplace you'd like to go?" Nathan's voice was a whisper in the quiet of the car. Catherine smiled and shook her head, surprised at how willing she was to let him take the lead. This was new for her, letting someone else make the decisions.

"No place special. Wherever you feel like going, I guess." Her face grew warm at the implication of her suggestion; a shiver of excitement tingled her nerve endings at the heated look Nathan gave her. He shifted in the driver's seat until he was only inches away from her. She leaned forward, pulled to him by some invisible force, and sighed when his lips rested ever so briefly against hers before disappearing. She swallowed her groan of disappointment, glad that the darkness of the car's interior hid the blush that flamed across her cheeks.

"Hmm." She heard Nathan's own sigh and wondered if he felt the same pull that seemed to grow stronger every time they were in each other's company. "Do you like music? Maybe dancing? The guys were supposed to meet somewhere not far from here later tonight. They're probably there by now. Would you mind going?"

"No, that sounds like it would be fun," Catherine said. Going to a public place would probably be the safest thing for her right now. At least there she wouldn't be able to give in to the growing temptation of throwing herself at Nathan.

He maneuvered the sports car through the streets of the city, her hand clasped lightly in his. Soft music surrounded them, lulling Catherine into a dangerous mood of comfort and desire. She watched Nathan from the corner of her eye, enjoying the chance to study him, wondering why she had tried to fight the attraction between them in the first place.

He was more than just attractive. He had a sort of boyish charm, a carefree attitude on the surface that hid the deeper parts he was slowly letting her see. The fact that he guarded them so carefully touched her, made her think of him as vulnerable though there was nothing defenseless about him. And he fit in almost anywhere, adapting to whatever was around him.

Tonight he wore an expensive suit that was expertly tailored to fit his broad shoulders, trim waist and muscular legs. On anyone else the look would have been too stiff, too forced, but not on Nathan. With hair that hung over the back of his collar, a nose that was just this side of perfect and the boyish chip in his tooth, he looked real. Approachable. The look fit him perfectly, but so did the careless manner in which he dressed in frayed jeans and a worn-out shirt.

He impressed her as down-to-earth, a picture

enhanced by her memories of seeing him with Matty. She took a deep breath and looked out the window, hoping that she wasn't making a mistake by becoming involved in a relationship with her son's hero. If they *were* in a relationship. She wasn't sure about their status with each other, if there even was a status. Which was her fault for always keeping *her* distance. From everything.

She let out another sigh and wondered when she had become so afraid to let other people in. When she had shut herself off from the world and become so afraid of living life.

"Penny for your thoughts."

"Hmm?" Catherine faced Nathan, surprised to see they were now parked in a paved lot at the intersection of two dimly lit streets. She wondered how long she had been lost in thought.

"There's a small nightclub a few doors down from here," Nathan said in response to her unasked question. "So, what were you thinking?"

"Oh." Catherine shook her head, embarrassed by the turn of her own thoughts. "Just wondering when life seemed to get away from me. There are times when I feel like I've been caught in some kind of time warp and…and why am I telling you this?"

"Maybe because you're beginning to like me?" Nathan's smile lessened some of the insecurity she heard in the question, but she didn't have a chance to answer him before he kissed her. She leaned into him and curled her hand behind his neck. A soft moan escaped her when he pulled away and rested his forehead against hers. A small smile played at the corners of his mouth as he stared into her eyes. "I'll take that to mean yes."

Catherine answered with a smile of her own, surprised that a part of her wanted to be honest with him, wanted to open up to him. He kissed her again, quickly this time, then opened his door and got out before walking around to open hers. It seemed the most natural thing for the two of them to walk hand in hand down the street. A whisper of warning played in the back of Catherine's mind, cautioning against letting down all her barriers too quickly. She pushed the traitorous thought away as Nathan opened the door to a dubious-looking establishment.

The inside wasn't much better than the outside. The club was nothing more than the first floor of a renovated row home, the walls stripped down to dark wood and old brick. A scarred bar ran down the far wall, the stools sparsely filled with customers. The remainder of the patrons, not more than a handful, were in the back of the club on a makeshift dance floor, swaying to the heavy blues music being played by a band pushed back into the far corner.

Nathan squeezed Catherine's hand and leaned down to whisper in her ear. She shook her head to let him know she didn't hear him and leaned closer.

"Is this okay?" A shiver raced down her back as Nathan's words came to her on a hot breath in her ear. She smiled and nodded, letting him lead the way to a small group at the end of the bar. The music stopped as they approached and Nathan made hasty introductions.

She vaguely nodded at each, suddenly uncomfortable when she realized she was the only date present.

"Has Alec been here?" Nathan asked one of them.

"Yeah. He's back in the courtyard."

Nathan nodded then leaned over to Catherine. "I'll be right back. I have some business to take care of with him."

She watched him walk away, suppressing the urge to beg him not to leave her alone. The urge grew when she turned around and noticed five pairs of eyes glued to her. Their scrutiny was oppressive, and Catherine wondered why the band had chosen now of all times to take a break. One of the men suddenly stood and motioned to his vacant stool.

"Here, you sit now." The deep voice was so thick with a Slavic accent that Catherine almost didn't understand him.

"Um..." Her voice refused to work so she hesitantly took the offered stool, conscious of the way her hemline drifted up as she sat. She pulled at the material, trying to cover more of her leg, and noticed several of the players watching her. She folded her hands in her lap and offered them a weak smile.

The scrutiny lasted for several more seconds, then quickly disappeared as the players circled around her, eager to make conversation, all talking at once. She looked from face to face, only catching a word here or there, not knowing what to make of it. Suddenly it was too much for her and she laughed, a clear, infectious laugh that surprised her.

"I think she finds us amusing."

"Not us, Ian. You. I told you women found you funny."

Catherine covered her mouth with her hand then turned and saw Nathan standing a few feet from her, a bright smile on his face as he watched her. Catherine's laughter caught in her throat when she saw the naked desire burning in Nathan's eyes.

The music started again, drowning out everyone around her as Nathan closed the distance between them. He reached out and curled his hand around hers, then gently pulled her from the stool, holding her closer than necessary.

"Let's dance." His voice was deep and husky, echoing the sultry notes of the song that vibrated around them. Catherine nodded as he led the way to the dance floor, where she stepped into his arms with no hesitation.

They stood outside her front door, the night-light casting a soft glow around them. Nathan shifted his weight, suddenly uncomfortable. He cleared his throat, about to speak when Catherine took the opportunity away from him.

"I had fun tonight." The words came out in a soft whisper, hesitant, as if the admission startled her.

"Me, too." He stepped closer. "I guess I'd better let you get inside before you freeze. It's gotten a little cold out."

"Yeah, it has."

Nathan noticed the way she ducked her head and the soft blush that blossomed across her cheeks. He reached out and clasped her chin with one hand, tilted her head up and leaned closer until his lips lightly brushed across hers. Heat instantly rushed through him, urging him to deepen the kiss, to give in to the desire that tore through him like a ragged wound. He groaned and pulled away, afraid of losing control.

Catherine pulled at her lower lip with her teeth before offering him a small smile. He knew the safest thing he could do right now was leave, just mutter "good night" and walk away. He opened his mouth to utter the words but couldn't force them past his lips. Instead, they just stood there, watching each other.

"I didn't think this would be so awkward," Catherine said with a small laugh, finally breaking the ice.

"I feel like a sixteen-year-old on his first date," Nathan admitted. He sighed and stepped back. "I should leave now."

"Um...would you like to come inside? For coffee, I mean?"

The invitation, whispered with so much hesitation, struck a nerve inside Nathan and unleashed ideas he didn't want to admit having. Watching Catherine standing there, so uncertain, so vulnerable, made him want to do nothing more than wrap his arms around her and protect her, keep her safe. The thought was like a punch in the gut, robbing him of breath and reason so that the only thing he could do was nod in response. A part of him wondered why he was agreeing. It was a dangerous move.

He followed her into the house, blinking against the

sudden brightness as she turned on the hall light. She offered him another small smile before leading the way into the living room.

"Um, you can just make yourself comfortable. If you want." She indicated a large sofa covered in a maroon-and-white country check. "I'll go put on some coffee."

Nathan watched her leave, again noticing how uncomfortable, how uncertain she seemed. He sat down on the sofa, leaning forward with his elbows braced on his knees and his hands clasped in front of him as he looked around the living room.

It was vastly different from his own place, which was decorated in a combination of modern abandonment, a term he used to describe the major lack of decoration in the condo. This place, or what he could see of it, was carefully decorated with warm woods and cheery colors, a combination of country accents meant to welcome. He noticed the odd spacing between some of the furniture and realized that while the house was decorated to welcome, it was also designed for a young boy in a wheelchair.

Instead of worrying him or scaring him, the thought unleashed another urge to protect. They had been through so much, Catherine and Matty, that they deserved to be taken care of, to have somebody else to lean on.

Nathan swallowed against the sudden anxiety balled in his gut and wondered if any part of his mind possessed the ability to reason. He decided it didn't because he was still sitting there when Catherine came back in.

She had removed her shoes and was walking barefoot, now wearing only nylons. No, Nathan corrected, she was wearing stockings. Which were a lot different than nylons. He remembered the feel of soft flesh against his hand and shifted on the sofa, clenching his fists more tightly. If he had any sense at all he would get up and leave while he could, before it was too late.

"The coffee should be ready soon." Catherine stood a few feet away, her hands clasped in front of her. She forced a small smile then started walking by him to the matching love seat.

"Oh, hell," Nathan muttered, knowing it was too late, that he had long ago lost all sense. He grabbed her hand as she sidled by him and stood up; her body stopped against his, all soft curves and sweet flesh. Catherine's breath left her on a surprised whisper as she looked up at him, her dark eyes wide as they searched his face. He saw the apprehension in them, and below that, a reflection of his own desire. His breath quickened as they stood there, their bodies touching.

"I—"

Nathan placed a finger against her lips, cutting off whatever she had been about to say. He lowered his finger to her jaw, caressed the delicate planes of her face before running his hand behind her head and pulling her even closer. Nathan's body tightened in response and still he made no move to kiss her, afraid he wouldn't be able to stop once he started. Afraid of how much control he lost around this one woman.

Catherine seemed to sense his hesitation and, looked baffled by it. The air around them thickened with desire as they watched each other. And still Nathan was afraid to do anything, afraid to break the spell, afraid of losing all control.

In the end it was Catherine who made the first move. She placed the flat of one palm against his chest and leaned up, briefly meeting his lips with a soft touch before pulling away. The quick contact shattered Nathan's hesitation. He pulled her tighter against him, lowered his head and claimed her mouth with a searing possession that left no doubt about how he felt.

A groan rumbled in the back of his throat as Catherine's arms slipped inside his jacket and wrapped around him. Her lips molded under his, her mouth opening under his gentle insistence. His tongue darted in, swept the heat of her mouth, then joined with hers in a wild frenzy. He dug one hand into her hair, gently tugging until it fell free from its knot and cascaded over his arm in a tumble of waves. His other hand dipped lower, feeling each curve of her body until coming to rest on the swell of her bottom. She sighed into his mouth as he pulled her even closer, tilting her hips into his until he was sure she knew the extent of his desire.

Nathan broke the kiss, felt a rush of hunger sear his veins at Catherine's groan when he dragged his lips along her jaw to her ear, then down her neck. He paused, waiting for some sign from Catherine. Things were going too fast but he was helpless to slow them down. The breath tore from him in a ragged rush when she pulled her trembling hands from his jacket and rested them on his shoulders, her fingers curling in his hair.

The soft touch of her fingers against his skin caused his control to waver then disappear, and he lowered his head, used his mouth and tongue to tease the soft flesh that peeked from the low neckline of her dress. Her body went limp under his touch and he braced her against his arm and turned, dropping onto the sofa so she was sprawled across his lap.

He lifted his head at the soft sound of surprise that escaped her, met her eyes and felt a hitch in his own breathing at the glazed passion in their dark depths. Time slowed, nearly stopped, as they stared at each other. Nathan lowered his head and again claimed her lips with his own, softer this time, slower, enjoying the way she molded herself against him. With his free hand he removed his jacket and tossed it to the floor.

He bit back a groan when Catherine pulled away and stared up at him, her cheeks flushed and her lips swollen from his touch. She watched him with those deep eyes, stripping away his outside layers until all that was left was a vulnerable core. Nathan tried not to squirm under her gaze and felt his heart slam into his chest when she offered him a shy smile and whispered two words that destroyed all control and hesitation.

"Not here."

Chapter Nine

Not here.

Catherine heard the words leave her mouth in a husky whisper but couldn't believe she actually said them. Never before had she said or done anything so forward, so blatant. Nathan's heart leaped under her palm. He lowered his mouth to hers in a hungry kiss that stole her breath as heat rushed through her body at his touch, spreading to dormant nerves.

She wrapped her arms around his neck and leaned into him, letting him know she didn't want him to stop. The breath left her again when she realized she was being lifted, that Nathan now stood with his arms wrapped securely around her. She pulled her mouth from his and felt a strange tingling in the pit of her stomach at the heated look he gave her. Knowing what he wanted, knowing she was about to cross her own self-imposed boundary, she motioned to the open doors along the hallway.

A blush heated her face when Nathan's gaze remained intent on hers, mesmerizing. She would have looked away, even tried to, but was stopped by the shake of his head and his whispered, "No." So she continued to stare into his eyes, felt the play of hard muscles and heated flesh against her body as he carried her down the hall and into her room.

There was very little light, just the reflection from the living room lamp coming down the hallway, but Nathan had no problem finding the bed, seemed to find it instinctively as he carried her to the middle of the room. Catherine waited for him to lower her to the bed, wondered briefly what would happen next and felt the first twinge of uneasiness. Her tongue darted out and licked her lips as she pulled her gaze away, unable to read the emotions in his amber eyes.

"Catherine, look at me."

She was helpless to ignore his whisper, touched by the thick huskiness of his voice, and slowly she looked up at him, felt herself drawn into his stare.

"Do you know how much I want you?" Nathan uttered the words against her lips on a warm breath that mingled with hers. Catherine's eyes widened, surprised at the intensity in his voice, at the heat in his eyes. And something else, something she was sure she wasn't meant to see. Vulnerability. Her breath caught in her throat as the last of her hesitation melted away and she reached up, suddenly hungry for more of Nathan's touch.

Catherine stilled, feeling the heat of Nathan's arms still wrapped around her. The air around them sizzled, giving her courage. She tugged his shirt free from the waistband of his trousers then reached up, gently undid the first button of Nathan's shirt, then the second and third until all the buttons were free. Biting her lower lip, she peered up at him, suddenly shy. The naked desire in his eyes urged her on and she gently, slowly, pushed the shirt from his shoulders and slid it down his arms, where it stopped at his wrists.

Her breath caught at the sight of his bare chest, muscular and toned with a sprinkling of hair across the center. She lowered her head and placed a gentle kiss over his heart, felt power surge through her veins at his swift intake of breath and the quivering of his muscles under her touch. Her hands roamed across his chest, around to his back, caressing, hungry for the feel of rigid muscles and hot flesh beneath her touch. Greed took over, forcing an urgency to her touch as her right hand drifted over his stomach, skimming lower until her fingers tugged on the waistband of his trousers, shyly ventured inside before darting back out.

"Oh." The word were a harsh rasp against her skin, muttered a second before Nathan pulled her tight against him and crushed his mouth against hers, demanding that she open for him, giving and taking with the same intensity. Cool air drifted across her back, followed by the burning touch of his hands as he released the zipper of her dress. She pulled her arms from the sleeves as he pushed the material down, shivered when the dress pooled around her hips.

There was a second of embarrassment as Nathan pulled away and looked at her, a second when she wanted to hide herself from his gaze. The embarrassment disappeared, replaced by a fluid warmth that radiated outward, the heat intensified under his stare. He leaned forward, dragged his lips from the corner of her mouth to her ear and down, bringing to life sensitive nerves, touching them, teasing them with his mouth and tongue. Catherine's eyes drifted shut as her head fell back, offering more of herself, an offer Nathan eagerly accepted.

Her body came more alive with each touch, each kiss and caress that he lavished on her. Her senses swayed and tottered under his onslaught, her breathing hitched as he released the clasp on the lacy bra she wore. A cry escaped her when his mouth closed over one hard nipple and she reached out, tightened her hold on his arms to keep from collapsing when he suckled first one breast then the other.

The sensation came over her all at once, the certainty that she was no longer in control, and she ruthlessly pushed the feeling away. She didn't want control, not when Nathan touched her like that. There was only greed and hunger, a need to feel all of him, a need to give herself up to his physical onslaught.

Catherine pulled back, felt his hot breath against her moist skin as he moaned in frustration and looked up at her. She licked her lips, briefly wondered what would happen later and decided she didn't care as she brought her mouth to his and inched forward, pressing closer until her body was crushed against his, bare skin to bare skin. A ribbon of sensation whipped through her and she leaned back, pulling Nathan with her as she toppled to the soft mattress.

A groan of desire floated to her ears but she wasn't sure if it came from her or from Nathan. He broke the kiss and pulled back only an inch, balancing himself across her as he tried to free his wrists from the shirt.

"Damn," Nathan muttered between clenched teeth and Catherine's mouth curled into a small smile at his frustration. She reached over, intending to unbutton the cuffs for him, then pulled back when he pushed himself to a kneeling position. "Oh, screw it."

There were two small popping noises, followed by a soft *ping* as the buttons flew from the cuffs and landed on the floor, quickly followed by the shirt. Catherine fought back the nervous giggle trying to break free. Nathan looked at her, one eyebrow raised as she pointed to the white fluff on the floor.

"Your shirt..."

"Oh, Catherine." He lowered himself beside her, propped his weight on one elbow as he watched her. "I don't care about the damn shirt."

The nervous giggle that threatened earlier disappeared under his heated gaze, replaced by hot awareness as he leaned over her and claimed her lips. Catherine melted under his touch, reached out to pull him closer and swallowed her frustration when he resisted then pulled away. The frustration disappeared as he ran his hand along her body and wrapped his fingers around the elastic of the lacy thong she had dared to wear. He shifted to his knees and pulled, dragging both the thong and her dress down past her ankles. He carelessly tossed them so they joined his shirt on the floor, then settled himself more comfortably at her feet, watching her with those intense eyes, making no move to hide his desire from her.

Catherine swallowed, waiting, then tried to sit up and remove the stockings. Two large hands clasped around hers, rough with calluses but gentle in their touch.

"Don't."

She blinked against the raw need she heard in his voice, looked up and felt something inside her tilt dangerously as their eyes locked. Catherine swallowed again and rose to her knees even as Nathan refused to free her hands. She leaned closer and pulled them from his grasp, lifted her mouth to his as her hands slid down his front and undid his belt. A murmur passed from his mouth to hers and she pressed herself closer, willing her hands to stop their trembling as she fumbled with the button and zipper of his trousers. Nathan broke their kiss and once again his hands closed over hers, stopping them but not pulling them away.

"Are you sure you want to do this?"

Catherine met his steady gaze and took comfort in the vulnerability she saw in his eyes, knowing it mirrored her own. She took a deep breath and nodded, not sure of the consequences that would come tomorrow, only knowing that she wanted this, wanted all he offered her at this moment, wanted it now.

Her nod unleashed whatever Nathan had been holding back. The desire in his eyes flashed and grew, engulfed her as he guided her hands in undoing his trousers and pushing them past his hips. Catherine felt the thick smoothness of his erection against the flat of her stomach, felt an answering wet heat between her legs. Nathan crushed his mouth to hers, taking and giving, feeding her own desire.

She lowered her hand, felt him throb under her touch as she held him, caressing and stroking until Nathan groaned and grabbed her hand, dragging it upward until it rested in the center of his chest. Her fingers brushed against his skin, felt the crisp hair under her touch as he gently lowered her to the bed and followed her down before kicking his pants to the growing pile on the floor.

He pulled her to him, tighter until they were flesh to flesh. Catherine leaned up and touched her mouth to his then ran kisses along his jaw and down his neck, eager for his touch, wanting him, wanting to touch him the way he had touched her. She pushed against him, rolling him to his back as she sprawled across him. She wanted him to feel the same need that coursed through her. She touched her mouth to his chest, dragged her mouth lower, across the hard flatness of his stomach and lower still until reaching the object of her search.

Nathan tensed under her touch and groaned as she closed her mouth over him. His hands played in her hair then suddenly tightened around her arms, pulling her back up then under him as he rolled over, trapping her with his weight. He stared at her, an unreadable expression in his eyes. Catherine licked her lips nervously then sighed when he kissed her, his hand running down the length of her body then back up, pausing at the juncture of her thighs.

A ribbon of pleasure curled through her and she cried out when Nathan eased a long finger into her. She felt him smile against her mouth as he continued to tease her with his finger, slowly until the pleasure grew and spiraled outward, then faster until Catherine's hips tilted under his touch, searching for more.

"Nathan..." She whispered his name, not sure why, couldn't think anymore when he removed his hand only to replace the touch with his mouth. Catherine arched her back under the intimate touch, surprised at the escalating sensation, stunned by the intensity. She took a deep breath, held it then blew it out in a long gasp; everything inside her tightened, searching but unwilling to let go just yet. "Nathan..."

"Shh." His whisper was a hot breath against the inside of her thigh, nearly as exciting as the feel of his mouth and tongue on her, inside her. Catherine gasped for breath, moaned when he pulled away, cried out in frustration when he leaned over the bed and shifted through the pile of clothes. The rational part of her realized he was pulling out a foil packet, was sheathing himself with the condom even as she fought the impatience of losing his touch.

Her impatience disappeared as Nathan repositioned himself between her legs and again lowered his mouth to her. The need built quickly, coiled tightly deep inside then shattered in a waterfall of colorful sensation. She arched under him, called his name and suddenly he was on top of her, covering her with his warm weight as his mouth dropped to hers. She arched her hips under him, searching, reaching for him before he grabbed her hands in his and held them over her head.

"Shh. Not so fast, Catherine." The words were a harsh whisper against her mouth and she arched her hips under him. "Oh, hell."

Catherine wasn't sure if he muttered the curse in frustration or in surrender, didn't care as he entered her in one swift move. Her reaction was immediate and shattering; she tightened around him and exploded again in a burst of pulsating fragments. She wrapped her arms around him and held on tight, nipped at his shoulder as wave after wave of pleasure crashed over her. There was a vague realization that Nathan hadn't even moved over her, just held her as she slowly resurfaced from the pool of feeling she was drowning in.

He lowered his head against hers and smiled against her mouth. Embarrassment coursed through her at the realization of how quickly and how thoroughly she had just climaxed, and she closed her eyes, turning her head away from him.

"Oh. That never…I mean…I don't…" Her words faded at Nathan's chuckle and she turned her face to his, surprised at the amusement that flashed in his eyes. He pressed a hard kiss against her mouth, still smiling.

"Catherine, don't apologize. Not for that. Ever."

His eyes turned serious as he stared at her, the intensity of his look enough to ignite the heat possessing her. "I don't do one-night stands, Catherine."

Her heart slammed into her chest at his words, bringing a hundred thoughts and questions to mind that she was afraid to ask, not sure what he meant. Instead she swallowed and shook her head, met his serious gaze with her own. "Neither do I."

"I know." He claimed her mouth in a searing kiss that left her reeling. He moved against her, slowly, quickly reawakening her senses with each thrust, pulling her into his rhythm. Catherine wrapped her legs tight around him and followed him to the pleasure he promised.

Nathan shifted against the warmth curled beside him and cracked open one eye at the unaccustomed sensation. A smile played on his lips as he gazed down at Catherine's sleeping form, tucked protectively under his arm, her hair spread in wild abandon across her pillow. He closed his eyes and pulled her closer, last night still vivid in his mind. Never before had he given so much of himself to a woman. Dread came from that last thought but he quickly banished it, unwilling to let a split second of hesitation ruin what had been the most intense night he had ever experienced.

They had made love two more times during the night, each time different, each time giving and receiving more than before. The intensity almost worried Nathan. So many things had clicked between them, surprising given the short and rocky time they had known each other. Minutes passed before she tensed beside him and he knew without looking that she was awake. He ran a finger lightly across her arm and propped himself on his elbow, dropping a kiss on her shoulder as he did. "'Morning."

Nathan fought the guilt that swept over him when she jumped in surprise at his voice and told himself that she wasn't accustomed to waking up next to someone. Possessiveness stole through him as Catherine rolled over, the sheet and blanket held firmly in place under her chin. She studied him for a second longer than necessary before offering him a weak smile.

"Oh. Um, good morning." She pulled back a bit when he tried to kiss her. He raised his brows in question, studying her.

"You don't sound too sure about that."

"No. I..." She shook her head and pushed herself to a sitting position, still clinging to the sheet. "I'm sorry. I just...I didn't expect you to still be here."

"I see," he said, not seeing at all. "Mind if I ask why?"

Catherine studied him for a full minute then lowered her head. He sighed and sat up, not bothering to cover himself with the sheet as he tried to peek through the curtain of her hair. A blush stained her cheeks; he turned so he was facing her, then curled one hand around her neck and pulled her to him until their lips met. The kiss he gave her was gentle and soft but he still felt the beginnings of desire stir inside him.

"Did you want me to leave?" He whispered the question against her mouth then held his breath until she shook her head. She finally met his gaze, her anxiety clear in her dark eyes.

"I'm sorry. I'm just..." She waved her hand around them and let it fall back into her lap. "I'm not used to this."

Nathan almost asked her if it was something she wanted to grow used to, then choked back the words. Instead he leaned forward and claimed her lips in another kiss, sighing when she melted against him. He tugged gently on the sheet then moaned when she let the cool material drop away from her heated flesh.

The kiss exploded between them with the same intensity of the night before. Nathan's hands drifted across Catherine's back, caressing before moving to the front where his thumb brushed against one tightened nipple. He wondered if their lovemaking would be the same this morning when a harsh noise screeched next him. He jumped back, one hand over his ear as he glanced at Catherine in bewilderment.

She scrambled to reach her nightstand, her hand fumbling across the cluttered surface until it slammed on a small brown object. The buzzing mercifully ended, followed by an unnatural quiet that echoed around the room. Nathan let out his breath and gave a questioning look at Catherine.

"Sorry. I can be a heavy sleeper sometimes."

Nathan watched the faint blush spreading across her cheeks. He placed his arm around her shoulder, pulling until she rested against him, her skin warm where it touched his. She sighed as his lips brushed her temple and curled closer, snuggling. Nathan held her, enjoying the feel of her body next to his and the comfortable silence that cloaked them. He pressed another kiss to her face then looked up, groaning when he saw the bright red numbers on the clock. Nine thirty-five.

"What's wrong?"

"I didn't realize how late it was. I should probably get ready to leave," Nathan muttered, knowing he should get out of bed. Instead he sunk deeper into the soft mattress.

"I thought you said you had to leave."

"I do."

"Oh."

Nathan ran his hand up and down her arm, felt her soft curves mold against him and tried to calculate how much longer he could put off leaving. He had practice in an hour and a half. The rink was less than thirty minutes away. Which left him just under an hour. Plenty of time, he thought.

He brushed a kiss against Catherine's soft lips, then a second and a third, ready to continue where they left off the night before when another thought ran through his mind and doused the stirrings of desire. He tensed and pulled away. "Do we have…I mean, what about Matty? Won't he be home soon?"

Her smile melted his tension and hesitation. She reached up and wrapped her arms around his neck, pulling him closer as she shook her head. "Matty's staying at Brian's all day."

"All day, hmm?" Nathan smiled, considered telling her about his conversation with Dr. Porter the night before, then forgot all about it as Catherine's mouth claimed his.

Nathan's heart rate soared as their passion escalated. His hands roamed over her body, enjoying the way she responded so openly to his smallest touch. Enjoying the way their bodies seemed to know each other so well. Enjoying the way each caress, each stroke, each murmured word fed their desire. He reached beside the bed, searching for another condom. His hand closed over the foil packet just as the phone rang.

Nathan groaned, heard Catherine's own sigh of frustration and decided to ignore the noise. On the third ring Catherine finally moaned and pulled away from him. She offered him a small smile of apology as she reached for the phone.

"It could be the office. Or a patient," she explained, yanking the phone from the receiver. Nathan sat up next to her and lowered his mouth to her shoulder blade, hoping it was a wrong number. "Hello? Oh, Brian, hi."

Nathan bit back his groan and leaned on one elbow, knowing that their time together had come to an end. He watched as her hair swung against her back, heard her voice as background noise and mentally calculated how many days it would be until they could be together again. He quickly changed the days to hours, surprised at how much he wanted this one woman.

"What? What happened?" Her sharp voice jolted Nathan from his fantasies and he straightened, suddenly aware of the tenseness that throbbed around

Catherine. He glanced at her face, saw her skin pale and her hand tremble. Her mouth moved but no words came out, just a breathy rasp. Nathan's stomach clenched with foreboding; something bad had happened.

He didn't even think about his next move, didn't consider the consequences as he reacted from instinct and took the phone from Catherine's shaking hand. He brought it to his ear as he pulled Catherine to him. Her skin had turned to ice. "Hello?"

"Who is this?" Dr. Porter's voice was flat and Nathan cringed at his tone. He took a deep breath and let it out.

"It's Nathan. What's wrong?"

"Oh, Nathan." A sigh echoed in the line between them, and Nathan wondered if that was a good sign or bad. "It's Matty. There was a small accident."

Nathan closed his eyes. "What happened? Is he okay?"

"He will be. He broke his arm skating."

"What?" Nathan felt Catherine tense against him and realized he had failed to keep the surprise from his voice. He cleared his throat and tried again. "Um, how?"

Another sigh came over the line and Nathan sensed the doctor's discomfort. The memory of Catherine's reaction the first time she had seen Matty on the ice came back in vivid clarity and Nathan inwardly cringed. He didn't want to be in the other man's shoes when Catherine found out.

"It was really all my fault, but that can wait. Right

now I'm worried about Catherine. How is she? My guess is panicked."

Nathan chanced a quick glance at the woman beside him, noticed her pale face, trembling lips and icy skin. He nodded, then answered with a quick, "Yes."

"They're getting ready to set his arm now, but I know Catherine won't be happy unless she's here. Is there… Nathan, she shouldn't drive herself, but she will. Would you be able—"

"Yeah, no problem. We'll leave now." Nathan hung up the phone. Catherine turned to face him, her eyes round with worry, and he gave her a quick hug. "Matty's fine. He broke his arm."

"He what? But how? What happened? Is he okay? What did they say? Oh, God, what if it's something else? What if the…" Her voice trailed off. Nathan watched as she tried to hide her fear. He pulled her to him, held her close and whispered in her ear.

"Catherine, he's fine. It's just a broken arm, that's all. Lots of kids get them."

"No, you don't understand." She pushed away from him, ran a shaking hand through her hair and stared up at him with wet eyes. "That's what happened when…Matty broke his leg, and that's when…how… they found the cancer."

Nathan's stomach dipped and tilted at the sight of her anxiety, and he suddenly understood what it must have been like for her. He sighed, ran his hand through his own hair and debated the wisdom of telling her exactly how Matty broke his arm. The idea left faster than it appeared. He had the impression that she wouldn't welcome the news, and he didn't want to be the one on the receiving end of her anger when she found out. But he didn't want her to worry needlessly the entire way to the hospital, either. He decided on a compromise.

"Catherine, it was an accident, not cancer. I'm not sure exactly what happened, but Dr. Porter himself said it was nothing to worry about. Now he wouldn't say that if it wasn't true, would he?" Nathan wasn't sure exactly how far her friend would go to protect her, and he hoped he hadn't just made up the biggest damn lie ever just to ease her worry.

"No. No, he wouldn't." Catherine took a deep breath, shook her head and tried to smile.

"Good. Now get dressed, and I'll drive you to the hospital." Nathan leaned over and grabbed his clothes from the pile on the floor, shaking the wrinkles from them when Catherine rested a still-trembling hand on his arm. He turned and looked at her, surprised at the emotion in her eyes.

"I thought...but you have practice."

Nathan shrugged and offered her a small smile. "It won't hurt if I miss one." *Much,* he added to himself. He saw the gratitude flash in her eyes, in the warmth of her smile before she pulled the sheet around her and climbed out of bed. Nathan followed her movements until she disappeared into the bathroom.

An insignificant fine and verbal chewing-out from Sonny LeBlanc was nothing compared to helping Catherine and Matty.

Chapter Ten

Catherine's tennis shoes squeaked against the polished floor of the corridor leading to the emergency room. Her fists balled against her sides, her nails dug into the skin; she was thankful for the pain, thankful for its diversion.

The lead ball in her stomach had grown during the ride to the hospital. Nathan seemed to understand how she felt and had simply reached over and held her hand, the warmth of his touch temporarily easing her anxiety. She was aware of him now, walking beside her, silently offering his support.

She wanted to accept that support, wanted to lean on him for strength, but part of her fought against it. Already she was questioning the wisdom of last night, wondering how things could change so quickly with the coming of a new day. Guilt grew inside her, consuming her, and she wondered how she could have possibly thought of anything besides Matty.

Matty, who was in the E.R. with a broken arm that he wouldn't have if she had been with him instead of with Nathan.

Catherine took a deep breath, held it to the count of three and released it slowly, hoping to calm her nerves. They reached the door leading to the emergency room. Catherine reached out to grab the handle but Nathan beat her to it. She looked up at him, so solid, so attractive. And wearing last night's clothes.

Her eyes drifted to the sleeves of the suit jacket, searching for the ruined cuffs of his shirt. A blush heated her face as she recalled exactly how the cuffs had been ruined. She suddenly wanted—needed—for him to stay behind, not to go any farther with her for fear of what everyone would think. Her son was in the hospital because she had been too busy enjoying herself instead of protecting him.

Catherine swallowed nervously and opened her mouth to ask Nathan to wait, but it was too late. Nathan was pulling open the door, holding it for her, looking at her expectantly.

She brushed by him, telling herself that the only thing that mattered was Matty as she briskly closed the distance to the triage station. One of the interns looked up from his report, gave her a quick smile and motioned down the hallway with his pen. "Hey, Doc. Matty's back in room four. They're almost done with the cast."

"Thanks, Steve." Catherine caught the widening

of the intern's eyes when he noticed Nathan behind her, and again she wanted to tell him to stay behind. Instead she merely walked down the hall, leaving it up to him to follow or not. His footsteps behind her told her he had chosen to follow.

She stopped in front of the door, took a deep breath and finally faced Nathan. "I think…I mean…it would probably be better if you waited out here."

He studied her, seeing too much. Catherine lowered her head, no longer able to look at him. She squirmed, debating whether or not to say anything else, then turned toward the door. Nathan's hand closed over hers before she could open it.

"Catherine, you didn't do anything wrong. This isn't your fault. You shouldn't feel guilty."

"Guilty? He's my responsibility and I…" Her voice cracked and she turned, looked at the floor, at his hand, at the wall behind Nathan. Everywhere but at him. "I need to see Matty." She shrugged off his hold and pulled the door open.

"I'll be here if you need me."

His words followed her into the room, creating a hollow feeling deep inside her instead of comforting her the way she knew he intended. She pushed everything to the back of her mind when her eyes rested on Matty.

He was sitting in the middle of the cot, a blanket covering him to the waist, his left arm held shoulder-high as a nurse finished wrapping it. A fresh cast encased the lower half of it, running from his hand to just below his elbow. Her heart sank when she looked closer and saw the cast he had chosen.

Plain white casts were a thing of the past. Patients had their choice of colors and styles, from solid neon to rainbow splashes, from favorite comic characters to favored sports teams. Matty's arm had been turned into an advertisement for the *Baltimore Banners*. She bit her lip, noticed the solid white strips in the exact center of the cast and knew that it had been wrapped in pieces in order for there to even be a plain section. For autographs, no doubt.

An irrational flare of anger spouted inside Catherine and she pushed it away. She took a deep breath and stepped closer to the bed, trying to smile when she saw Matty's grin.

"Hey, Mom. Check out the cast. Isn't it cool? Shelley did it up for me special, so I can get everyone to sign it." Matty held his arm out for her inspection. She nodded over it, flashed a thankful smile at the nurse, then turned to Brian.

"What happened?"

"Everything is fine. It was just a little accident."

"'Little accidents' don't cause broken arms, Brian. Is everything else okay? Where are the X-rays? I want to see them."

"Catherine, everything is fine. The X-rays are fine."

"I want to see them. Now."

Brian stared at her then grabbed a large envelope from the corner table and handed it to her. She pulled out the films, held them against the light board on the wall beside her and studied them, aware of Shelley leaving the room.

"Just a hairline fracture of the radius. Nothing else,"

Catherine muttered to herself as relief washed over her.

"Which is what I said."

She pulled the films off the board and stuffed them back in the envelope. "Yes, you did. So what happened then?"

"How did you get here?"

She almost answered the question before realizing it had been a deliberate ploy to change the subject. She pursed her lips together and studied Brian, noticed how uncomfortable he was and how he refused to meet her eyes. Catherine glanced at Matty and noticed that he had suddenly become preoccupied with the blanket covering him from the waist down. She had the distinct impression that both of them were hiding something.

"Does somebody want to tell me what happened?"

"It wasn't his fault, Mom. Really it wasn't." The words rushed from Matty's mouth, accompanied by his patented look of puppy-dog innocence. Catherine pursed her lips again and looked from one to the other, waiting. Silence greeted her.

"What happened?"

"Matty, do you want to go wait—"

"I want to know what happened, and I want to know now." Catherine's clipped words filled the room with even more tension as she fought to control her irrational fear. Matty fidgeted, failing to hide his eagerness to be anywhere but there.

"We went ice skating this morning and—"

"You what?" Brian flinched at her raised voice and

lowered his eyes to the floor. She took a deep breath, trying to keep her anger from her voice and failing. "You took him ice skating? Without my permission? After knowing how much I'm against it?"

Catherine blew another deep breath between her clenched teeth, ran a hand through her hair and paced in circles. "Why, Brian? You *know* how I feel!" She pointed to Matty's arm. "*This!* This is why I don't want him skating! He's not ready for it!"

"Mom, it was an accident."

"It was my fault, Catherine."

She stopped her pacing, looked from Matty's red face and wet eyes to Brian's stubborn stance and determined frown. "I don't care. That's it. No more skating."

"Catherine!" Brian's raised voice stopped her. Her head whipped around in his direction and she stared at him, saw the anger in his eyes and opened her mouth for a retort. Her mouth snapped shut with an audible click at his next words. "It was my fault, Catherine. I tripped and fell, and knocked him over, and that's when he broke his arm."

The silence surrounding them after Brian's confession was louder than their voices had been. Catherine bit her lip, feeling like she had just been betrayed by her best friend.

She *had* been betrayed by her best friend.

"You broke my son's arm." Catherine squeezed her eyes closed and fought to replace the hurt with anger. "That's just great. Wonderful. Fine. Matty, let's go."

"No!"

Catherine whirled at Matty's outburst, staring at

him in shock. He never talked back to her, never. "Excuse me?"

"It was an accident, Mom. I'm okay. See?" He slid off the cot, his broken arm cradled next to his chest.

"Hey there, kiddo. Nice cast." Nathan's steady voice echoed around the room, creating an unnatural stillness in the aftermath of the outbursts. Catherine tensed, feeling his eyes boring into her back. She ignored the impulse to turn and order him from the room, knowing it would only make things worse, knowing she had no right to take this out on him.

"Nathan!" Matty's eyes widened as he looked past Catherine, a bright smile on his face. She clenched her teeth and curled her fists in anger and frustration when Matty walked right by her without even looking. His gait was steady and she realized that anyone who didn't know about the prosthesis would be unable to tell he used one from the way he walked.

"Nathan, this isn't..." Her words froze in her throat, choking her when she saw the cool look he tossed her way. His eyes remained steady on hers, assessing, before he looked away and gave Matty his full attention.

"Well, check this out. I never knew we had our own line of casts. That's pretty cool."

"Yeah, and see how Shelley wrapped it? So I can have people sign it in the middle. You want to sign it?"

Nathan's answering laughter filled the room, a direct contradiction to the icy tension hovering in all four corners of the small cubicle. Catherine shifted uncomfortably, chanced a glance at Brian to see his reaction and noticed that he was engrossed in studying the crease of his shirtsleeve.

"Of course I'll sign it. Just tell me you didn't do that on purpose so you could get autographs." Matty laughed and smiled when Nathan leaned over to ruffle his hair. A flash of jealousy pierced Catherine at her son's reaction to the gesture, knowing that Matty always pulled away when she did the same thing.

"No. It was an accident. Uncle Bri…I mean…" Matty glanced at Catherine and Brian then lowered his voice, but not low enough that he couldn't be heard. "Uncle Bri doesn't know how to skate and he fell on me."

"Yeah, I heard." Nathan looked up and stared hard at Catherine, his smile gone. She squirmed under his direct gaze, knew he was telling her that her shouting could be heard outside. Her face heated and she looked away, hurt, angry and now embarrassed. "So, you got a pen I can sign that thing with?"

"Oh. No. Don't you have one?"

"Sorry, kiddo, fresh out of pens. You want to go see if they have something on that big desk I saw out there?"

"Nathan, I don't think—"

"No, it's okay." Nathan fixed her with an unreadable expression, one that filled her with even more anxiety because she couldn't understand it. She fidgeted then shook her head.

"Nathan—"

"We'll be fine, won't we, Matty?" Nathan ruffled her son's hair again then led him out of the room without a backward glance. Catherine watched their disappearance, surprised at the sudden emptiness she felt. She blinked against the sting of tears in the back of her eyes and wrapped her arms around herself, wondering if she would ever feel warm again.

"Well. That was fun." Brian muttered the words under his breath, loud enough so she could hear them. He busied himself with cleaning up a side cart, refusing to look at her.

"What's that supposed to mean?"

"Oh, Catherine, c'mon. Don't you think you're overreacting?"

"Overreacting? Brian, you took Matty skating without my permission, knowing perfectly well how I feel about it. *You* broke *my* son's arm!" Catherine paced in circles, motioning wildly with her hands as she tried to calm her breathing. "I feel like my best friend betrayed me!"

Catherine's voice cracked as a tear spilled from her eye, and she wiped at it, angry, furious, wanting suddenly to do no more than take that anger out on something. Anything. She spun around, surprised at the strength of her emotions, not wanting Brian to see her, afraid of how out of control she looked.

"You want to be pissed at me, fine. You've got every right. It was a stupid mistake, I shouldn't have done it and I'm sorry. Sorrier than you know. Hell, I'm pissed at myself. But everything else..."

Catherine fingered the smooth edge of the metal table in front of her, felt Brian's eyes on her but refused to turn around, refused to ask him what he meant. The silence stretched for minutes before he let out a deep breath and spoke.

"I'm the one who's guilty here, Catherine. Not you. Don't use this as an excuse to shut down again."

"Excuse me?" Catherine whirled on him, her eyes wide, her face heated with anger and disbelief. She couldn't have heard him correctly. "Tell me I didn't just hear that."

"Are you afraid of the truth, Catherine?"

"What are you talking about?"

"The guilt is written all over your face. Even Nathan could see it. Don't let this spoil something that could be good for you, Catherine. Don't use this as an excuse to hide away again." Brian's voice was soft and full of sympathy, bringing tears to her eyes when she realized he spoke the truth. She did hide, because it was easier that way. But that didn't mean she wanted to admit the truth, even to herself.

"I don't hide, Brian. I have responsibilities, and they come first. They have to. Once they're taken care of, then maybe I can enjoy life." Catherine's voice broke and she frantically blinked back the tears that were threatening. She felt moisture on her face and knew she had failed. Brian took a step toward her, sympathy and regret etched clearly on his face.

"Catherine..."

"No." She backed up a step, shaking her head as he reached for her. "No. I'll be fine. I just need to get Matty home."

"Catherine—"

She shook her head again, pivoted on her heel and

pulled open the door, ignoring the curious looks from the meandering staff as she concentrated on walking a steady line to the desk. Steve looked up at her and she tried to offer him a weak smile.

"Where's Matty?"

"Matty? He, um, he left."

A pit opened in Catherine's stomach and filled with a blast of cold air. She fought back the panic, swallowed, took a deep breath. "What do you mean, he left? Left how?"

"With Mr. Conners."

"When?"

"Five minutes ago. He looked upset. From, well, you know."

"Oh, God." Catherine took another deep breath, ran her fingers through her hair and squeezed her head between her hands, turning in a small circle while a hundred thoughts swamped her. "Not this. No more. I can't handle this."

"Catherine, what is it?"

She turned at the sound of Brian's voice and reached out for him. "Matty left with Nathan."

"What?" Brian looked at her then turned to face Steve. He shifted under their combined stares, finally shrugging.

"Matty was upset and asked Nathan to take him home."

Catherine tried to reduce her near-hysteria to inconsequential worry, telling herself that Matty was safe with Nathan. But why would he leave without telling her? She took a deep breath, then another, and briefly considered which one she wanted to yell at first before deciding that neither of them deserved it. The whole thing was her fault. She should have seen how upset Matty was. She shouldn't have overreacted—to Matty's broken arm, to Brian. To everything.

Catherine turned to Brian, ready to ask him for a ride home when he pulled the car keys from his pocket and motioned for her to follow him.

"Mom's going to be angry at you for doing this, won't she?"

Nathan took his eyes from the road to glance at the boy sitting next to him. He then turned his attention back to the traffic. *Angry* was an understatement. Nathan just shrugged and offered Matty a carefree smile. "No big deal."

"I shouldn't have asked you." Matty's miserable whisper hit Nathan straight in the chest, unleashing an emotion he had no business feeling. It was one thing to be pals or to joke around, but another thing altogether to start feeling so protective.

"Hey, kiddo, don't sweat it. It'll work out." Nathan tried to make his voice light and winced at how flat the words sounded. Matty sighed and leaned his head against the passenger window, visibly worried. "Besides, I think she's already mad at me. This won't make any difference."

"Why is she mad at you?"

"I have no idea." It wasn't a complete lie. Nathan knew Catherine well enough to figure out that she was suffering from some serious guilt about Matty's broken arm. What he didn't know was how much of her guilt would turn into regret, and if she would blame him or just herself.

A soft moan caught Nathan's attention and he turned to look at Matty, noticed the way he was cradling the broken arm against his stomach. He called himself a fool for not realizing sooner that Matty would be in pain. "Are you okay?"

"Yeah." Matty swallowed then nodded. "It's just a little uncomfortable is all."

Uncomfortable hell, Nathan thought. Judging from his pale and sweaty face, the arm was a lot more than just uncomfortable. Nathan pursed his lips then eased the car into the turn lane.

"Hey, Matty, how about going to my place? It's closer and you could lie down for a bit until your mom picks you up."

"Okay." Matty was unusually quiet. Nathan looked over and noticed the pained look on his face. The protectiveness he felt earlier grew, and Nathan's anxiety grew right along with it.

He needed his head examined.

Matty had fallen into a restless sleep by the time Nathan pulled into the parking lot of his complex. He let out a sigh and waited, watching the slow rise and fall of Matty's chest.

"Perfect. Now what?" Nathan leaned over and gently pushed on Matty's leg. Still nothing. He shook his head, got out of the car and went around to the other side, slowly opening the passenger door so Matty wouldn't fall out. He bent down and scooped the sleeping kid into his arms, wincing at the pull in his knee. Matty stirred, looked at him through half-closed eyes.

"Nathan?"

"Shh, kiddo. Go back to sleep." A knot formed in Nathan's stomach when Matty wrapped his good arm around his neck and rested his head on his shoulder. Nathan kicked the car door closed, careful not to jostle Matty as he walked.

The first thing he was going to do when he made it inside was get Matty comfortable. The second was going to be a phone call to Catherine to let her know where Matty was. And the third…

Well, the third was going to be another phone call, this one to a shrink because there was no doubt in Nathan's mind that he needed his head checked.

Chapter Eleven

Bzzz. Bzzz.

"Go away." The sleepy mumble tumbled from Nathan's mouth as he rolled over and tried to get comfortable.

Bzzz. Pause. *Bzzz. Bang. Bang. Bang.*

Nathan groaned, wondered what the irritating noise was, wondered why his bed suddenly seemed so much smaller and harder.

Bang. Bang.

The loud noise dragged Nathan from the gray depths of hazy sleep. He opened his eyes, squinting at the surroundings that were barely more than shadows in the dim light, and realized he had fallen asleep on the sofa. The banging was more insistent this time, and he wondered why someone was trying to beat his door down. Memory swam to the surface of his mind as he sat up.

Matty and his broken arm. Bringing him here.

Catherine.

The reason for the banging noise was suddenly clear. Nathan stumbled to the door, looking at his watch and groaning at how much time had passed since he brought Matty here.

"Oh, hell." His hand closed around the cold knob, twisted and pulled just as Catherine raised her hand to knock again. She lost her balance and stumbled as the momentum carried her forward. Nathan reached out to steady her.

"Where's Matty?"

"He's sleeping..." Nathan's voice trailed off as Catherine pushed by him, squinting her eyes in the darkness. Nathan reached over and flipped the wall switch; soft light from two end lamps chased the shadows back to the corners. He was about to close the door then stumbled back when Brian walked in.

"Where?"

"Where what? Oh, Matty." Nathan rubbed his hands over his face then straight back through his hair, grimacing at the dryness in his mouth. He couldn't remember the last time he had fallen asleep in the middle of the day. "He's in my room."

Catherine turned and walked through the living room to the short hallway, peeked through the open door with an audible sigh of relief. She looked back at Nathan with an unreadable expression before walking in, leaving him and Brian alone.

Nathan shook his head and walked to the kitchen, desperate for something cold to drink to wake him up.

"You shouldn't have left the hospital with Matty."

Nathan turned to see that Brian had followed him into the kitchen. He opened the refrigerator door, studying the shelves for a full minute before grabbing a carton of milk. "He was upset and asked to leave. What was I supposed to do?"

"Well, you could have told his mother for starters."

Nathan gave Brian a look that left no room for doubt about his thoughts on that idea. He brought the open carton to his nose, sniffed, then frowned at the sour smell and put it back.

"Or you could have taken him to his own house."

He ignored Brian, letting him have his own one-way conversation as he continued his search for something to drink.

"Dammit, the least you could have done was call Catherine and let her know."

"I did. There was no answer so I left a message. Twice. And then I paged her. Still no answer." Nathan pulled the pitcher of water from the door of the refrigerator and grabbed a clean glass from a cabinet. He poured a glass and drained it in one long swallow, refilled it and drank again.

"Oh." Brian shifted his weight from one foot to the other then leaned against the counter and studied Nathan. "I guess she forgot her pager."

"Guess so." Nathan drained his third glass of water and placed the near-empty pitcher in the sink, ready to refill the reservoir so the water could be filtered.

"So. Is Matty okay? Is his arm—"

"His arm hurts like hell but he's afraid to admit it because of his mom." A concern that Nathan completely understood, especially after seeing how protective—how overly cautious—Catherine was when it came to Matty. "Other than that, he's fine. He took one of the pills they left out for him at the hospital not long after we got here, and he's been sleeping ever since. And I even made sure to put ice on his arm."

"I see." There was a short pause, filled only by the sound of running water. Brian cleared his throat and Nathan prepared himself for the next barrage of questions and comments. "You, um, don't seem too happy. I didn't think having Matty for such a short time would have been such a big inconvenience."

"Oh, for crissakes. I don't believe this." Nathan slammed the faucet off then turned and fixed Brian with a harsh glare. "Matty is not an inconvenience. Far from it. He's probably the most easygoing kid I've ever met and...and why am I even explaining this to you?"

"I see."

"Somehow I doubt that." Nathan leaned against the counter and crossed his arms tightly in front of him, staring at a spot on the floor as a still quiet permeated the room.

"Oh, I don't know. My guess is that Matty got to you."

Nathan looked up in time to see a small grin lift the corner of the doctor's mouth. He shook his head and grunted, not sure how to respond, not sure if a response was even necessary. Saying that the kid got to him was one of the biggest understatements Nathan had heard in a long time.

Matty *had* gotten to him, in ways he didn't want to think about. His strength and positive outlook was a contradiction to everything the poor kid had been through. *Poor kid.* The words echoed through Nathan's mind. Matty could never be described as a "poor kid." If anything, he could set a positive example for many adults Nathan knew.

"They're a package deal, you know."

Nathan grunted again and looked up, not surprised to see Brian studying him with a carefully blank expression. He finally met the doctor's stare and softly gave voice to the thought that had been spinning through his mind. "Yeah, well...I don't think Catherine's ready for any kind of deal, if you ask me."

Brian shrugged and casually looked around the kitchen. Nathan wondered what he was looking for but didn't ask. He had no desire to play host, afraid that this wasn't a social call, afraid that Catherine's guilt and sense of responsibility would pull her away before they had a chance to start anything.

"Catherine's been through a lot, and most of it on her own. She's not accustomed to being with anyone. Try not to hold that against—" Brian stopped midsentence, interrupted by a muffled *beep, beep, beep.* He swore softly under his breath and pulled a small pager from his trousers pocket. He glanced at it then offered Nathan a weak smile. "The hospital. I need to go."

Nathan watched the doctor walk out of the kitchen and he wondered where the conversation had been heading when another thought occurred to him. He pushed off the counter to follow Brian then nearly collided with him when he turned the corner.

"Nathan, I hate to ask this, but is there any way… Would you be able to take Catherine and Matty home?"

"Uh, I don't—"

"Great, thanks." Brian turned back around and headed for the door before Nathan caught his breath enough to protest.

"I don't think she'd want—"

"She'll get over it, don't worry." Brian tossed him a look that Nathan didn't understand then stepped into the hallway, closing the door behind him. Silence followed, leaving Nathan stunned. He stared at the empty spot where Brian had been only a second before then released his breath through pursed lips, suddenly feeling like he had been set up. Again.

"Wonderful." Nathan placed fisted hands on his hips and shook his head, wondering where his common sense had gone. He was still standing there a few minutes later when Catherine emerged from the bedroom, pulling the door closed behind her.

"Matty's still sleeping…." Her voice trailed off as she came to a stop a few feet away and looked around. Nathan clenched his jaw against the frustration he felt when she avoided looking at him. "Um, where's Brian?"

"Gone."

"Gone?" Catherine's face visibly paled as she finally met his eyes. The look of despair on her face unleashed a mix of emotions in Nathan that he didn't want to examine.

"Yeah. He got a page and left."

"Oh." Catherine continued to stare at Nathan, obviously uncomfortable, and he recognized the morning-after regret, along with her guilt. She shifted her weight from one foot to the other, her downcast eyes focused on the floor. Nathan noticed how her hands fidgeted, nervously playing with the crease of her slacks before clenching each other. "Um, did he say when he was coming back?"

"He's not."

"He's…what do you mean, he's not?"

"Just what I said." Nathan turned away from her, from the anxiety in her eyes and the small tremor of uncertainty that edged her nervous words. The spacious living room with its vaulted ceiling suddenly seemed small and suffocating. He took a step toward the kitchen, stopped, then made a half turn toward the hallway before realizing escape to his bedroom was also impossible. The spare room would have been an option if not for all the weight-lifting equipment and hockey gear that cluttered it, and he had no desire to lock himself up in the spare bathroom. Maybe the loft would offer some escape….

"May I borrow your phone, please?"

Nathan tensed at the cool formality in her voice. Irrational anger flared through him at her ability to smother her emotions when his own were always so close to the surface. He stopped his search for escape and stared at her. "Why?"

The question caught her off guard. Her mouth opened and closed silently as she stared at him through narrowed eyes. Nathan bit back an oath when she raised her chin a notch, a sure sign of the stubbornness that streaked through her.

"So I can call a taxi." Her coolness lowered the temperature in the room by a few degrees.

Nathan studied her, looking for signs of the warmth he knew she possessed, and suddenly realized it was all an act. The slight trembling that shook her delicate hands was disguised by clenched fists; the sheen of moisture in her eyes was replaced by an icy glare.

Yes, it was definitely an act. From the beginning, the facade he had noticed had been erected for protection, a barrier against an outside world that wasn't always kind. The insight jolted Nathan like contact with a live wire, hard and biting.

So what did he want to do about it? Let her continue with her barriers, or take a chance and crash through them?

The saner part of his mind told him to just let it go. To take the easy way out and point her to the phone.

"No." The single word that fell from his mouth caught him by surprise and sent a silent groan through the part of his mind that was thinking clearly. The other part, the part that possessed entirely too much emotion for his own good, breathed a sigh of relief and gave a quiet shout of delight at the expression that crossed her face.

Again, Catherine's mouth opened in silent protest. Nathan smothered the grin that wanted to break free at the sight of her indecision and uncertainty. He turned toward the kitchen, hoping he knew what he was doing.

"Then how do you suggest we get home?" Her voice, so close behind him, wasn't as cool or certain as before. Nathan shrugged, then slid the pocket door of the kitchen closed and threw the small lock, effectively trapping her inside the room with him.

A flush of pleasure shot through him as Catherine sputtered her outrage. He could hear her breathing, sensed her indecision as she paced a few steps behind him. Nathan finally turned and looked at her. Her brown eyes glowed with irritation as she motioned wildly with her hands. He cocked an eyebrow in her direction and bit back a smile when she stepped closer, the flush on her face growing bright.

"What are you doing? And how are we supposed to get home?"

"Catherine, I'll take you home. No need to worry, okay?"

Just like that, the fight and apprehension evaporated from her. She shook her head, though Nathan wasn't sure what she was denying. Catherine stared at him for a long minute then slowly closed the small space between them. She fidgeted then swallowed audibly, not looking at him.

"Nathan, I..." The words trailed off in a choked whisper and she tried to take a step backward, only to be stopped when he folded his arms around her and pulled her closer. He tilted her chin up and searched her face, gazing into her eyes.

"Catherine, you don't need to worry, okay? And you don't need to feel guilty, or act like we did anything wrong." Her eyes briefly met his, wide with uncertainty and emotion before she looked away. The body he held in his arms was stiff; he could feel a tremor pass through her as she fought to keep her distance, if not physically then at least emotionally.

"I…I don't…" Nathan tightened his hold around her and once again tilted her head so she was forced to look at him. His breath hitched at the emotion in her eyes. He gentled his hold, glad when she didn't pull away.

Quiet seconds stretched before he noticed the moisture filling her eyes. He held her close, ignoring the squeeze in his chest when she relaxed against him and rested her head on his shoulder.

He refused to look too closely at the comfort he felt at just holding her, of having her in his arms. There would be time for that later, he thought. For now, he just wanted to enjoy the feel of her body tucked close against his, wanted to enjoy the sensation of protection that surged through him at the trust she showed in the simple act of wrapping her arms around his waist.

"Nathan, about this morning…" Her words were muffled against his chest. The warmth of her breath seared his skin through the cotton T-shirt and Nathan's jaw clenched at his body's instant reaction. He shifted and gazed down at Catherine, saw the anxiety in her eyes.

"Shh. Don't worry about it."

"No, I have to." She pulled away from him, looked around before facing him again. "I didn't mean to act distant. It's just everything with Matty… I'm sorry."

The apology hung in the air between them and Nathan knew how hard it had been for her to offer it.

She stood in front of him, watching, waiting. Seconds ticked by as they stared at each other before Nathan offered her a small smile.

"You weren't too distant. Guilty, maybe." Nathan hurried on when disappointment crossed her face. "But I understand, Catherine. I do."

"How can you? I don't understand myself!" The pain that flashed in her eyes was unbearable and Nathan wanted to do nothing more than reach out to her again. He sensed that it wasn't time yet so he remained still, watching as she fought some silent battle. "I just… God, I don't know what to do anymore! Matty's changing. I'm changing. Nothing is the same and it scares the hell out of me. It scares me that Matty might get hurt again and there's nothing I can do about it."

"Catherine, you have to let him grow up."

"I know that! Don't you think I know that? But it's so hard. I don't want him hurt, and part of me is so afraid that I've already hurt him by being so protective. I mean, what if I've made things worse for him?"

"Catherine—"

"Let me finish!" Nathan winced, surprised she sounded so frantic, so desperate. He took a step forward then stopped when she held up one hand to hold him off. "Please, let me finish. This is so hard for me. You have no idea how hard." She took a deep breath, released it on a ragged sigh but remained silent.

Nathan sensed that she was struggling with something, felt her indecision and frustration and helplessness. He bit back an oath and suddenly closed the distance between them, wrapping his arms around her as she muttered a small protest. "Catherine, stop. You don't have to explain. You don't have to apologize."

"But I do! What if I made things worse for him? What if I keep making things worse? I'm so afraid that..."

Nathan felt something tighten in his stomach. He swallowed hard, willing her to look at him. "Afraid of what?"

The air around them thickened, crackled with tension as time stretched. Nathan held his breath as he searched her eyes and waited. "What are you afraid of, Catherine?"

"Everything." The word fell from her mouth, full of agony and ache. Her throat worked silently as she met his gaze. "Of everything. Of Matty, of you. Of this."

The vulnerability on her face went straight to his chest. A fist closed around Nathan's heart and squeezed, constricting until his lungs ached from it. He took a deep breath, felt the pain ease as they stared at each other in the charged silence. There were words he could say to ease her fear, words he wanted to say but he choked them back, afraid of what she would say. Hell, he was afraid of what he might say himself.

Instead he lowered his mouth to hers, gently rubbed his lips against hers in a soft kiss meant to reassure, to take the place of the unformed words stuck in his throat. What was meant as gentle comfort quickly escalated out of control, erupting into a frenzied mating of breath and tongues, of roaming hands and pounding heartbeats. Nathan's arms tightened around her, lifted and molded her pliant hips against his as he caught the soft groan that escaped her with his mouth.

Out of control. The phrase echoed through his mind, accusing, warning. Nathan ignored it, could think of nothing but the soft woman in his arms as he pulled his mouth from hers, dragged it along the narrow column of her throat. Catherine's knees buckled and she tumbled against him as her head fell back.

He leaned down, wrapped his arms around her thighs and lifted. A tortured sound ripped from his chest when her legs wrapped securely around his waist and he fumbled against the counter, turned then gently eased her onto the cool surface. He ignored the sharp clink of canisters rolling against each other, ignored the rush of emotion that mingled with the warning in his head, focusing instead on the sweet, hot flesh under his mouth.

"But Matty—" Catherine's voice was a ragged whisper in his ear. He dragged his mouth back up Catherine's neck, felt her chest heave against his as he gently nipped her earlobe.

"The door's locked and he's sleeping. We're okay."

"Are you sure?"

Nathan nodded then inhaled sharply at her smile as her hands tightened their hold around his neck, tugged at his hair and forced his mouth back to hers. Their eyes met for a second, caught and held as the passion flared between them.

Their mouths crashed together, hungry and feeding. Nathan's hands roamed over her, touching, searching. He silently cursed the barrier of her shirt, reached down and pulled the blouse from her slacks before pulling it over her head and tossing it aside, quickly following it with her silk bra. Nathan pulled away, let his eyes feast on her creamy skin. His groin tightened painfully, viciously, as he gazed at her.

Catherine raised her hands and he brushed them away when she would have covered herself. He reached out and gently cupped her with his own callused hands, felt the warm flesh mold under his touch. Catherine sighed sharply as he lowered his mouth and closed his lips around one taut nipple and suckled and teased.

She moaned again, dug her fingers into his shoulders and pushed him away. Nathan looked at her through glazed eyes, realized she was dragging at his shirt. He stepped back and peeled the shirt off in one quick move, stepped closer and enjoyed the feel of bare flesh pressed against bare flesh.

He wanted her. Oh, how he wanted her.

His tongue swept the inside of her mouth and danced with hers as his hands dropped to the waistband of her slacks. In seconds he was tugging at the material, easing her pants and underwear down around her hips as she wiggled against him.

He wanted her. Bad enough that he would take her right here, on the kitchen counter.

Guilt niggled at the back of his mind as he pushed linen and silk down her legs, letting the garments fall at his feet. Catherine deserved better than cold granite. He wanted to treat her to a downy mattress, to smooth silk that rivaled the softness of her skin. The guilt ebbed and flowed through him, fighting with the heat of Catherine's hands wandering over his burning flesh, hesitant and teasing.

Her touch grew bolder, drifted down over the flat of his stomach before easing into the waistband of his sweat shorts. He tightened his arms around her nude body and lifted her from the counter. His breath quickened as she wrapped her legs around him, molding herself against his erection, opening herself to him, pushing against him. It would be so easy to reach down, to free himself and drive wildly inside her instead of waiting.

He gazed into Catherine's face and saw his own urgent need reflected in its warm depths. He bit back a curse and kissed her. Balancing her against the counter, he reached down and pulled at his shorts, swallowing her groan as he sprang free between them.

Catherine pulled away, breaking the kiss as her hips searched for him. Almost too late he remembered what he was forgetting, and held himself away from her. "Catherine, wait. Wait…." His hoarse whisper was nearly lost in the combination of their breathing. He sat her on the counter, gave her a lingering kiss before pulling away.

Nathan shook his head to clear it, motioned for Catherine to wait as he frantically searched the kitchen table. His hand closed around his leather wallet and he hastily opened it, grabbing the foil packet and dropping everything else in his haste to return to Catherine. Their mouths met in a heated frenzy as he quickly sheathed himself with the condom.

His arms closed around her, pulling her close as she rocked against him. Teeth nipped at moist skin; their breathing echoed around them, pulling them deeper into the mist of passion as Catherine lowered herself fully onto him. His jaw clenched and his breath hitched at the hot tightness that clamped around him. He lowered his head, caught Catherine's mouth with his own as they found each other's rhythm and matched it.

Her arms twined around his neck as his hands closed over the firmness of her bottom, guiding her, holding her against him as he thrust into her. Burying himself. Deeper each time. Her back arched, offering herself. Nathan lowered his head, pulled the taut peak of one nipple into his mouth, sucked it greedily.

Thrust. Bury. Their movements faster, frantic and urgent.

"Nathan…"

Catherine's legs tightened around him, squeezing, holding. He thrust again, felt her shatter around him. He captured her mouth with his, swallowed her cries of pleasure as she continued to shatter around him. One more thrust and his own cry of pleasure was lost in the frenzied mating of their tongues.

Seconds went by as he gentled the kiss, finally

pulled away and looked at Catherine, breathless. Embarrassment flushed her cheeks but she met his gaze squarely. A grin spread across his face and was answered by her own tentative smile.

"I feel like I should say something but I don't know what." Her soft admission touched him, and he searched for something heartfelt to say.

"How about 'wow'?" The words were out before he could stop them. Catherine stared at him in shock before a soft laugh escaped her. Nathan felt his grin widen then falter as guilt rushed through him, and he suddenly, clearly, understood the reason for Catherine's reaction that morning.

As clearly as the soft voice of a nine-year-old boy calling him from his bedroom.

Chapter Twelve

Nathan bit back an oath as mortification washed over him. He glanced at Catherine, who fixed him with an absent look that was quickly replaced by dawning horror. Nathan's heart clenched. He leaned forward and pressed his lips hard against her cold ones. He wasn't surprised when she pulled away.

"Catherine, don't. Don't close up again."

"Oh, God. What..." Her trembling words faltered as she stared at him, as she looked down and noticed that her legs were still tightly wrapped around his waist. Nathan swallowed, thought fast as he tightened his hold on her.

"Catherine, don't. Listen to me. It's okay. It's going to be okay." Nathan pivoted so she was resting against the counter, clenched his jaw against the flare in his knee. The pain was nothing compared to what she obviously felt.

Matty's small voice called out to Nathan again. He gave Catherine one last look, then turned toward the closed kitchen door. "Uh, I'll be right there, Matty. Just stay right there." *Please, God, stay there.*

Nathan took a deep breath, gently eased away from Catherine and tried not to feel the loss too deeply. He was a moron. A complete idiot.

He rushed around the kitchen, scooping clothes from the floor and hastily pulling them on. His arm caught in the sleeve of his T-shirt and he nearly ripped it in his haste to smooth it over his chest. He sat Catherine's pile next to her.

"Catherine, look at me." He ran his hands lightly over her arms then cupped her face until her dazed eyes slowly focused on him. "It's going to be okay. I'll take care of Matty. You stay in here and get dressed."

Nathan reached down and grabbed her clothes, shoving a piece into her shaking hand. His face flamed in embarrassment when he saw it was her underwear. Stupid. So stupid. He planted a quick kiss on her stiff lips then walked out of the kitchen.

The door to his room was still closed. He took a deep breath, shoved his hands through his hair and prayed he didn't look as guilty as he felt before pushing it open and walking in. Matty was still lying in the center of the bed, his arm propped on a pillow. The boy suddenly looked smaller, more vulnerable.

Guilt and humiliation quickly replaced his short-lived relief when Matty turned his head and offered Nathan a strained grin. Great, just great. *The kid's lying here in pain and you're in the other room doing the wild thing with his mother.*

Nathan pushed the thought away, offered Matty a stiff smile as he walked closer to the bed. "Hey, kiddo. How are you doing?"

"Okay, I guess. My arm still hurts a little."

"Well, you didn't expect to go turning somersaults so soon after breaking it, did you?" Nathan took some comfort in Matty's expression then eased himself down on the bed, careful not to disturb the elevated arm. "So is everything okay?"

"Yeah. I just kinda forgot where I was at first."

You're not the only one. "Hmm. I know how that one goes."

A comfortable silence settled over the room as Nathan watched Matty's eyes drift shut, then pop back open. He reached out and smoothed a damp lock of hair from the boy's forehead. The contact sent a river of warmth crashing over Nathan and he snatched his hand away, shocked at the sensation.

"I'm thirsty." The words were a sleepy mumble that unleashed more warmth in Nathan. He pushed the feelings away as he leaned over and poured Matty a glass of water from the pitcher on the bedside table, then helped him up so he could drink. "Is Mom here? I thought I heard her voice."

"Uh…mmm…" Nathan cleared his throat and started over. "Uh, yeah. She's in the kitchen, um, fixing something to eat." *Brilliant, Conners. That's a new way to put it.* He sighed and mentally shook his head, turning his attention back to Matty when the boy shifted and stared up at him with innocent eyes.

"Is she mad at you? For bringing me here, I mean."

Nathan blew a deep breath through pursed lips and shrugged, not sure how to answer the question. He shifted on the bed and fluffed the pillows behind Matty before helping him lean back.

Catherine watched them from the doorway, her heart constricting painfully when Nathan brushed Matty's hair from his forehead with a soft touch. The look of adoration that crossed her son's face brought tears to her eyes and she blinked them back mercilessly. What was with her lately that she was so prone to crying? Too much change, too fast. That had to be the reason.

"Well, is she?" The impatience in Matty's voice as he repeated the question brought a faint smile to her lips. She took a deep breath and crossed the threshold, causing Nathan's head to turn in her direction so fast she feared he would get whiplash. She saw the different emotions flash through his eyes: confusion, gratitude, guilt, uncertainty. A charge of awareness flashed between them before she shifted her gaze to Matty.

"No, Matty, I'm not mad. Not too much, anyway."

"Mom, don't be mad at Nathan. Please. It was my fault. I asked him to, he didn't make me. Really, it was my fault." Matty's rush of words and the desperation in his voice as he pleaded with her had Catherine crossing the room with hurried steps. She leaned over and gave her son a quick, reassuring hug, careful not to jostle his arm, careful not to overreact to the sight of the slender limb encased in colorful plaster.

"Hey, it's okay. Shh. I'm not mad, Matty. It's okay." She crooned the words in a comforting whisper, breathed a sigh when Matty's body relaxed under her touch. She straightened and offered him a small smile. "Next time, just make sure I know where you're going. You had me worried."

"I'm sorry. I just…you and Uncle Bri were arguing and I didn't like it so I asked Nathan to take me home and—"

"I know. And I'm sorry. I shouldn't have said what I did to Brian." Catherine took a deep breath and sat down on the bed when Nathan moved over to make room for her. Her eyes darted to his and another jolt shot through her, this one different from the sexual awareness that had passed between them earlier.

There was something almost comforting about the three of them being together like this. Her throat constricted and she quickly cleared it, looking away while she pushed the feeling aside and focused on finding the right words to comfort Matty. "Listen, I'm sorry about this morning. I shouldn't have said what I did. I was upset and I overreacted, and I said some things I shouldn't have. To everyone."

Nathan shifted on the bed next to her and she knew without looking that he understood the apology was for him, as well. Matty glanced from her to Nathan and back again, then smiled with an innocence Catherine knew was all show.

"So you're not mad at Nathan anymore, either?"

There was entirely too much calculation in the words. She bit her tongue and wondered what he was up to. Instead of questioning him, Catherine just sighed and ruffled his hair. "I told you I wasn't. So are you up to going home now?"

"Home?" The catch in his voice was followed by a dramatic sigh as he leaned his head back on the pillow. He closed his eyes, an exaggerated grimace crossing his face as he shifted in the bed. "I…my arm hurts, Mom. Can I just sleep some more?"

Catherine covered her mouth with her hand, hiding her smile as Matty uttered a heartbreaking moan. She turned her attention to Nathan and saw the corner of his mouth twitch.

"Don't you think you'd be more comfortable in your own bed?" Her question was greeted by silence, slowly followed by a sleepy murmur from Matty as he turned his head away from them. But not before Catherine noticed the tiny grin that curled his lips. A warm hand closed over her shoulder and she turned to see Nathan shake his head.

"Just let him sleep," Nathan whispered, winking slowly in her direction. He gave her shoulder a comforting squeeze then stood. "C'mon. I think we need to talk, anyway."

Sweat popped out on the palms of her hands and her heart skipped a beat at his words. Talk. Yes, they needed to talk. But she wasn't sure what she wanted to say, what she should say. Catherine leaned over and brushed a light kiss across Matty's forehead then followed Nathan, making sure she closed the door to the bedroom.

Nathan grabbed her hand and led her the short distance to the living room before turning her in his arms and lowering his mouth to hers. She stiffened briefly, afraid to surrender to the sensations swarming over her. Nathan sighed against her lips and stared down at her with an unreadable expression.

"Listen, about earlier, it was an unbelievably stupid move on my part. I wasn't thinking straight. But I don't regret it for a minute, Catherine, and I'd probably do the same thing given a second chance."

"Nathan—" He cut her words off by placing a single finger against her lips, gently.

"Not yet. Just think that over for a few minutes." He removed his finger, took a step back to put distance between them and smiled. "So, can I get you anything to drink? I think I might have some wine around here. Or soda. Definitely water."

"Water's fine."

"Good. Now just sit down and make yourself comfortable. I'll be back in a minute."

Catherine watched as he disappeared into the kitchen, then fought the blush that spread across her face at the recent memory. It *had* been a stupid move, on both their parts. But it had also been an incredibly exciting encounter that still had tremors pulsating along her nerves. She took a deep breath, blew it out between pursed lips and shook her head.

What was she supposed to do about it now? she wondered. Put it out of her mind? Easier said than done.

She brushed the hair out of her eyes and walked over to the bookcase against the far wall. There had been too much on her mind when she first got here that she hadn't taken in any details, so she took her time with them now.

The first thing she noticed was that Nathan's place was exceptionally neat in a bachelor sort of way. No piles of clothes, no careless stacks of magazines or empty pizza boxes. She wasn't sure what she had expected of the loft condo, but it wasn't the neatness and simplicity surrounding her.

Furniture was minimal: a comfortably overstuffed sofa and a recliner, both covered in a neutral leather upholstery. A single magazine lay open on a glass-and-chrome coffee table. She looked closer and smiled absently at the latest issue of *Sports Illustrated,* open to an article on the NHL. Of course.

A free-standing chrome lamp perched near a glass end table. An identical lamp was tucked behind the recliner, and a magazine rack rested next to it on the floor. A quick glance told Catherine that it held more sports magazines.

The most impressive piece of furniture, and what had first caught Catherine's eye, was the combination bookcase and entertainment center that took up the entire back wall. A television and stereo sat prominently in the center section, flanked by a collection of various CDs and DVDs. The left section held an assortment of books and magazines, a spattering of knickknacks and a few framed snapshots. The far right section was nearly identical except for the two shining trophies displayed on a top shelf.

Admiration went through her when she stepped

closer and read their inscriptions. She then studied the smaller snapshots scattered on the shelves. One showed Nathan and his teammates celebrating on the ice; another captured his crooked smile as a blazer-clad official presented him with one of the trophies sitting on the shelf.

There was a surprising similarity to the pictures. Most were informal candid shots of Nathan with his teammates taken over the years. There were different faces, different uniforms, but the same relaxed, jubilant smiles. Catherine looked closer, surprised to see that the only picture of Nathan by himself was the one of him accepting the trophy. Unusual for someone who had obviously enjoyed a successful career.

Footsteps echoed behind her and she jumped, turned to see Nathan watching her from a few feet away. She cleared her throat and fought the sensation that she had been caught snooping. "I, uh, I was just looking at the pictures."

Nathan raised an eyebrow in her direction, smiling, then closed the distance between them and handed her a glass of water. His eyes scanned the shelves behind her, a flash of emotion sparking in their amber glow then disappearing. "Nothing much to look at if you ask me."

"Oh, I don't know. I'm surprised there aren't more of you, though." Nathan shrugged then looked away, and Catherine had the sudden impression he was embarrassed. She studied him as she sipped her water. "The trophies are impressive."

Nathan turned back to her, his eyes intense before

he looked away. He made his way to the sofa and she wondered why he seemed embarrassed. Turning back to the pictures, she realized the small collection covered a wide span of years. The corner of her mouth turned up in a smile when she noticed one of the pictures had obviously been taken during his teen years. "So how long have you played hockey, anyway?"

"Too long." A long sigh accompanied the words and Catherine looked at him in astonishment. She saw him rubbing his knee, noticed the speed with which he removed his hand when he realized she was watching. Nathan was making an obvious effort to pretend nothing was wrong.

"So how long?"

"Catherine, when I said earlier that we needed to talk, I didn't mean about my hockey career." Nathan patted a section of the empty sofa, motioning for her to sit next to him. She bit the inside of her lip and tried not to notice the play of muscles under his shirt or his well-defined legs. She might as well have told herself not to breathe.

She had just as much success trying to relax by telling herself they were only going to talk. The look of amusement Nathan gave her didn't help, either.

"Tell you what. You stop looking so frightened and come over here, and I'll tell you whatever you want to know about my playing hockey."

"Am I that obvious?" She forced the words through a suddenly dry throat, wincing when they came out as little more than a croak. Taking a sip of water didn't help.

"For the most part, yes. Sorry."

Warmth spread across her face and she mumbled in embarrassment, but at least she finally made her way to the sofa. She carefully sat, making sure there was ample space between them, then uttered a noise of surprise when she sank into the soft cushions. More heat rushed to her cheeks as she struggled to hide her small fumble with the overstuffed cushions, unsuccessfully if Nathan's chuckle was any indication.

"Now what was your question?"

"My question?" Catherine looked at him in confusion, gave her head a little shake to clear it enough to remember. "Oh. I was just wondering how long you've been playing hockey."

"Twenty-three years if you count them all, ten years if you just count the major league."

"Twenty-three years?" Catherine stared at him in openmouthed shock. "But that would mean you started when you were…how old were you when you started?"

"Six. Don't look so shocked. That's not really young."

Catherine shrugged, not willing to admit her ignorance about such things. She had never been one to go out for sports, choosing instead activities that exercised her mind. Geeky activities. She wondered why that suddenly bothered her. It had been the truth, after all. Not that she hated physical activities. It was just that she preferred to curl up with a good book, to kick off her shoes and watch a relaxing movie instead of getting her body drenched with sticky sweat.

The hair prickled on the back of her neck as Nathan

watched her with an intensity that curled her toes. She cleared her throat and briefly met his gaze before looking away, suddenly uncomfortable. Suddenly? Catherine nearly laughed. It seemed she was always uncomfortable around Nathan.

"So did you have any other hockey questions for me?" His voice was too soft, too husky. She frowned, wishing she could think of something, then reluctantly shook her head. "Good. Maybe we can talk about something else now."

"Like what?" The words flew from her mouth in a panicky screech, causing a mischievous grin to spread across Nathan's face. Catherine tried not to stiffen when he reached over and wrapped his arm around her, pulling her closer. Her back felt as if it had been fused into an unbreakable column, though, and she heard Nathan sigh a tired sigh.

"Catherine, relax. I'm not going to bite."

"I know. Sorry." She straightened, willed her body to relax and succeeded only slightly. But at least she didn't pull away; she gave herself credit for that. Apparently so did Nathan because he offered her a small smile before shifting closer to her. He studied her in the silence. Catherine swallowed and took another sip of water.

"Better now?" Nathan smiled again, reached out and pushed a strand of hair behind her ear. Catherine ignored the shiver that raced through her at the touch. "I meant what I said last night. About not doing one-night stands."

"Um, oh."

"'Oh,' hmm? You know, this would be a lot easier if you actually participated. Maybe said a word or two."

Catherine knew the words were meant to tease, meant to lighten the conversation, but she still couldn't relax. She didn't know where the conversation was heading or what Nathan expected from her. That was probably the worst, the not knowing. She took a deep breath and downed the last of her water.

"I don't know what to say. I mean, I didn't expect any of this to happen." I don't even know what *this* is, she thought to herself. She looked down and realized her hands were fidgeting. She wished she hadn't put her empty glass on the table.

"So what were you expecting?" The question was a whisper, full of emotion Catherine couldn't interpret. She turned toward Nathan, felt her heart lurch at the look in his eyes. Awareness flared between them, spreading a warmth through her that was almost as painful as the realization that suddenly gripped her.

She was falling for Nathan. Had already fallen. Hard.

Warning bells rang loudly in her ears but it was too late. What had happened to the barriers she so carefully erected around herself? When had Nathan chiseled away at them a piece at a time until they no longer offered protection?

There hadn't been a specific occasion, she realized. Instead, it had been a gradual attack, slowly over the past few months. Fear threatened to suffocate her. She had fallen for him. Against all of her own precautions, the man sitting across from her had worked his way into her heart and latched on.

"Catherine, what were you expecting?" Nathan repeated the question, drawing her attention back to their conversation.

"I don't know. I don't think I was expecting anything. None of this." She waved her hand back and forth, motioning to the two of them. "This wasn't supposed to happen."

"Why not? Catherine, look at me." Nathan cupped her chin in his hand, gently turned her so they were facing each other. His voice grew soft, husky. "There was something there that first day I met you, and I think you know it."

"I thought you were a jerk." The words popped out before she realized she was going to say them, and her eyes widened in disbelief. The embarrassment eased some at Nathan's soft chuckle. She fumbled with an apology but he waved it away.

"I had already figured that one out. Believe it or not, I do catch on quick." The laughter faded from his eyes, replaced by a deep warmth that sent more warnings through Catherine. "I know I'm not the only one who thinks there's more to this. I can see it in your eyes even though you try so hard to hide it."

"Nathan—"

"Shh. I'm not going to force anything on you and I'm not going to push you in a direction you don't want to go. But I'm not going away, either. I don't want to, and I don't think you want me to." His eyes searched hers, probing, before he lowered his head. She leaned in to his kiss, touched by the emotion it conveyed. She tried to hide her disappointment when he pulled away.

"I don't understand you." Catherine searched his face, looking for a hidden agenda and finding none. Instead, he met her stare, an eyebrow cocked in expectation as one corner of his mouth turned up in that boyish grin of his.

"What's not to understand?"

"It's just, most guys would never say anything like that. I always thought men were supposed to be more…I don't know, closed, I guess."

"Or hardheaded?"

Catherine laughed at his choice of words, knowing they were closer to what she meant. Nathan smiled and pulled her closer, tucking her securely against him.

"I'm just as hardheaded as the next guy, but I'm not stupid. I don't believe in playing games. If there's something I want, why not go after it? Why take the chance of losing it? I learned a long time ago that going after what you want is a helluva lot better than waiting until it's too late."

Catherine let his words sink in, tried to figure out their exact meaning without looking at them too closely. It was too much to absorb all at once. Part of her wanted to ask if his words reflected deeper feelings. But she remained quiet, lost in her own thoughts as she rested her head against his chest.

Tension eased out of her, aided by Nathan's gentle caressing of her arm, by the slow rise and fall of his chest under her head. She heard the echo of his heart, a strong, steady beat, lulling in its rhythm, comforting in its strength.

"I wanted to thank you, by the way."

"Thank me for what?" His voice was a deep rumble under her ear, soothing and relaxed.

"Brian and I went to the practice rink first today. Why didn't you tell me you would be fined for missing practice?"

Nathan stared down at her, offered her a quick grin before easing her head back against his chest. Catherine felt him shrug under her. "There were more important things to worry about."

"More important to me, you mean."

"No, to me, too. I've kinda gotten attached to Matty. The kid grows on you, you know?"

Catherine smothered a laugh. "You mean like a fungus? I'm sure Matty would be overjoyed to hear you say that."

"I didn't mean—"

Catherine straightened, placed a finger over his mouth to cut him off. "I know you didn't mean it that way. And I know how much it meant to Matty. He's become attached to you, too."

Nathan shifted against her, the expression in his eyes serious as he looked down at her. He placed a light kiss against her forehead then offered her a reassuring smile. "He's going to be fine, Catherine. He's a lot stronger than you think."

"I know. It's just going to take some getting used to, after worrying about him for so long." She dropped her head against his shoulder and let her eyes drift closed.

"Just take it one day at a time. Things will work out."

Chapter Thirteen

Catherine jumped to her feet with the other 19,000 people surrounding her. She looked down at Matty and felt a smile spread across her face that had nothing to do with the *Banners'* goal. Matty was hopping up and down, waving his pennant with enthusiasm. Nathan's jersey hung on his small frame, still too big for him, but he no longer looked lost in it.

Or maybe she was just starting to see her son for the healthy boy he now was. Catherine sat down as the game resumed, sneaking a glance at Matty. He *did* look different. More self-confident, more enthusiastic and outgoing. Just another nine-year-old boy attending a hockey game. People didn't even notice his prosthesis, especially when it was hidden by his jeans.

Catherine shook her head, amazed at how well and how fast he had adjusted to it. A finger of guilt crept over her but she shrugged it away. Yes, she had been wrong to make him wait, she knew that both as his mother and as a doctor. But that was in the past and there was nothing she could do about it now.

She realized suddenly that Matty wasn't the only one who was different, who had changed in the last few months.

"You're deep in thought. Not a good sign." Brian's voice was close to her ear, startling her.

"Just good thoughts."

Brian motioned to Matty, who was sitting on the edge of the seat, all his attention focused on the game. "He's fine, Catherine. No more worries."

"I know. That's what I was just thinking." She turned back to face the ice as the crowd cheered for Alec's last save, and she clapped with everyone else as the puck was moved to the opponent's side of the ice. She held her breath, leaned forward to watch as the players passed the puck back and forth until Nathan received it and took a shot on goal.

A groan went up from the crowd as the goalie fell back, pulling the puck out of the air before it crossed the line. An official blew the whistle, signaling a stop in play. Catherine turned back to Brian as the players drifted to center ice.

"This is turning out to be a pretty good game."

"A good game? Catherine, this is unbelievable! Look at the score, will you? Four to two. And it's only the second period!" Brian's eyes sparkled as he waved around them, and Catherine laughed at his obvious delight. She hadn't realized what a big fan he was. Or how big a fan she was becoming herself.

The tickets had been another of Nathan's treats, just one of many in the last few weeks since Matty had broken his arm. Tonight they were in the club level, being treated with pomp and circumstance Catherine had trouble associating with ice hockey. She gave up trying to determine how much was normal attention, and how much was arranged by Nathan.

She glanced again at Matty, down at the special orange pass he wore around his neck that matched the ones she and Brian had. The passes would allow them access to the locker rooms after the game. Why Nathan had provided them was something she could only guess at. They had made several trips down there over the last few weeks, as well as social outings with the other players. She doubted if they were strangers to anyone working with the team.

Her attention swung back to the game while her thoughts traveled forward to what the night might bring.

Nathan yanked at his soaked jersey, pulling it over his head with a wince and tossing it on the bench before sitting down. He needed to take off his pads and skates, and all the other equipment that suddenly seemed to weigh so much. But for right now, all he wanted to do was sit back and take a break.

"Nice game, Nathan, but you're going to be sore tomorrow, for sure." Alec tapped him on the head with the blade of his stick, then tossed it on the floor before sitting down. The groan that escaped him echoed Nathan's feelings exactly.

"I don't think 'sore' covers it. I feel like I've been run through a meat grinder with dull blades." Nathan removed his skates and socks, wincing at the dull pain that throbbed along his left side, from his shoulder all the way down to his knee.

"Yeah. That was a helluva hit you took. How's the knee?"

"About as good as the rest of me—which is not so good." Nathan pulled the chest pads and T-shirt over his head, then twisted sideways to survey the damage. His breath came out in a hiss when he saw the series of dark bruises on the side of his chest and leg. Alec let out a low whistle.

"Oooh yeah, you are definitely going to be hurting tomorrow. Better go soak in the whirlpool before you stiffen up."

"I think it's a little late for that." Nathan's words came out in one long grunt as he stood and stripped off the rest of his gear. "Listen, Catherine and Matty are supposed to meet me down here. Can you keep them company while I soak?"

"Yeah, no problem." Alec watched Nathan with a speculative gleam in his eye. "So just how serious are you two, anyway? You've been seeing a lot of her lately."

"I don't know. Halfway serious, I guess. I'm not pushing her anywhere, though, just taking it one day at a time."

Alec raised his eyebrows in disbelief and snorted

before turning away. Nathan grabbed a Ping-Pong ball off the table next to him and threw it at Alec, hitting him in the head.

"That was for the smart-ass comments you were thinking," Nathan explained when Alec faced him with a questioning look. He ducked as the ball was thrown back at him, laughing as he made his way to the whirlpool room, doing his best not to limp.

He eased his body into the whirlpool, leaned back and closed his eyes as the swirling water closed over him. Blissful silence settled over him. He had just started relaxing, allowing the sounds of the water to lull him, when a loud bang startled him. Nathan jumped, cursing silently when he saw Sonny LeBlanc looming over him, beefy arms folded across his wide chest.

"How's the knee?" Sonny's voice was deceptively soft, instantly putting Nathan on alert. He gave Sonny a cursory look before turning away.

"Fine. A little stiff. Nothing that won't go away."

"I want it checked out."

"I said it was fine. Leave it alone."

"Get it checked out or I'll put you on injured reserve."

Fury bubbled through Nathan. He took a deep breath and glared at Sonny. His clipped words fought their way through clenched teeth. "I said it was fine."

Sonny stepped closer and pointed a large finger at him. "And I said get it checked. Don't push me, Conners. I don't need you screwing yourself up, not this close to the finals."

The two men locked eyes, waging a heated battle of wills. Nathan looked away first. "Fine. I'll get it looked at."

"And I don't mean by that doctor you're seeing."

"Wait a minute. There's no need—"

"I mean it, Conners. Get somebody else besides her. I don't want you charming her into thinking nothing's wrong."

Nathan nearly laughed at Sonny's assessment of Catherine, knowing he couldn't be more wrong. She would be the first to bench him if she thought there was a problem, charming or not, but he didn't see the point in telling Sonny that. Instead he leaned back in the tub and offered him a grunt of assent, knowing Sonny was serious about pulling him.

He thought Sonny was finished talking and apprehension knotted his gut when he let out a long sigh and took a seat on the side of the tub, his expression more serious than feral. "Have you given any thought about next season?"

The question was like a punch, instantly putting Nathan on the defensive. He glanced at Sonny, swallowed back more apprehension at the look on his face. "Thought about what?"

"About your playing. You do a good job of hiding it, and some days are better than others." He paused, leveling a serious look at Nathan. "But we both know your knee's not what it used to be, and that it's not getting better."

Leave it to Sonny to get right to the heart of matters, Nathan thought. Something dangerously close to fear raced through him and he did his best to push it away. "The knee's fine."

"That remains to be seen." Sonny stood and walked toward the door, pausing to stare at Nathan again. "You need to think about it, Conners. And then think about this. We need a new training coach next year. If you want it, the job is yours."

"No."

"Just think it over."

"I'm a player, not a coach."

Long seconds ticked by before Sonny responded, his voice quiet and thoughtful. Nathan turned and felt an unknown emotion sweep through him as Sonny fingered the scar that ran down his face. "I used to say the same thing."

Nathan sat in the whirlpool for long minutes after Sonny left, no longer feeling the water that rushed over him, no longer feeling the dull throb of pain along the left side of his body. He was numb. Empty. Almost detached.

Fury and frustration seeped into him as Sonny's words played through his mind. Everything was fine. He was playing strong. Christ, he had even scored twice tonight! His knee was fine, nothing more than an occasional pain. Nothing that couldn't be expected with the grueling practices and hard play that were part of his daily life.

Everything had been fine until Sonny showed up and started talking nonsense. And that's all it was, pure nonsense.

"Dammit!"

Nathan balled one hand into a fist and slammed it against the tile wall. He hit the wall again, barely feeling the impact against the flesh of his hand. "Dammit!"

Sonny was wrong. Everything was fine.

Catherine smiled absently at something Alec said, glanced at her watch then sighed. It was getting late, way past Matty's bedtime. If Nathan wasn't ready soon, they'd have to leave. She already would have if it had been a weeknight.

Youthful laughter caught her attention and she turned, smiling again as she watched the Ping-Pong game Matty and Alec were playing. Catherine stood, knowing she should get Matty ready to leave. She just wished Nathan wasn't taking so long showing Brian around.

"Hey, Matty, are you almost ready to leave?"

"Mom, we're still playing! Besides, Nathan's not back yet."

"I know, but it's way past your bedtime, kiddo. You've got a long day tomorrow." Catherine fixed Matty with her sternest maternal glare before he could protest again. His eyes rounded in feigned innocence and he poked out his lower lip just far enough to make it convincing. She shook her head.

"But, Mom..."

"Better do what she says, Matt. Looks like she means business to me. I certainly wouldn't want to tangle with her." Matty giggled at Alec, letting them know how ridiculous his words sounded. Catherine flashed a grateful smile at Alec then walked over to where she had put their coats. She was just shrugging into hers when

Nathan and Brian turned the corner, both of them looking serious.

Nathan offered her a tired smile as he closed the short distance between them. His arms came around her in a quick hug and he pressed a kiss against her lips before stepping away. She still wasn't accustomed to his public displays of affection, and her face heated at the attention. She offered him a quick smile that faded when she saw how tired he looked.

"Are you okay?"

"Yeah, I'm fine. Just tired."

Catherine studied him some more then turned to Matty and motioned for him to put on his coat. The expression on his face clearly said he was doing it against his will.

"Hey, Nathan, are we still going to go for ice cream?"

"I think we'd better skip on that tonight." Catherine's voice was firm, but she was still surprised when he didn't offer any protest. Going out for ice cream after the games had become a small ritual with them, something she knew Matty looked forward to with excitement. She wasn't sure if it was the ice cream, the time spent with Nathan or the attention they always seemed to attract. Knowing Matty, it was probably all three.

"You're not heading home, are you?" Nathan's quiet voice caught her attention, and she turned to study him. His eyes were hooded, strained. She noticed for the first time that he looked worse than tired. He looked drained, physically worn out. Part of her wanted to reach out and feel his forehead to see if he was coming down with something. She rammed her hand into her pocket before she could do just that, knowing that the action would be too motherly and embarrassing.

"I was thinking about it. It's past Matty's bedtime."

"Catherine, why don't I take Matty home with me? You can pick him up in the morning." She turned and frowned at Brian, wondering what he was up to. He usually asked her first before offering something like that. She opened her mouth to reply but saw something in Brian's eyes that made her stop. She saw a similar look in Nathan's eyes before he turned away.

Something was going on, but she had no idea what. She chewed on her lower lip, trying to ignore Matty's pleas.

"Um, okay. But you go straight to bed when you get there, young man. Understand? And I'll be over early to pick you up." Was it her imagination, or did Nathan seem to breathe a sigh of relief at her agreement? She glanced at him again, frowning, but couldn't see anything in his tired eyes.

Brian gathered the rest of Matty's things then led him out of the locker room. She watched them leave, surprised at the sudden silence that arrived with their departure. She noticed for the first time that Alec was also gone and that she and Nathan were the only two left.

"Now what's going—" The question was interrupted when Nathan's mouth closed over hers in a kiss that nearly buckled her legs. She wrapped her arms around his neck, partly for support, partly to be closer to him.

"I have been wanting to do that all night." Nathan's warm breath caressed the side of her neck as he held her close, gently rubbing her back with his hands. She breathed deeply and rested her head against his chest, enjoying the feel of simply being near him. It was a sensation she could quickly become accustomed to. Was already too accustomed to.

Catherine remained in his arms for a few more minutes then reluctantly pulled away and looked up at him. She thought she saw despair in his eyes, frowned when it disappeared behind a worried look. "Is something wrong, Nathan?"

The minutes ticked by as Nathan stared down at her. The intensity of his eyes sent a flurry of heat shooting through her, nipping at her nerve endings until her entire body hummed.

"I just needed to be with you tonight." His voice, husky and strained, washed over her. Their eyes locked and sent another jolt shooting through Catherine when she glimpsed the emotion and raw need reflected in their golden depths. Her breath caught in her throat and she swallowed, pulling away to put the slightest distance between them.

"Are you sure nothing's wrong?"

"No, just tired." Nathan watched her in silence and she couldn't help but feel like there was something else he wanted to say. His lips twitched briefly but anything he might have said was interrupted by a muffled banging from somewhere else in the locker room. He shook his head and offered her a small smile. "I think we're about to have company."

The door swung open as the words left his mouth. A middle-aged man wearing industrial blue coveralls struggled with a cleaning cart and bucket of water, then looked up in surprise. Heat flooded Catherine's face and she felt like a teenager caught making out in a dark corner of the high school gym.

"Sorry, Mr. Conners. Didn't realize anyone was still here."

"No problem, Gary. We were just leaving, anyway." Nathan squeezed her hand again before releasing it, then bent down to pick up the small gym bag he always carried with him. After he slung it over his shoulder, his hand settled on the small of Catherine's back as he guided her toward the door.

Heat from his touch already radiated through her, spiraling outward to tingle the endings of each nerve. Catherine swallowed and let him guide her outside. She thought of asking him where they were going then decided against it, knowing already that he would take her back to his place for the night.

Just as she knew that neither of them would get much sleep in the upcoming hours.

Chapter Fourteen

Catherine hated Mondays. Not for a specific reason, just the principle of starting a new week of hectic activity. But today was worse. Worse than worse.

She had overslept, something she couldn't remember doing anytime recently. The lost thirty minutes had wreaked havoc with her schedule. Matty had missed the bus so she had to drive him to school. She was late for the single surgery scheduled for today, which, fortunately, was a minor arthroscopy. The time she lost on that spiraled out to her patient rounds, which rippled even further to affect her afternoon appointments at the office.

Catherine glanced at her watch then impatiently jabbed at the elevator button again. She cursed the thirty-minute block of time that had started it all, then cursed the alarm's snooze button, the bus driver who refused to wait and every single red light she'd encountered. Her list extended to include slow elevators by the time the doors opened with a soft whoosh.

Who was she kidding? She could point blame wherever she wanted but it wouldn't change the fact that she was the one responsible for the day's upheaval. Catherine absently hit the button for her office floor then slouched against the panel wall. What was with her? She never overslept. Never.

Guilt raked cold fingers over her. She had overslept to catch up on the sleep she missed Saturday night. And the other two nights last week that had been spent with Nathan.

She rubbed a hand across her face as if the single action could brush away the tiredness that refused to let go. The late nights had to stop. She needed sleep and a clear mind.

The elevator stopped at her floor and she stepped off, trying to recall her appointments for the afternoon. Just a few, if she remembered correctly.

"You finally made it!" Gwen offered her a quick smile as she turned the corner. "Your two o'clock is waiting in room three, and your two-thirty is in the reception area. I told them you were delayed in surgery."

Catherine glanced at her watch then moaned. Well, it wasn't like people actually expected to be seen by a doctor on time. Never mind that she was usually more punctual than the patients. "Thanks, Gwen. Just give me a couple of minutes."

She pushed through the door of her office and closed it behind her, sagging against it for the briefest moment before moving to her desk. She tossed her lunch on the cluttered surface then rooted through a drawer for aspirin, which she tossed back with the water Gwen had placed there earlier. Obviously much earlier. A grimace spread across her face as she swallowed the warm water.

There was a short rap on her door which she acknowledged with a soft grunt. Gwen poked her head in and quickly looked her over. "You look exhausted."

"I am exhausted." Catherine shrugged into her lab coat.

"Well, if it's any consolation, you only have the two appointments today. Your three o'clock just canceled."

"Thank God for small favors. Any other messages?"

"A few lab results came back, all fine. Brian called to say he'd pick up Matty. And Nathan called but no message."

Catherine bit back a sigh when she remembered she was supposed to have called him earlier about tonight's game. Once again he was getting tickets for her and Matty. She'd just have to cancel. No more late nights, not until her system caught up.

Her first patient, an elderly woman with the unlikely name of Jane Smith, was recovering from hip surgery. The progress she had made was astounding and the appointment should have taken no more than fifteen minutes, but was delayed because the woman liked to talk. Incessantly. Catherine waited for a pause in her story then explained she had another patient to see. Miss Jane had trouble concealing her disappointment and reluctantly left the office, telling Catherine she wasn't looking at all well.

Tell me something I don't already know. Catherine blew a strand of hair from her eyes and proceeded to the next patient, an elderly man with arthritis who, unlike Miss Jane, preferred to remain silent. She was in and out of the exam room within fifteen minutes, breathing a sigh of relief when she was finally able to sit behind her desk and lean back in the chair.

The silence of the office wrapped around her and her eyes drifted closed. Guilt nagged at her but she ruthlessly squashed it. There was no harm in enjoying the solitude, nothing wrong with letting her eyes relax. Nothing pressing waited for her, just a few reports to dictate. Nothing that couldn't wait.

She leaned farther back in the chair, her head resting comfortably on the padding. She would keep her eyes closed for a few more minutes, for one of those power-naps everyone always talked about. A few minutes, that was all she needed.

Nathan listened to the message for the third time then slowly placed the receiver back on the hook, trying to hide his frustration and impatience. Catherine hadn't returned his call, and there was no answer at her house. He could page her, but what was the sense in doing that? He didn't want her to call back on the locker room payphone. Not that he wouldn't be there to answer it, of course, since he wasn't playing tonight.

He let out a heavy sigh and rested his forehead against the cool metal of the telephone. Sonny had made good on his promise, much to Nathan's surprise. Six hours earlier he had shown up at the practice rink for game-day skate, had avoided Sonny's questioning stare and performed well. Two hours ago he dressed with his teammates and went out on the ice for warm-up, still avoiding Sonny but thinking he was in the clear when the coach let him go. He had honestly thought Sonny had forgotten all about their talk the other night, until thirty minutes ago when a stone-faced Sonny approached him.

The coach stopped in front of him, slowly looked him up and down then shook his head. Just a small side-to-side motion of his head followed by words that only Nathan could hear.

"You're a scratch tonight, Conners." Sonny walked away, leaving Nathan to stare after him in stunned silence. A part of him wanted to chase after the coach but he didn't. Sonny had warned him the other night and Nathan had ignored him. This was Sonny's way of letting him know he meant business.

"Dammit." The expletive rushed out of Nathan on a frustrated sigh. In the background he could hear the crowd go wild as the intro music blasted through the arena. His team would be hitting the ice right now, stepping onto the slick surface into the spotlights, lining up for the national anthem. Nathan swallowed against the sudden tightness in his chest.

"Dammit!" He hit the wall above the phone with his fist then turned away, ripping his jersey off as he moved to the bench. He was supposed to dress and go into the stands, mingle with the fans and smile and pretend that nothing was wrong.

Nathan clenched his jaw as he peeled the remaining pads off with a ruthless desperation and flung them to the side. Screw it. He was in no mood to mingle with the masses. Did they honestly think he could go out there with a cheery smile and pretend nothing was wrong? Sonny was threatening his career, his whole *life,* dammit! There was no way he was going to go out there and pretend nothing was wrong.

He grabbed the gym bag and yanked it from his locker, pulling out ripped jeans and a faded T-shirt, opting for comfort instead of the casual dress clothes that hung in the locker. What else could they do to him if he just left? He was already scratched for tonight, probably for the next game, as well, if he knew Sonny, so screw team policy.

Nathan threw the gym bag over his shoulder, grabbed his keys from the locker shelf then slammed the door, taking obscene pleasure in the hollow echo it made in the deserted locker room. The sound of the horn blaring in the arena filled the empty room, muted but still loud enough to drown out the echo of the slamming door. Nathan gritted his teeth, knowing he should be happy that the *Banners* had scored so quickly. He was happy. But he was also resentful as hell. Dammit, he belonged on the ice right now. That could have been his goal. He reached out to open the locker door then slammed it again.

He rested his forehead against the door and shut his eyes. He had to get out of there. If he was smart, he'd go straight home and work his frustrations out on the home gym. Maybe run a couple of miles on the treadmill until his anger was gone.

Yeah, right. He'd be on the treadmill all night before his anger disappeared. The last place he needed to go was home. He thought briefly about going to Catherine's then quickly dismissed the idea. Matty was home, and Catherine had made it clear that their relationship had certain boundaries in front of Matty. Holding hands and the occasional kiss were permissible, but no overnighters with Matty present. Nathan respected her for that, but right now it only added to his frustration.

It looked like he was going home to work things out on the weights. After a drive, though. A night ride through the streets of Baltimore would go a long way to relieving the stress that knotted his shoulders and tightened his neck.

Nathan sped out of the parking garage, not going in any particular direction. He was in a sour mood tonight, his thoughts lingering in the past instead of focusing on the here and now. Instead of thinking about what might happen.

He didn't want to think about what lay ahead, about the very real possibility that this could be his last year playing. Dammit, he still had a lot to offer, was still a good player regardless of his knee problems. Sure, it had set him back a little at first, but he had worked hard to get back. It would probably never be a hundred percent, but he could get it close. Just a little more work…

Who was he kidding? He *had* worked at it, pushed himself beyond his limits and he could still feel the difference, knew he'd never be back to his old self. He had gone as far as he could; if he pushed further, he'd only do more damage. He knew it, and Dr. Porter had confirmed it the other night when Nathan asked him to do a quick check on it after the game.

He could finish this year out with minimum problems. It was mid-March. The regular season ended the beginning of April. The *Banners* were in first place in the Southeast Division and guaranteed a spot in the run for the Cup. There was no doubt in Nathan's mind that they'd go all the way, which meant playing until June. Playing a game every other night, playing through injuries, ignoring the pain. All for the privilege of raising Lord Stanley's Cup over his head. It was a price he—like everyone else—would gladly pay.

As for next year…he didn't know. He'd asked Brian about it the other night. Things didn't look to be in his favor, though.

Nathan muttered an expletive under his breath and cranked up the stereo volume. George Thorogood blared from the speakers, piercing the night as he maneuvered the small car through the Baltimore traffic. Cold air whipped past him, clearing his head as all thought disappeared behind him into the night.

* * *

Catherine woke in time to see the shadowed figure looming over her. The scream building in her throat was cut off by the large, callused hand over her mouth.

"Shh, it's me." The hoarse whisper was close enough to her ear that she could feel the moist heat of breath against her cheek, smell the faint scent of stale beer. The fear that had momentarily frozen her released its grip and she lashed out with her fist, connecting with something hard and bony. A loud *oomph* escaped the intruder as he stumbled backward. Another grunt broke the silence as she kicked out with her foot.

She thought she heard her name but dismissed it, thinking it was surely her imagination as she flicked on the bedside light and grabbed her alarm clock for use as a weapon. Her eyes blinked against the sudden bright light, then blinked again at the huddled figure on the floor next to her bed.

"Nathan?" He was kneeling close to her feet, bent over far enough that his forehead rested on the floor. One arm was wrapped firmly around his stomach; his free hand covered his nose. She called his name again.

The seconds stretched around them. Nathan's harsh breathing finally returned to normal as he slowly sat up. His deep amber gaze rested on her, one dark eyebrow raised in question.

"Are you going to clock me, too?"

"What?" Catherine stared at him, thinking he must have gone mad, then realized she still held the alarm clock up, ready to wield it as a club. She placed it on the nightstand then turned back to him. "What are you doing here? How did you get in?"

"Your back door was unlocked." A small groan punctuated his words as he slowly stood, alternately rubbing his nose and his stomach. He stepped closer to the bed and looked down at her, a crooked smile turning up one corner of his mouth. Catherine glanced down, realized she was wearing only a T-shirt and struggled to pull the hem lower over her legs. Nathan's hand reached out and closed gently over hers.

"Don't." His voice had turned quiet, a husky whisper in the silence that surrounded them. She swallowed, trying to clear the last of the sleep from her head. Nathan closed what little distance remained between them and placed one knee on the bed beside her, trapping her between his legs, trapping her with the heat of his body and the sparks flying between them. Sleep and passion fought for control of her senses, blocking out coherent thought as his lips came down to claim hers. Catherine fell backward, felt Nathan ease his body over hers until they were nestled in the overstuffed mattress and jumble of blankets.

It was the faint taste of beer on his tongue that brought her fully awake, the faint scent of it on his breath as he nuzzled her neck that told her things were not as they should be. Catherine pushed gently against him until he reluctantly propped himself on his elbows and stared down at her.

"Nathan, are you drunk?"

"No."

"But you've been drinking?"

"Yes."

"What are you doing here?"

"I wanted to see you." Nathan dipped his head and dragged his lips along her jawline, sending a jumble of sensations through her. Catherine caught her breath, held it, let it out in a rush as she pushed against him once more, this time rolling out from under him. It wouldn't be quite as easy to give in to temptation if there was distance between them.

She heard Nathan's soft groan of frustration but he didn't follow her. Instead he shifted more comfortably on the bed, stretched his long legs out and folded his arms under his head, watching her with an intensity she didn't quite understand. Catherine moved back on the bed and curled her legs under her.

"What's wrong?"

"I was getting ready to ask you the same thing. Nathan, what are you doing here?"

"I told you, I wanted to see you."

"But it's..." Catherine trailed off to look at the clock then uttered a small moan of disbelief. "Nathan, it's two o'clock in the morning! You break into my house—"

"The door was unlocked."

"—and scare the life out of me, then tell me you just wanted to see me? Didn't you think about the time? Couldn't it have waited until morning? I'd think the least you could have done was called!"

"I tried to call. First I left a message at your office that you never returned, then I tried calling earlier this evening and there was no answer. I didn't think you'd appreciate me calling this late at night."

Catherine stared at him in disbelief. He didn't move, just lay back on her bed, looking comfortable, looking too much as if he *belonged.* His eyes locked on hers with an expression of boyish innocence and something else that threatened what was left of her common sense. "You didn't want to call this late, but you had no problems with breaking into my house?"

"The door was unlocked."

"Nathan!" Catherine shot off the bed in frustration. She felt like she was beating her head against the wall, trying to figure out what was going on. Why would Nathan sneak into her house at two in the morning? And why wasn't she more upset at seeing him there?

Every grain of sense told her she should ask him to leave, that his being here wasn't right. Matty was in his room down the hall, sound asleep. There was no guarantee that he wouldn't wake up. What if he found Nathan here? Catherine strengthened her resolve, ready to tell him that he had to leave.

She turned to face him and the words died in her throat. He was sitting up now, his hands clasped together and hanging loosely between his knees. There was a desperate look in his eyes, a tortured haunting that impaled her with unexplained grief. She looked away for a second then turned back, not surprised to see his eyes clear of all expression.

"Did you watch the game tonight?" Nathan kept his voice carefully even, neutral. Catherine frowned, remembered they were supposed to go to the game but hadn't. Guilt smothered her.

"Uh, no. No, I didn't get a chance to see it. I was tired. There've been too many late nights and—"

"We lost."

"Oh." Catherine didn't know what else to say. Surely this couldn't be the reason for his sudden visit, for the look she had glimpsed in his eyes moments earlier. Even the best teams had to lose a game now and then.

"I didn't play." The three words were flat, toneless. The absence of emotion in Nathan's voice and the blank look on his face told a bigger story. "Do you know why I didn't play?"

Catherine shook her head. She was pretty certain it had something to do with his knee, but she remained silent.

"Because I'm a wash-up. A has-been."

"Oh, Nathan…"

"It's the truth. And all because of this damn knee." He shook his head then slowly pushed himself off the bed, unfolding his long body in a single fluid movement. Catherine felt the tension rolling off him as he paced back and forth in front of her. "Sonny told me after the game the other night that he'd scratch me unless I got another clearance from the doctor. He wants to make sure that it's not more screwed up than it is."

"Which doctor did you see?"

"I didn't. I didn't think Sonny was serious. He made his point tonight by pulling me."

Silence descended on the room, cloaking them in an eerie quiet. Catherine wrapped her arms around herself, suddenly chilled. "Not playing tonight doesn't mean you're a wash-up. It sounds more like two people butting heads than anything else." Her statement was met with a derisive snort from Nathan. He ran one hand through his hair, mussing it up, then turned to look at her with a quick shake of his head.

"No, there's more to it than that." He paused, fixing her with another unreadable stare. "You know, I left the arena tonight with no idea where to go. I drove around for a while then stopped at some no-name bar to watch the game and have a few drinks. I planned on going home when I left there, had really planned on it. Instead, I found myself sitting in your driveway and not knowing why at first. I know now, though."

Catherine shivered at his intensity and hugged herself tighter. The tension coming off him grew thicker as he stepped closer, not stopping until less than a hand's-width of space separated them. Catherine opened her mouth to speak then shut it when nothing more than a pitiful squeak came out. She swallowed and tried again. "So why did you come here?"

"Because I need to see you."

Chapter Fifteen

"You need to see me?" Catherine repeated his words in a hoarse whisper, an unreadable expression on her face. Nathan watched her, wondering at the sudden emotions that passed through her eyes. He knew he had been drinking but he was hardly drunk. His words shouldn't have caused her so much confusion.

"Yes, see you," he repeated. He reached out with one hand and rested it on her shoulder, thinking to pull her closer, to hold her until he could find some way to convince her to let him spend the night. Instead of leaning into him, though, she stiffened and pulled away a little, surprising him.

"Oh. I, uh, hadn't planned on seeing you until tomorrow." Nathan heard the wariness in her voice and frowned. Maybe he had more alcohol in his system than he realized, because he seemed to be missing something. He ran a hand through his hair, trying to decide if he should start over.

"I didn't want to wait until tomorrow."

"Oh. Um, why not?"

"Why not?" He sounded like a parrot, he realized. He shook his head and stepped toward her, not liking the fact that she stepped back when he did. He took a deep breath and let it out in a frustrated sigh. "Because you'll be at work tomorrow, then I'll be busy later, that's why. And I wanted to see you now."

"Oh." She sounded less excited than he had hoped. He watched, not liking the way she wrapped her arms protectively around her middle or the way she wouldn't look at him.

"Okay, so maybe it wasn't a great idea. I'm sorry. But you don't have to look so appalled. I just wanted to see you, to hold you. That was it." His earlier excitement at seeing her faded, and he did his best not to slump in disappointment as Catherine finally looked at him through the strands of hair covering her still-sleepy eyes.

"You just wanted to see me? You didn't want me to look at your knee or clear you or anything, right?"

"Clear me?"

"Yes. So you can go back to playing."

"What?" Nathan made no effort to keep the disbelief from his voice. He shook his head, trying to refocus, trying to follow her train of thought. He watched her for a few seconds, saw the uncertainty reflected in her eyes and the small frown that creased her forehead. "Hell, no, I don't want you to clear me! What on earth ever gave you that idea?"

"You said, I mean, you said you didn't play tonight, that you needed to be cleared, and then you showed up here and broke in—"

"The door was unlocked!"

"I just thought..." Her voice trailed off, her eyes focused on the floor in front of her. Nathan wasn't sure if he wanted to close the space between them so he could hold her or knock some sense into her.

"Catherine, I would never ask you to do something like that. I have a doctor, remember? Getting cleared to play again is not something I'm worried about. Next year may be a different story, but, well, never mind about that."

"Then why are you here?"

Nathan stared at her in blank surprise. Surely she had been listening earlier and had to know he wanted to be with her. Hadn't he told her that already, when they were on the bed together? Too much talk, that was the problem. He had never been much at talking, and this was why—it did nothing but cause problems. Better to let his actions speak for him.

He closed the distance between them in two long strides and pulled her to him. Her mouth dropped open in a surprised *O* and he used her shock to his advantage, lowering his head and claiming her lips in a hungry kiss that damn near buckled *his* knees. Masculine satisfaction raced through him when her body melted into his. Her hands reached for him, fisting into the thin material of his T-shirt as her tongue eagerly met his.

Nathan swallowed her small moan with a hunger that was out of control. His hands roamed lower, past the hem of her shirt, down to the bare silkiness of her thighs. Catherine moaned again as his hands moved back up, skimming her body, grabbing the hem of the cotton shirt and dragging it up, breaking the kiss so he could pull it over her head and toss it to the floor. She was bathed in the soft light from the lamp and he grew even harder at the sight of creamy skin and soft curves and rosy flush.

Catherine tried to cover herself but he reached out to stop her, holding her hands firmly by her sides so he could see her more fully. A look of uncertainty crossed her face then slowly disappeared when he smiled at her a split second before lowering his head and closing his mouth over one taut nipple. Her hands escaped his and threaded themselves in his hair, his name tearing from her mouth in a ragged whisper.

This was what he had come for. To feel her body mold itself against him, to lose himself in her. He broke away again, more satisfaction speeding through him at her groan of displeasure. Within seconds his clothes were scattered on the floor and Catherine was back in his arms, their bodies flushed together, her hands roaming wildly over his heated flesh as if she couldn't get enough of him.

He knew the feeling, felt the frustration at the realization that he would never get enough of this one woman. His hands closed around her hips and lifted until her legs wrapped around him, searching for him, rubbing against him. He tightened his grip, stopping her before she could close over him. He smiled against her mouth, shook his head and walked backward until his legs touched the edge of the bed.

"Not yet, sweetheart. Not yet." He collapsed onto the soft mattress, carrying her down with him, moaning when she straddled him. His earlier idea of sweetly torturing her body until she begged for mercy disappeared. Their mouths melded together, their tongues mating wildly, their hands frantic on each other's body. Nathan grabbed her hips, guiding her, swallowing her cry as she impaled herself on him. A moan escaped him as she tightened around him, taking him all in, filling herself. Fear tightened his chest when he realized he would never have enough of her. They could stay like this for the rest of their lives and it still wouldn't be enough.

Then the fear was gone, replaced by something more essential as Catherine rode him wildly, her breath coming in little gasps that grew with her pleasure. Nathan guided her hips, met each of her movements with a wild thrust until his name was ripped from her throat on a ragged scream. She tightened around him, grasping and pulling, treating him to the most exquisite torture he could imagine. Nathan turned, rolling with her until he was on top, clenching his jaw against the unbearable feeling of her legs wrapped around him. His hips thrust and he buried himself deep inside her, withdrew and thrust again. Again, until his own control shattered and his muffled cries mixed with Catherine's.

Moments passed, or it may have been hours before

his left leg cramped. He muttered a quiet oath, and reluctantly rolled off Catherine to stretch his leg. He felt a telltale wetness on her upper thighs when he moved and this time didn't bother to keep his oath silent.

"What?" Catherine's voice was sleepy, dreamlike. He looked down at her, took in her tousled hair and the contented smile curving her full lips. His mind was suddenly filled with an image of a child that would look just like her. Nathan held his breath, waiting for the fear to follow the image. None came, which frightened him even more.

Oh, man. Yeah, he had it bad.

"Is something wrong?" Catherine propped herself up and studied him, concern chasing the sleep from her eyes.

"No, nothing. Nothing's wrong."

"Are you sure? You looked a little pale for a second."

"I'm fine. Nothing to worry about." Nathan laid back against the pillow and tucked her head securely in the crook of his shoulder. There was no fear, only a contentment as calming as a sedative. He dropped a kiss on the top of her head and closed his eyes, smiling as she wrapped her arms around him and rested her head against his chest.

Hot coffee. Sizzling bacon. Something spicy.

The smells curled around Catherine, so thick with flavor she imagined she could see them. Her stomach rumbled in protest against the sensory onslaught and she stretched, not wanting to ruin the dream by awakening but knowing she had to.

Her eyes opened slowly. Light streamed in through the curtains. She stretched again then bolted upright.

The smells were still there.

She frowned, knowing something was wrong but unable to immediately place it. A smile replaced the frown as the memory of last night came back. Nathan sneaking into her house, their wild encounter, falling asleep wrapped in his arms…

Nathan.

Oh, God. Nathan was still here, cooking breakfast. He had spent the night. With Matty home. Catherine glanced at the clock on the nightstand. seven a.m. She bolted out of bed and searched for a robe as muffled voices floated through the closed door.

She found them in the kitchen, standing next to each other by the stove. Nathan was holding a small frying pan filled with beaten egg above the flame, manipulating it with a spatula. Chopped onion, tomato, cheese and ham were piled in small bowls on the counter next to him. He was talking in a quiet voice to Matty, telling him how to judge when the egg was ready, helping him add the different ingredients.

Catherine stared in shock. Nathan Conners was in her kitchen, teaching her son how to make omelets.

Matty turned and saw her in the doorway, a wide smile splitting his face. "Hey, Mom. Look who came over this morning. We're making breakfast for you."

"I…I see that." The words tumbled from her mouth as Nathan faced her, a hunger in his eyes she knew had nothing to do with the food he was cooking. She clutched the robe more tightly around her as her skin warmed under his gaze. "I, uh…I didn't expect to see you here."

"I was in the neighborhood and decided to stop by."

"Yeah, Mom. I heard the doorbell ring and you were still sleeping and I wasn't gonna answer it until I saw who it was then I let him in. And now we're cooking."

Catherine raised her eyebrows, her hearing overloaded at Matty's rush of words. Nathan shrugged, a barely noticeable motion of his shoulders as if to say…she wasn't sure what. All she knew was that for some reason Nathan had left—or at least pretended to leave—so he could make a surprise visit. To cook for her and her son.

The gesture was touching, surprising. And terrifying. She wanted to ignore the liquid warmth that ran through her. Just like she wanted to ignore the softness in Nathan's eyes and the small grin that touched his lips.

It was too much to handle this early in the morning.

"I've got coffee ready for you here." Nathan pulled a mug from the under-the-counter rack and poured the steaming brew into it. She watched as he added just enough cream and sugar to suit her taste, all without asking. He stepped around Matty and handed her the mug, their hands momentarily touching. She mumbled a thank-you and sipped, closing her eyes as the first jolt of caffeine kicked in.

So he knew how she liked her coffee. Big deal. He probably saw her fix it herself a hundred times. At least a dozen. Or maybe just once or twice. It meant absolutely nothing.

Nathan set three plates on the table and motioned with a grand gesture for everyone to sit down and eat. Omelets, bacon, toast, juice…it was an impressive spread. And more than Catherine usually fixed for breakfast. She ate most of it in silence, watching the interplay between Matty and Nathan, enjoying the sounds of their playful conversation as they talked between bites of food.

Almost like they were father and son. Like a family.

The last bite of food hit Catherine's stomach like a slab of concrete and settled there. She wrapped her hands around the mug of coffee, seeking warmth to thaw the chill creeping through her veins. Dangerous thoughts. Thoughts that could only lead to trouble. She didn't want to think of their interplay, didn't want to recognize the bond growing between them.

It was too late. The two of them were already like a family. Maybe the three of them were. Looking back, there were times when they all certainly acted like it.

Catherine gulped the hot coffee, hoping the heat would burn away the ridiculous thoughts swirling through her mind. It was too early in the morning for wishful thinking. Dreams were only supposed to happen at night, during the safety of sleep.

Nathan sat on the exam table, afraid to breathe as Brian Porter looked at his knee. He flinched when the doctor manipulated the kneecap from side to side, then cursed himself for the telltale movement when Brian looked at him curiously. The exam ended and then the only sound in the room was the scratching of pen on paper as Brian scribbled notes in his file. Nathan's nerves stretched tight in proportion to the growing silence until he couldn't take it anymore.

"Well?"

Brian placed the clipboard on a small table and sat on the wheeled stool, studying Nathan in silence. "There's swelling and tenderness with lateral movement. Your range of motion is good considering the condition of the kneecap. Your muscular strength is excellent, which will only help."

"But?"

"But your kneecap is deteriorating." Brian flipped through the oversize file in front of him, searching. He pulled out a set of X-ray films, glanced at them in the overhead light and chose two. He placed them on the lightboard, turned it on and motioned for Nathan to stand next to him. He pointed at the first one with a stylus he removed from his coat pocket. "This was the X-ray we took before your surgery. You can see some irregularities on the underside, small patches of roughness. The front was nearly smooth." He tapped at the second film.

"This is from today. You can see the underside shows quite a bit of roughness. That shouldn't be there—I smoothed it during your surgery. And if you look here, the front is beginning to show the same roughness. Not as much as the underside, but it's there."

Nathan squinted at the films in front of him, trying to pick out the patches Brian was pointing at. He had no idea what he was looking at. "So what's that mean? You need to operate again, to go in and smooth them out? That's something that could wait until the end of the season. Give me enough time to go through rehab..." Nathan's voice trailed off, a funny feeling in his gut when Brian let out a weary sigh.

"Nathan, you have arthritis in your knee."

"Arthritis? How can I have arthritis? I just turned thirty for chrissakes. Arthritis is something you get when you're old!"

"It's not just for old people. And it sometimes happens after surgery. You've had two so far. But that isn't the only thing that's causing the deterioration. The amount of trauma your knee is exposed to, the amount of wear and tear..." Brian removed the glasses from his face, cleaned them almost absently before putting them back on and leveling a serious gaze at Nathan. "Your knee needs to be replaced."

"Replaced?" Nathan repeated mechanically. His breath left him suddenly and he slumped against the exam table. "Replaced? So what does that mean? I mean, you replace it and then what?"

"Nathan, I don't think you understand. The damage isn't substantive enough to warrant a replacement right now. Even if it did, I'd be hesitant to do it. With a replacement, you could expect to go ten, maybe fifteen years before needing another. With moderate activity."

Nathan stared at Brian, stunned. He couldn't have heard right. There was no way he could have heard right. "You mean to tell me with all the technology today, you can't fix a knee?"

"Unfortunately, no. I could go back in, smooth it out again, but each time would just weaken the knee more."

"But what about…I mean, what…" Nathan couldn't finish the sentence, could barely make himself complete the thought.

"Playing?" Brian sighed and took a seat again. "Finishing this year shouldn't be a problem. Next year, I don't know. Maybe, maybe not. The rate of deterioration, the amount of wear and tear your knee is subjected to—it's hard to say."

Hard to say. The words floated around him like a bad nightmare as he stood against the exam table, too stunned to move. There was no guarantee he could play next year.

There was no way he would accept that.

He didn't know anything *except* hockey. It wasn't just how he made his living, it was how he lived his *life.* And Brian Porter just told him it was *hard to say* if he'd play next year.

Nathan rubbed at the bridge of his nose, hard, as if the pressure could relieve the sudden splitting inside his head at the simple words. *Hard to say.* Like it wasn't a major deal. Nathan felt like he had just been cross-checked from behind and was reeling across the ice, out of control, shooting straight for the boards.

Porter was wrong. He had to be wrong. He'd get a second opinion. Go see another specialist. There had to be someone out there who knew something Porter didn't. He'd just find somebody else, get that second opinion, pretend this whole visit never happened…

"Nathan? Are you listening to me?"

"What? No, I…no." He faced Dr. Porter, saw the concern in the eyes behind the glasses. Saw the pity. Nathan pushed away from the table, shaking his head. He didn't need pity.

"This isn't the end of the world. You're still young, healthy. And in a few years, who knows? Maybe we'll know more by then, be able to do more. In the meantime, there's nothing stopping you from doing what you normally do now."

"Except play."

"Except play." Brian stood, studying Nathan with a quiet intensity. "I don't think planning to continue next year would be a wise thing to do. Your knee won't be able to handle the continued stress. In the end, it would only make things worse."

"You don't think? So what are you saying here? That I *shouldn't* play next year, or that I *can't* play next year?"

"I'm strongly advising against it."

"Advising? Not ordering?"

"Nathan, I think you should take a day or two to think about what I said. I know it's nothing you want to hear, but it's something you do need to come to terms with." Brian rummaged through a plastic tray containing assorted leaflets, pulling two from the pile. Nathan ignored the doctor's outstretched hand and instead he shoved his hands deep into the pockets of his sweat shorts. "Sure, I'll think about it."

"I think you should take these, look them over."

"No, that's okay. I'll pass."

"Nathan..." Brian's voice trailed off, filling the room with a stubborn silence that was broken by a short rap at the door. Nathan continued to stare at Brian, his chin tilted defiantly.

Catherine stepped into the small room, her attention focused on a chart in front of her. "Brian, I'm sorry to interrupt but..." She looked up, her surprise plain on her face. "Nathan. What are you doing here?"

Nathan stiffened, suddenly wishing he was somewhere else, realizing he should have made the appointment with Brian when Catherine wouldn't be in the office. How could he have been so stupid? He should have known he'd end up running into her.

"Just thought I'd have Brian look at my knee." The words escaped in a rush, sounding hollow and false. Why, he didn't know—it was the truth. Maybe not all of it, but close enough. Catherine looked at Nathan, then at Brian, before her eyes drifted down and settled on the leaflets in Brian's hand. Nathan reached over, snatched the papers and shoved them in his pocket.

Catherine stared at him, the clipboard in her arms held protectively against her like a shield. He noticed the distancing in her eyes when she spoke. "What's going on?"

"Nothing. Brian was just looking at my knee. Like I said."

"Nathan..."

He closed the distance between them, almost knocking Brian over in the process. He placed a quick kiss on Catherine's lips then stepped into the hall. "It's nothing, Catherine. I have to go. See you tonight."

Nathan scurried down the hall, the leaflets burning a hole in his pocket as surely as Catherine's stare burned a hole in his back.

Chapter Sixteen

Catherine tightened her hands on the steering wheel and looked around at the crowded parking lot, reconsidering. She didn't have to do this now. She didn't have to do this at all.

She didn't *want* to do this at all.

She took a deep breath and stepped into the mild March weather, squinting against the glare of sunlight. She had to do it now, to get it over with before she lost her nerve. Things had gone too far, especially after Matty's stunt last night.

The chill of the ice rink hit her as soon as she opened the doors, seeping into her bones. Close to a hundred fans were seated on the bleachers, cheering on the players during the practice. Catherine almost lost her resolve at the sight of so many people but she firmly ignored the urge to turn and run.

She glanced at her watch. The practice should be over in a few minutes. Catherine took another deep breath and walked over to the stanchions that blocked the access to the ice and locker room. She chose a spot off to the side next to a set of machines that sold soda and juice and waited.

The knot in her stomach tightened and grew, and again she wondered if she was doing the right thing. She squelched her doubts, knowing that Matty had to come first. And being with Nathan had suddenly put Matty in danger.

The image of Matty careening down the driveway on a skateboard was still crystal clear, and enough to nearly make her lose what little food she had eaten. The skateboard was a gift from Nathan—a gift that sent the wrong message.

Someone jostled her from behind, pushing her up against the soda machine, and she looked up. It was a pair of younger girls, maybe in their late teens, pushing through the crowd to get closer as the players made their way to the table. Catherine noticed the jerseys and calendars in their hands, saw the predatory gleam in their eyes as a few players stepped forward.

She tried to rein in what remained of her patience as more eager fans pressed closer, forcing her to the back of the crowd. Catherine gritted her teeth and tried stepping closer, only to stop when Nathan finally made his way to the roped-off area. A few young girls rushed forward, smiles on their faces as Nathan greeted them with that boyish grin of his.

What am I doing?

Catherine took a step backward, suddenly unsure of herself. She didn't want to do this. She *had* to do this. She had to. Matty's health was at stake. She had already made her decision; why was she suddenly second-guessing herself?

Taking a deep breath, she skirted the edge of the crowd, slowly making her way to the front. She reached her destination just as Nathan posed for a picture with a fan, his arm draped casually around the girl's shoulder. A flicker of surprised amusement crossed his face when the girl turned to kiss him. He gently shrugged away from her with a good-hearted chuckle that left the girl sighing dreamily.

Catherine folded her arms tightly around herself, surprised at the small glimmer of jealousy—and remorse—she felt. Nathan turned to greet someone else, his eyes scanning over her, just someone in the crowd. Catherine knew exactly when he realized it was her, saw it in the slight widening of his eyes.

He did a double take, a blush turning his face crimson as he met her stare. His mouth opened briefly then snapped shut. The fans scattered about him didn't seem to notice and kept calling out to get his attention. Nathan waved at them absently, pushing his way through until he stood directly in front of her.

"Catherine, what are you doing here?"

"We need to talk, Nathan."

He shifted his weight from one foot to the other,

his height exaggerated by the addition of the skates. Catherine tilted her head up to watch him, noticed how uncomfortable he seemed as he gestured back to the young girl who had kissed him. "That wasn't what it looked like. I mean, I didn't even know—"

"Not about that."

"Oh." His relief was obvious. He shifted again, his look turning from discomfort to confusion. "Then about what?"

"About Matty. And the skateboard you got for him."

A frown crossed Nathan's face, then he reached out and closed his hand gently around her arm, leading her away from the crowd that was closing in on them. He turned her so his back shielded them from the curious onlookers and leaned closer. "I'm not sure I follow you, Catherine. Why are you so upset?"

"A skateboard, Nathan? What were you thinking?" She forced the words through clenched teeth, knowing they weren't the words she had come here to say. Her insides knotted painfully and she opened her mouth to get it over with but she couldn't, not with Nathan looking at her like that.

"Listen, this isn't a good place to talk. Too many people." Nathan glanced behind him, motioning to the growing crowd. "How about if you wait here until I'm finished cleaning up and then we can go get something to eat?"

"No."

"Oh. Um, okay. Then how about we meet later? I can bring pizza for dinner or something."

"Fine."

"Fine? Catherine, is there something else I should know?"

"No."

"Are you sure?"

No, I'm not sure. About anything. But she didn't say the words out loud, just nodded, afraid to say anything else. He had already broken through her defenses once before she realized it and made her trust him. My God, she had been having ridiculous thoughts of them actually becoming a family!

Only to find out that he wasn't as dependable and responsible as she thought. She should have stuck with her first instincts and stayed away from him, before it was too late.

Before she had fallen in love with him.

Oh, God, how could she have let such a thing even happen? She knew better, but she had let it happen anyway. She had grown to depend on Nathan, to let go of her own misgivings and trust, when she knew better than to depend on anyone but herself.

Catherine looked down at the hand on her shoulder, realized Nathan was speaking to her in quiet tones. She tilted her chin up with a carelessness she didn't feel and leveled a blank look at him. "I'm sorry, I didn't hear you."

"I asked you what time I should bring the pizza over." Nathan paused, fixed her with a steady stare that made her feel like he was reading the very depths of her soul. His eyes narrowed slightly as he studied her, seeing too much. A flicker of something unreadable flashed in his gaze and he shifted subtly closer to her. She suppressed the urge to cower and hide from that penetrating gaze.

"Six will be fine."

"Okay, then. I'll be there around six." He shifted on his skates and motioned absently behind him. "I need to get going. If you need me to bring anything else, just give me a call."

"Fine." Catherine backed up when she realized Nathan was stepping closer for a quick kiss. A sharp stab of pain pierced her chest at the look of confusion in his eyes, and she turned away before she could do something stupid, like change her mind.

He might have called her name but she couldn't be sure, since any sound was drowned out by the loud crashing of the panic bar as she hit it before rushing out the front door.

Nathan sat in the car and stared at the neat rancher in front of him. His stomach churned suddenly and he blamed it on the combination of smells of pepperoni pizza and fresh flowers. *Nothing* was wrong, even though every nerve in his body screamed out that something bad was about to happen.

So the skateboard had been stupid. He knew that even before he got it for Matty. He'd apologize and everything would be fine. But Catherine seemed upset about something more, had looked like she had been about to break into tears right before she bolted out of the practice rink. He didn't know what was going on, and part of him was afraid to find out.

The same part that was afraid to admit how deeply he cared for her. He wouldn't yet say it was that damned *L* word, but he was afraid it was close.

Liar.

He mentally flinched as his conscience hurled the accusation at him, but he didn't deny it. Didn't agree with it, either, but he'd sort that out later. Instead, he took a deep breath, grabbed the pizza and flowers and got out of the car.

Nathan smiled a little when he imagined the wide grin that would spread across Matty's face when the kid noticed the pizza box. He rang the doorbell, realizing he was enjoying these little moments with them more and more. It was a time he looked forward to, almost as much as the time he spent on the ice.

God, what a thought.

He shifted the box on his arm and waited, wondering what was taking them so long to open the door. Nathan reached out to push the buzzer again then stepped back, startled, when the door was pulled open by a somber-faced Catherine. His smile of greeting died at her expression.

"I, uh, brought the pizza." It was an asinine thing to say, so obvious that a blind man would have noticed, but the look of anxiety and determination on Catherine's pale face had caught him so off guard he was almost speechless. She stepped back and barely motioned for him to come in. His stomach churned again. The house was too quiet. "Where's Matty?"

"At a friend's."

"Oh." He followed Catherine into the large kitchen

and placed the pizza box on the table. The flowers were still clenched in one hand and he turned to give them to her only to realize she wasn't looking at him. He cleared his throat and waved them absently, hoping to get her attention, to bring a smile to her face. "I brought these, too."

She finally turned toward him, her face completely blank as her gaze darted from his to the flowers he was waving like an idiot. His hand dropped to his side as Catherine folded her arms across her chest and stared at a spot somewhere behind him.

"Nathan, this isn't a good idea." Her words were cool and precise, distanced and hollow. He swallowed against the growing dread in the pit of his stomach and forced a smile.

"What? The pizza? We can always get something—"

"Not the pizza. This." She finally looked him in the eye, fixed him with a stare that was completely devoid of all emotion. Nathan glanced away, searching for something to distract him from that blank look and the irrational fear it gave him.

"'This' what?" His own voice was steady, carefully neutral, betraying none of the anxiety that suddenly swamped him as he tossed the flowers on the table beside the pizza.

"This…whatever this is between us. It's not a good idea."

"It's not?"

"No."

"And why is that?" Nathan's voice was calm, almost

as flat as Catherine's. It surprised him because inside he was seething. He wanted to rail at her, to force her to show some kind of emotion. To shatter the veneer of cool poise that surrounded her. Underlying the anger he felt were deeper emotions: confusion, pain. Betrayal. He forged ahead before Catherine could answer, tossing another question at her. "And what exactly do you think is between us?"

"I…I don't know."

Nathan grunted in disbelief, shaking his head as he turned away and walked out of the kitchen. He stopped and leaned one shoulder against the doorjamb, his gaze focused on the several prints carefully arranged on the dining room wall, copies of antique herbs framed in old gold-tone frames. Formal. Safe.

I don't know.

Catherine's answer echoed in his ears. A safe answer. Like everything else that surrounded her. He took a deep breath and slowly let it out, trying not to think about how fast she had given that answer. He refused to believe she really didn't know what was between them. He *couldn't* believe it. Not after everything that had passed between them in their time together. Not after yesterday morning.

He took another deep breath and turned back to face her, studying her for any reaction or sign of emotion. "So what is this all about, Catherine? Why the sudden change of heart?"

"There hasn't been any change of heart."

"Really? There wasn't anything wrong yesterday."

Catherine again folded her arms across her chest and studied him, making him feel like an intruder under that analytical gaze. "It doesn't matter."

"It doesn't? What's going on, Catherine?"

She pursed her lips, blew out a breath and suddenly waved her hand, dismissing his question. Or dismissing him. Maybe both. "A skateboard, Nathan?"

Nathan ran a hand through his hair, wondering why she seemed to be overreacting so much. "Okay, I'm sorry. The skateboard was a stupid idea. I didn't think. I'll take it—"

"He was trying to jump a ramp last night! His leg is bruised from where he jammed it against the prosthesis."

Nathan's stomach flip-flopped in fear. "Oh, God. Is he okay? Was he hurt?"

Catherine paused, studying him. He thought she was going to reach out for him, reassure him, but she pulled back at the last minute and looked away. When she turned back, her face was an expressionless mask, devoid of all emotion. "He's fine. But giving him the skateboard wasn't a very responsible thing to do, and it set a bad example."

"I said I was sorry. I wasn't thinking. I'll talk to him."

"It's not just the skateboard, Nathan. It's you."

"What?" Nathan ran a hand through his hair in frustration, trying to control the barrage of emotions simmering in his gut. Something was very, very wrong. He took another deep breath, trying to clear his head. "I don't understand."

"What kind of example are you setting for Matty by playing when you shouldn't be? Do you think it's healthy for him to see you risking yourself every time you go out on the ice? He looks up to you, Nathan, and he's going to end up following your example. I can't let him do that!"

Nathan stood still, stunned. "What are you talking about?"

"I'm talking about the fact you shouldn't be playing hockey anymore. Your knee can't handle it."

"Nobody said I should stop playing."

Catherine stared at him, outwardly calm when inside chills raced through her at the sudden change in him. His voice was deadly quiet, his face a stony mask that hid emotions she could only guess at. She dug her nails into the palms of her folded hands and fought to keep her voice even.

"Who are you lying to, Nathan? Me? Or yourself? I know what Brian told you yesterday." Not because Brian had told her, though. Because she had looked at the open files in the exam room. She hadn't meant to, was only straightening the room when she happened to see them. So she had looked, driven by a strong need to discover the truth. Because Nathan would never tell her.

He couldn't even admit it to himself. That much was obvious from the way his whole body stiffened. The dim light reflected the hardness in his eyes, mirrored by the coldness when he spoke. "Nobody said I should stop playing."

Catherine studied him for a second longer then

looked away, feeling lost and empty. She shook her head, her words almost a whisper when she finally spoke. "This is why it can't work, Nathan. You can't even admit to yourself that it's time to quit. I need to think about Matty. He shouldn't be looking up to someone who pushes himself to the point of irreparable injury."

"Excuse me? You're going to put this off on your son? Use him as an excuse?" He walked back to the kitchen table and fingered the bouquet of flowers, then gave a short laugh before facing her. "Now look who's talking about admitting the truth to themselves. That's the great Dr. Wilson for you. So noble and self-sacrificing. Maybe you should think about the example you're setting, always holding yourself back."

"How dare you!"

"No, Catherine, how dare *you.* I really thought we had something going. Christ, I was even starting to think of us as a family. Matty means the world to me, and for you to turn around and accuse me of setting a bad example..." Nathan's voice cracked and he cleared his throat. "What a crock."

A sudden piercing stabbed Catherine in the breastbone as Nathan's words hit her with the force of a physical blow. She sucked in a breath that stuck in her throat. Her mouth opened and closed but no sound came out. She imagined she could hear a rending tear coming from her chest when she noticed the naked emotion in Nathan's eyes. "What...what did you say?"

"I said it was a crock." Nathan stared at her, his eyes blazing with emotion. He continued fingering the flowers, then finally picked them up with one hand. It struck Catherine as an absent gesture, as if he wasn't even aware he was doing it. "You know, you're right. This won't work. I'm not perfect. Too bad that makes me a bad example in your eyes."

"Nathan—"

"Forget it." His words came out in a whisper. He looked down at the bouquet of flowers in his hands as if he just realized he was holding them. A distant look flashed in his eyes and he shook his head before holding them out to her, a final offering she refused to accept. Nathan carelessly tossed them back onto the table. "Have a nice safe life, Catherine. I hope you find the perfection you're looking for. Tell Matty I said goodbye."

The silence between them was charged with unspoken words, accusations and denials. Catherine swallowed back her tears and thought about denying his words, couldn't because she knew they held some truth. She thought about telling him how she really felt, what was really in her heart and how much that scared her.

The moment, and the chance, was lost when Nathan shook his head a final time and walked past her. His footsteps echoed in the unnatural quiet of the house, ringing with a finality that paralyzed Catherine with regret.

She heard the rattling of the doorknob, heard the whisper-soft creak of the front door opening. The noise broke her paralysis and catapulted her into action. Her feet moved of their own accord, dragging her out of the kitchen. Uncertainty gripped her when she realized she didn't know what she was going to say, didn't know *why* she was running after him.

She was running after him because she loved him. But then it was too late. A closed door greeted her just as she turned the corner of the empty hallway. Nathan was gone.

Catherine reached for the knob, imagined she could feel the heat of his touch still on the metal, like a living thing. Nothing was stopping her from turning the knob and throwing open the door. Nothing was stopping her from calling out to him, telling him that he was right, she had been holding back.

Because she was afraid.

Because she loved him.

The sound of an engine turning over drifted through the closed door, followed by the squeal of tires as his car pulled out of the driveway. Catherine sagged against the door, defeated. She had come so close to chasing after him. Stupid.

It was better this way. Better for a clean break before things got too out of hand. Before she really lost her heart. She wiped the wetness from her face and kept repeating the words to herself, over and over, hoping she'd eventually believe them.

Chapter Seventeen

"You look like hell."

Catherine looked up from the report she was trying to write, surprised to see Brian standing in her office. She hadn't even heard him come in. "Thanks, Bri. I knew I could count on you to make me feel better."

"Just doing my job." He shut the door behind him, walked toward her then lowered himself into one of the chairs and propped his feet on the edge of the desk. Catherine raised her eyebrows but said nothing, just moved a pile of papers before he could knock them to the floor. She turned her attention back to the report, determined to ignore him.

"Somebody sent me three tickets to tonight's game," Brian finally said as he studied his finger-nails. Catherine knew without asking that he was talking about the *Banners'* playoff game. She pretended to ignore Brian.

"I thought maybe you and Matty—"

"No."

"Catherine, Matty misses him—"

"I said *no.* No more, Brian. Just drop it."

Silence filled the room. Her vision swam and she realized she didn't even know what she was writing anymore. A sigh hitched in her chest and she finally tossed the pen down.

"How long are you going to make yourself miserable?"

"Who said I'm miserable?"

"Come off it, Catherine. Everyone can see you're miserable. You haven't been sleeping. You look like the walking dead."

"Thank you, Brian. Thank you very much. I don't need this from you, okay?" Catherine leaned back in the chair and ran her hands through her hair in frustration. "I'm fine. Matty's fine. Everyone is fine so please, just mind your own business."

Brian pinned her with a glare that was so unlike him she physically recoiled from it. "No, everyone is not fine. If you want to ignore how you've been lately, that's up to you, but Matty doesn't even look like the same kid anymore!" His features softened as he paused, thinking. "And Nathan is just as miserable as you are. Maybe more, if that's even possible."

Catherine blinked, hard and fast, then focused all her attention on the mess that had accumulated on her desk. She leaned forward in her chair and went through the piles, trying to organize everything, knowing it was hopeless since she couldn't really see what was in front of her.

An image of Nathan the last time she saw him came to mind against her will. She remembered the haunted look in his eyes, the brief glimpse of raw emotion that she nearly missed seeing before he ruthlessly hid it behind an impenetrable wall. She sucked in a deep breath and let it out slowly, trying to fill the emptiness that had been inside her. "Brian, it's over. Not that there was anything there to begin with. Just let it go."

"Catherine..."

She looked up at Brian and saw the sympathy on his face. She didn't want or need sympathy. All she wanted was time. Time to get over everything, time for things to return to normal. Was that too much to ask?

"Then what about tonight? At least let me take Matty."

"Brian—"

"It'll be good for him, Catherine. In spite of what you think, the way you and Nathan are acting is tearing that poor boy apart. Is that what you want?"

"You know it's not."

"Then let him go. Let him have one night out away from everything. It'll just be the two of us. He can even stay the night, let you have some time to yourself."

The last thing she needed was more time to herself but she suspected Brian already knew that. If she said yes, she would be caving in, contradicting every reason she had for not seeing Nathan again. If she said no, she would look spiteful, like she didn't care about Matty. It was a no-win situation.

Catherine suspected Brian knew that, too, and mentally cursed him for knowing her too well. She ran a hand through her hair again and let out a weary sigh. She didn't have a choice.

"Fine. Take him to the game. But that's it, Brian, just the game." She pushed away from the desk and stood, jamming her pen into her coat pocket as she leveled her sternest glare at Brian.

"Now what else would we do?"

"Brian, I mean it. The game, and straight home. No stops afterward." She held his gaze until he sighed and nodded.

It wasn't until she was finished with the last patient that she realized he had never actually agreed with her.

Nathan sat in the locker room after the game, an ice pack held to his broken nose. He had played well, scored twice, had even hoped that Catherine was watching the game from home. Now, as he shifted on the padded table and winced as pain shot through him from at least a hundred different places, he couldn't care less if she had seen the game or not.

"All right, lemme see." A hand appeared in Nathan's peripheral vision, moving forward until it grabbed the ice pack and took it away. Another hand tilted his head back until the face of the trainer came into view. "How many fingers?"

"Get lost, you moron. It's a broken nose, not a concussion." The words were nasal and tired, a direct reflection of how Nathan felt. All he wanted to do was go home and soak.

"Such appreciation. How's the cut?"

Nathan fingered the small slice below his eye and shrugged. It was a cut. A few stitches probably wouldn't hurt but there was no way anyone was getting near him with a needle. The butterfly bandage would do the job just as well. "Fine."

"How about the nose?" The trainer squeezed the bridge of Nathan's nose, causing him to wince. He batted away the offensive hand and put the ice pack back in place.

"It'll be fine as long as you leave it alone." And it would, Nathan knew from experience. They had one day off before flying to Pittsburgh to finish the series. One more win, and they'd move to the conference finals. Then the Cup.

There was no doubt in Nathan's mind that they'd go all the way. That *he* would go all the way. All it had taken for his game to pick back up was that first goal tonight. Once he scored that, they had been unstoppable.

He had been unstoppable.

The trainer finished his poking and prodding then made his rounds through the battered and bruised. Nathan limped into the shower for a steaming soak that did little to ease his aches. He was in the process of buttoning his shirt and getting ready to leave when Sonny came over to him.

"Good game, Conners. About time."

"Hmm." Nathan didn't bother replying, knowing that Sonny didn't expect—or want—an answer.

"You got visitors. I'll send them back."

Nathan's fingers fumbled on the last button and he drew his head up sharply but the coach was already gone. Damn. It had to be Brian and Matty; he had seen them in their seats earlier. But he wasn't sure if he was ready to deal with Matty one-on-one yet. What would he say to him? What had Catherine told him?

He didn't have time to wonder more than that before Matty's excited voice broke through the grunts and groans that floated through the locker room. Nathan forced a smile on his face and turned to greet Matty and Brian; the smile turned real at the laughter in Matty's voice when he ran up to him and stopped just short of giving Nathan a hug.

"Geez, Nathan, you look like somebody whupped you good!"

"Yeah? Then you must not have been watching very close." Nathan reached out and ruffled Matty's hair, surprised at how good it was to see him again, surprised at how much he had missed him. It wasn't a good sign. He drew his hand back and met Brian's eyes, trying to read the expression hidden behind the doctor's glasses. "Doc. Nice to see you again."

"Nathan." Brian nodded a short greeting then inclined his head to Nathan's leg. "Looks like things got a little rough out there tonight. How's that knee holding up?"

"Fine. Good." He shifted uncomfortably, unsure

about what to say. "So, um, how were the seats? Everything okay?"

"The seats were cool. The best ones yet," Matty answered. He tilted his head and fixed Nathan with a curious gaze. "Mom didn't want to come, though."

"Matthew!" Brian's harsh whisper echoed around them. Nathan guessed that Matty had been told not to bring up his mom but it was inevitable. Nathan waved Brian's correction away.

"No, it's okay." He turned to face Matty, trying not to squirm under the kid's clear gaze. "I didn't really think your mom would come, even though I hoped…well, I didn't think she'd be able to make it. She's probably busy and all."

"She's not busy, she just didn't want to come."

"Oh. Um, yeah, well, you know how it goes." Nathan took a deep breath, surprised at the pain that sliced through him with the brutally honest words. "So. Your mom knows you're here?"

"Yeah. But Uncle Brian had to really talk her into letting me come. And she didn't want us to come back here, either, but I made Uncle Bri bring me."

"Matty, I think we should probably leave now—"

"No. No, it's okay." Nathan straightened, tearing his gaze away from Matty's, away from the confusion in the boy's eyes. He shifted his attention to the gym bag on the bench beside him and absently shoved some things into it, needing a minute to sort through the jumbled thoughts whirling in his mind.

Catherine didn't want to come to the game because she didn't want to see him. Nathan supposed he really hadn't expected anything different. But she let Matty come, though she didn't want her son seeing him, either. Nathan had no idea what to make of that, if it was a good thing or a bad thing. Hell, he probably shouldn't read anything into it, especially if Brian had talked her into letting Matty attend. He should just cut his losses before anything else happened, move on. Get over it. Get a life. Something. Anything.

"How come you don't like my mom anymore?"

Nathan's head shot up at the soft question, so full of misery his breath caught in his chest. *Oh, damn.* This was exactly what he hadn't wanted. How the hell was he supposed to answer a question like that?

Nathan looked at Brian and saw the discomfort on the doctor's face. "Brian, could you give us a minute here?"

"Yeah, sure."

He watched the doctor walk away then sat on the bench and motioned for Matty to sit next to him, trying to find the right words as the two of them got comfortable. Nathan took a deep breath and let it out slowly, wondering exactly what Catherine had told Matty and what he should say.

"Um, why do you think I don't like your mom anymore?"

"Because you never come around and do things. Mom said you guys weren't friends anymore."

"Oh. Um, well, yeah. Maybe." Nathan cleared his throat and tried to figure out how to explain adult relationships to a nine-year-old boy. "Have you ever been friends with someone before then not been friends?"

Matty seemed to consider that for a minute then slowly nodded. Nathan breathed in a sigh of relief, thinking maybe this would be easier than he thought. "Well, it's kinda like that I guess. Your mom and I were friends, and now we're, um…not."

"Oh. How come?"

"How come?" Nathan repeated the question stupidly. So much for easy. "Well, I guess we just had different ideas…I mean, well, we just like different things. I guess."

Matty nodded, as if he understood exactly. He sat on the bench, bent over with his hands clasped loosely between his legs. Like Nathan. Seconds ticked around them and Nathan used the time to clear the lump forming in his throat.

"So just because you and Mom aren't friends anymore doesn't mean we can't be friends, does it? 'Cuz I still want to be friends." Matty's voice was thick with misery and he choked back tears. Simple words, spoken with a boy's innocent honesty. Pain ripped through Nathan's chest. He didn't think, just acted, reached out and put his arm around Matty's thin shoulders and pulled him closer, the lump in his throat growing bigger and choking him as Matty slumped against his shoulder.

"I still want to be friends, too, kiddo." Nathan had never spoken truer words but in some deep part of him, he knew he was setting them both up for a hard fall. A clean break would be easier for both of them. He couldn't bring himself to do it, couldn't bring himself to hurt Matty that way.

He had no idea what to do next, or what to say, but as Matty's arms came around him in an innocent hug and tears seeped through Nathan's shirt, he realized he didn't care. He would do anything for the boy in his arms, and if that meant finding a way to stay friends in spite of Catherine, then so be it.

The look of sympathy on Brian's face when he came in a few minutes later told Nathan that it was going to be one hell of a lot easier said than done.

"Stay away from my son!"

Nathan blinked at the tornado of fury that hurtled through the partially opened front door. He stared dumbly at the empty hallway then turned to face Catherine, who was now standing behind him. Her hands were fisted on her slim hips and her breathing was heavy with the indignant anger that flashed across her face. He slammed the door shut, his own temper simmering.

He was not in the mood for this. Maybe in five minutes, when the double dose of pain medication kicked in, he might be able to handle it, but not right now.

"Do you hear me? Stay away from Matty!"

"Yeah, I hear you. The whole damn building hears you. Anything else you want to scream while you're at it?" Nathan pushed by Catherine and went down the hallway to his bedroom. He needed to pack, to get his things together so he could collapse for a few hours' rest before leaving for Pittsburgh.

His knee was on fire, his nose throbbed and the cut

beneath his eye stung. Every single bruise acquired during the last game had been awakened during this afternoon's practice. He had been looking forward to the relative peace of his condo and now he wasn't going to get even that.

"I told you I didn't want you near him, but you had to see him anyway, didn't you? All day he's been slinking around the house, heartbroken and near tears because he thinks you're his friend!" Catherine's voice followed him into his room. Nathan turned and ran into her, she was so close behind him. He stepped around her and pulled clothes from his dresser drawer.

"Yeah, well, I'd like to think I am."

"No! You aren't. You can't be."

"Then you explain it to him. You tell him why we can't be friends." Nathan threw the pile of clothes into a duffel bag and faced Catherine for the first time. His heart lurched at the panic etched on her pale face and he bit back the sharp retort he wanted to hurl at her, taking a deep breath to calm the raging emotions that wanted to break free inside. "Listen, I know you have a real problem with me, *Doctor,* but I happen to like your son and I'm sure as hell not going to twist that poor kid's emotions into a knot because you have issues."

"How dare you! *I* have issues? *I'm* not the one who can't face reality! *I'm* not the one who's living in some dream world, afraid to accept the truth!"

"Really? Could have fooled me." Nathan winced when she flinched at the harshness of his words. Any other time, he would have left enough alone, would have stopped while he was ahead, but the medicine was finally doing its job. A synthetic calm poured over him, insulating him, numbing him. He was pleasantly detached from everything and reveled in the feel of it.

"What is that supposed to mean?"

Nathan stepped toward her, forcing her to step back. He ignored the panicked look on her face when her back hit the wall. He braced one hand on either side of her face and leaned closer, leaving mere inches between them.

"It means that you would rather shut yourself away from the world than grab the chance to live your life because you might get hurt." Nathan dipped his head closer, brushed his lips briefly against hers. "It means you're too afraid to accept my…an offer of love and I don't know how to change that. Wish to hell I could, but I can't."

He dropped his lips to hers once more, felt a warmth explode deep inside him and quickly pulled away. His head swam for a minute, though whether from his physical reaction to Catherine or to the medication, he didn't know. "And…it means I'm really buzzing on painkillers right now and not thinking straight and you should leave. You really need to leave before I say or do something that'll get me in deeper than I already am."

"Nathan…"

"Not now, Catherine. Just leave. Please." He stumbled to the bed and slowly sat on the edge before letting himself fall backward. He closed his eyes against the brief dizziness then opened them and stared at the ceiling. Muffled footsteps came closer, paused, then moved away. An eternity later he heard the front door open and close. He shut his eyes against the noise, wishing he could shut out the pain that had accompanied the soft, muted *click.*

Catherine leaned over the open dishwasher and shoved the last pot inside, briefly fighting with it until it cooperated and sat snugly in the bottom rack. She added detergent then slammed the door shut, giving the machine a dirty look.

She never used to have trouble with things. Up until six months ago, life had been fine. Maybe a little plain and boring, but quiet and sane. Safe. Then in walked Nathan Conners and everything changed.

Catherine grabbed the sponge from the kitchen sink and wiped the already clean countertop. Who was she kidding? Life before meeting Nathan had been miserable. There had been Matty's diagnosis and treatment, the fear he couldn't be healed, the fear he would get sick again and she would lose him. She had gone for "safe" because she was too afraid of anything else.

Well, that pattern had definitely changed these last few months. Matty was better, he was using his prosthesis like he had been born with it. He was playing sports, for crying out loud. He laughed and joked and smiled. Except for the past week. This past week he had been miserable. And it was her fault.

She tossed the sponge in the sink then walked over to the kitchen doorway. Matty was curled up on the sofa watching television, the volume so low Catherine couldn't hear it. She didn't need to hear it to know the hockey game was on.

Matty jumped guiltily and switched the channel when she walked into the living room. The studied look of feigned innocence on his young face added to her own guilt and misery. She swallowed both emotions and sat down next to him, shifting so he could prop his good leg in her lap.

"The Discovery Channel, hmm?"

"Uh, yeah."

"So…what's the score?"

"Three to two." Matty blurted out the answer. His mouth dropped into a wide *O* that he quickly tried to hide then he started coughing. Catherine held her breath. The coughing stopped and he wiped the tears from his eyes before looking at her again. "I mean, um, what score? To what?"

"Nice try, kiddo." Catherine studied him closely for a minute, trying to decide if he was flushed from coughing or if he was getting sick. She wanted to reach out and feel his forehead but hit the recall button on the remote instead.

The hockey game blared to life on the screen in front of them. She nudged the volume button and soon stereo sound accompanied the action on the ice. The camera panned in on the players' bench and suddenly Nathan was in the living room with them, his face looking worse than it had a week ago when Catherine barged into his house. She tried not to wince at the image, tried not to think of the bottle of

Percocet she had seen on his hallway table on her way out.

"He's playing pretty good." Matty whispered the words hesitantly, as if he was afraid to say anything about Nathan. Could she really blame him after the way she had acted?

"He looks awful."

"Well duh, Mom. He's a hockey player."

"Oh." As if that explained everything. Then again, maybe to Matty, it did. Catherine sighed and nudged the volume back a few notches so they could talk. "You know, Nathan and Alec and all of those guys really push themselves when they play. I mean, even past the point where it's safe."

"Mooooommm!"

"Matty, I'm trying to explain something to you." Catherine bit back a reprimand when he rolled his eyes at her, trying to decide the best way to explain. She took a deep breath and plunged in. "You can see how beat-up they are. And how tired. They're pushing themselves now, but tomorrow will be worse for them. Just because they're doing it doesn't make it right."

"Mom, I know that."

"You do?"

"Yes, Mom. I'm not stupid, you know. I'm not going to do something that'll hurt me." He rolled his eyes again and turned back to the television set. "Besides, Nathan already explained the same thing to me, only he did it better than you."

"He did?"

"Uh-huh. And so did Uncle Brian and Alec. Everyone's afraid I'm gonna do something stupid and hurt myself, the way Nathan keeps doing to his knee when he plays."

"I see." Catherine leaned back against the sofa and studied Matty. Watching him was a lot easier than wondering if she had just heaped one more mistake on top of a hundred others this week when it came to dealing with Nathan. "And when did everyone give you all this advice?"

"Mom..." Matty broke off and coughed again, this one rattling his thin chest. Catherine immediately felt his forehead, frowning at the heat that greeted her palm, frowning even more when Matty pushed her hand away. "Stop babying me!"

The anger in Matty's voice was a slap across her face and she sat back, stunned and hurt. His dark brows were drawn together in a tight frown, his arms folded tightly across his chest as he studied the television with unwarranted intensity.

"I didn't realize I was babying you."

"You are. Stop it!" Matty yelled and pushed himself up from the sofa, his face flushed. "Stop treating me like a baby! I'm a kid like all the other boys I know, so stop treating me like a baby!" He stormed away from her, ignoring her calls.

Catherine watched as he disappeared down the hallway, his gait a little stiff because of the prosthesis, his back held straight. The door to his room slammed shut, echoing around her. She stared at the empty hallway, startled, not sure what to do.

Should she go after him and talk to him? Give him some time alone before talking to him? Just let him go? She didn't know what to do. Matty didn't have temper tantrums. Matty was well-behaved. Matty didn't throw fits. Usually.

So what had changed?

The only change was her refusal to let him see Nathan because she had been afraid he was setting a bad example. Only Matty already knew that—because Nathan had told him.

Catherine looked back at the empty hallway, grimacing against the pain in the pit of her stomach, a bitter pain that came with the realization she had made one error after another. Just one more mistake in a long list of many.

She needed to fix this mistake. Maybe then, everything else would return to normal. If she fixed just this one thing, maybe she could have her old life back.

Her nice, quiet, *safe* life.

Chapter Eighteen

Nathan took a deep breath and started counting, actually made it to three when he realized the trick wasn't working and cursed. He glanced in the rearview mirror then quickly checked the intersection for oncoming traffic before blowing the red light, ignoring the sound of blaring horns as he sped by the waiting traffic. It was a stupid move but he didn't care.

The ride to the hospital was taking too long. He didn't have the time to wait for traffic; his nerves were in no condition to wait. Not when he was less than a mile away.

His heart thudded painfully and he swallowed against the strange sensation, rubbing his chest as if that would actually ease the pain. It had only gotten worse since the trainer had given him the note after the start of the third period.

Matty at hospital. Emergency.

No time noted, no details. Just those four cold words.

Nathan didn't know who had called to leave the message, or how the trainer had been persuaded to deliver it during the game.

Drenched in a cold sweat that had nothing to do with physical exertion, he showed the note to Sonny and told the coach he was leaving. Even though his voice left no room for argument, he had been surprised that LeBlanc had let him go without even a minor disagreement. Probably because the *Banners* had been up by two goals and Nathan hadn't been playing very well, anyway.

He wheeled into the emergency room driveway with a squeal of tires and pulled into the first open spot he saw, not caring that it had a reserved sign posted in front. Let them tow the damn thing away. That was the least of his worries right now.

Absently pocketing his keys, his long strides quickly ate up the short distance to the entrance. He nearly collided with the automatic sliding doors in his hurry to rush in.

If he was this frantic, how bad was Catherine?

Images rushed through his mind and he pushed them away. He didn't want to think about what dark thoughts must be going through her mind, not when he didn't even know what was wrong.

He paused in the busy waiting room, surprised at

how crowded it was. And how quiet. A few people glanced in his direction but for the most part they ignored him, too wrapped up in their own worries to be concerned about a newcomer. Nathan swallowed his discomfort and walked over to a large, circular desk beneath a sign that read Information. The older woman looked up at him with a blank expression. "May I help you?"

"I'm looking for Matthew Wilson."

The woman glanced at him then busied her fingers on the keyboard in front of her. A frown marred her wrinkled features as she hit a few more buttons then looked back at him. "Your relationship to the patient, sir?"

"Uh, friend. I'm a family friend."

"I'm sorry, sir, but the patient is listed in PICU. Only immediate family is allowed."

"PICU?"

"Pediatric intensive care unit."

The bottom of Nathan's stomach dropped open and let in an icy blast of cold fear. He took a deep breath that lodged in his throat, choking him. Nathan had assumed that there had been some kind of accident, that Matty would be in the E.R. getting patched up. He thought the anxiety that gripped him when he had been handed the note would lessen when he reached the hospital.

His hands tightened on the edge of the counter, the sharp corners digging into the flesh of his palms as his anxiety and fear intensified until it nearly doubled him over with pain. What the hell had happened to Matty? What was wrong with him?

Nathan ran a shaking hand through his hair and shifted on his feet, searching the E.R. waiting room as if an answer could be found somewhere. Still, at a loss, he turned back to the woman.

"Um, I got a message to meet the family here. Is there a way to go up to see them? Talk to them?"

"I'm sorry, sir, no. Only immediate family—"

"I *am* family! Matty's mother and I are engaged!" The outburst caught the attention of a few people close by, who stopped to stare at him. Nathan wasn't sure what had prompted the lie and didn't really care if it got him up to see Matty. But the woman appeared unaffected because she continued to stare at him with passive indifference.

He took a deep breath and leaned over the information desk, hoping to intimidate her with his size, wishing he had showered and changed into better clothes instead of throwing on frayed jeans and a T-shirt. Not that he would have taken the time, and not that the intimidation was working in either case. "Listen, just call up for Dr. Porter. He knows who I am."

"Sir, I'm sorry but—"

Nathan slammed the flat of his hand against the desk. "Will you just call, for crying out loud?"

"Is there something I can help with here?" The subdued voice came from behind Nathan, startling him. He turned to face a man in his late twenties, wearing blue scrubs and a lab coat. The man looked first at the woman behind the desk then at Nathan and there was a flash of recognition in the dark eyes.

"I'm trying to see my fiancée's son and she's saying I'm not allowed to go up, that only immediate family is allowed."

"Hmm." The man walked around the desk and glanced at the screen. "Matthew Wilson? Catherine's son? He's here?"

"Yes."

The younger man studied Nathan a little more, his brows drawing closely together. "You're Nathan Conners, aren't you? I thought I recognized you." The man grabbed a file from the desktop then looked back at Nathan. "You probably don't remember me. Steve Murray. I was working a few months ago when Matty broke his arm."

"Um, yeah, okay." Nathan couldn't recall one way or the other and didn't really care. "Listen, about Matty..."

"I'll walk you up." Steve scribbled a notation on some papers, closed the file and tossed it back on the desk, then motioned for Nathan to follow him. "So, Catherine's your fiancée, hmm?"

"Uh, I..." Nathan jammed his hands into his pants pockets and shrugged. "Um, I wasn't sure how else to—"

"Don't worry about it. I won't let on."

Nathan followed him to a set of elevators, thankful for the man's silence during the ride to the fifth floor. His breath hitched and the knot in his stomach grew when the doors finally opened onto a small, informal waiting room decorated in bright colors. Two corridors stretched out on either side, closed off from the waiting room by oversize wooden doors. Notices were posted on both doors, reminding visitors that a security pass was needed for entrance.

He stepped off the elevator then hesitated, not sure where to go or what to do. Steve tapped him on the shoulder and pointed to the waiting area. "Why don't you wait over there, and I'll go back and see what I can do." Nathan nodded then chose an overstuffed seat, shifting uncomfortably while he waited.

Brian walked out minutes later, a frown marring his face. Nathan rose, folded his hands in front of him, then quickly unfolded them and jammed them in his pockets. He took a deep breath and let it out in a rush when Brian approached him.

"How's Matty?"

"He should be fine."

"Should? What's wrong with him?"

Brian shifted his weight from one foot to the other and studied Nathan through his glasses, the frown creasing his smooth face. "Matty has very bad pneumonia. His immune system is still weakened, so it could get worse."

"But I mean, it's just pneumonia, right? That doesn't kill anyone." Nathan's voice cracked. The fear he had tried so hard to push away rushed forward and swamped him, uncovering emotions and feelings he hadn't wanted to acknowledge, had tried to ignore. He raked a hand through his hair, not surprised to see how badly it was shaking.

"He should be fine. We'll know more later. Nathan, are you okay? Do you need to sit down?"

"Huh? Uh, no, I'm fine. What about Catherine? How is she?"

"Catherine is putting on a brave face, as usual. Did you want to go back and see them?"

"Can I? They told me downstairs that only family..."

"Sure, come on." Brian led the way, opening the door by swiping a card into a special reader. Nathan followed, his attention on the floor until the door closed behind him. There was a change in the atmosphere and he looked up suddenly, his footsteps faltering before he stopped.

The corridor was painted in bright colors broken by cheerful paper decorated with different cartoon characters. The scheme was at direct odds with the hulking medical equipment that lined the hallway, and with the somber faces of visitors and staff. Nathan peered into one of the rooms and immediately wished he hadn't. A small child was on the bed, tubes and machines hooked up to different body parts. Mechanical bleeps drifted into the hallway, sounding like a clock ticking away life's minutes.

Brian tugged on Nathan's arm, pulling him farther down the hallway. "Matty's room is down here."

They passed a few more doors, finally stopping at one that was partially closed. Nathan realized Brian was trying to gauge how he would react. Nathan took a deep breath and nodded, hoping he could handle whatever was behind the door.

He wasn't prepared and he reached out for the doorjamb to steady himself, staring at the small, still figure in the bed. He almost thought Brian had led him into the wrong room, had to look twice until the blurry image in front of him wavered then focused, turning into a shadow of the boy Nathan knew.

Nathan released his hold on the doorjamb and took a hesitant step into the room. Catherine stood next to the hospital bed, her arms wrapped tightly around her middle. She was so absorbed in staring at Matty that she didn't seem to notice anything else. He cleared his throat, suddenly feeling like an intruder and wondering if he should just leave.

"He looks so small and helpless. And I'm not even allowed to hold him." The strangled whisper came from Catherine, hoarse and full of a mother's desperation. Nathan hesitated again then stepped closer, narrowing the distance between them.

"Is there anything..." Nathan's voice cracked and he took a deep breath, not finishing the sentence.

Catherine sensed his hesitation, looked first at Matty then at Nathan and shrugged, a tired gesture that relayed her weariness and worry. "He's on medication. And the oxygen. If it gets too bad, he might need a ventilator. But right now, no. There's nothing to do but wait. Just wait."

She turned back to the bed and stood there, looking lonely and afraid. A woman so used to doing for herself and for everyone else, a woman used to not having anyone there for her. All of Nathan's uncertainty, all of his hesitation and doubts disappeared in less time than a heartbeat.

He stepped forward and wrapped his arms around

her from behind, gently pulling her into his embrace. Catherine stiffened at first then leaned against him, allowing him to hold her. She turned and buried her face in his chest, her small shoulders shaking. He squeezed his eyes shut and held her tightly, brushed his lips against her hair. He said nothing, knowing there was nothing he could do except hold her. And he had never felt so helpless, so inadequate, before in his life.

"Oh, God, Nathan, I don't know what to do."

"Shh, it's okay. I'm here. I'm here." He whispered the words in her ear, over and over as he gently rocked her. He led her to the upholstered armchair positioned near Matty's bed, lowered himself into it then pulled Catherine onto his lap. She was as limp as a rag doll when she settled against him and tucked her head against his shoulder. All he could do was hold her and rub his hand across her back in small circles.

Again Nathan wanted to say something, to do something, but he didn't know what. Frustration warred with his own fear and in the end he did the only thing he could do. He held Catherine.

And prayed.

For the woman in his arms, and for the little boy lying helplessly in front of him—the boy who had become a son to him.

Catherine winced at the sharp pain in her neck, fighting to stay in the safety of the darkness, knowing there was something waiting for her in the light, something she didn't want to face. The darkness slowly gave way to grayness and she shifted again, not yet ready to confront whatever waited for her.

"Matty!" Reality catapulted her into consciousness and she bolted upright, tearing herself from the shackles of sleep. Eyes wide, she frantically searched around her, fear forcing her heart to race. Matty's flu, the pneumonia, the hospital...

Her panicked gaze rested on the hospital bed in front of her, on the small figure tucked securely in the center. Matty's chest rose and fell with each breath. Each clear breath. She studied the rise and fall, counting, listening.

"He seems to be breathing a lot better," a quiet voice whispered. Catherine's head snapped to the right. Nathan leaned against the wall at the foot of the bed, his arms loosely crossed in front of him. His wrinkled T-shirt was only partially tucked into his faded jeans; his hair was tousled, as if he hadn't had the time or inclination to do more than run a hand through it. Stubble covered his chin and jaw.

Catherine remembered falling asleep in his lap, lulled by murmured words of comfort she couldn't recall. She didn't realize he had planned to stay with them all night, was only slightly surprised that he did. She cleared her throat and pushed herself up from the chair, fighting the stiffness that wanted to immobilize her.

"He seems to be. Has the doctor been here yet?"

Nathan shook his head and slowly straightened from the wall, his gaze remaining on Matty. "Just a nurse. Brian was here, then went to get some coffee.

The nurse said the doctor would be in soon." Nathan finally turned to face her, and Catherine was surprised to see the red rimming his eyes. "I thought you might need a little more sleep."

"Thank you. I can't believe I slept, though." Catherine looked back at Matty, at the steady rise and fall of his chest, and some of the fear left her. She took a deep breath and turned back to Nathan. "You don't look like you slept much."

Nathan shrugged, a gesture that seemed forced somehow, too casual. "I'll manage."

"But what about—" She was interrupted when the door opened behind her. Brian muttered a weary greeting as he walked into the room and placed a tray filled with large, steaming cups on a utility table against the wall. He passed the cups in silence; Catherine wrapped her hands around the warmth but made no move to sip from it, her attention riveted instead on the carefully schooled expression that masked Brian's face.

"Dr. Gardner is on his way in with some test results."

The fear that had eased only moments before flooded back. Catherine's hands shook and she forced herself to keep hold of the cup instead of letting it fall. The normal morning sounds of a hospital floor faded, replaced by a loud buzzing in her ears.

Don't overreact. Take it easy. He's fine. He'll be fine. Catherine repeated the words over and over until they became an echo, until she could hear them whispered in her ear. Then she realized they *were* being whispered in her ear.

Nathan was behind her, his hand a reassuring warmth on her shoulder. Catherine swayed and nearly leaned into him, seeking his reassurance, but stopped herself. She couldn't fall to pieces, not now, not when she needed to be strong. His hand dropped from her shoulder when Dr. Gardner entered the room.

An elderly man with a slight build and tufts of white hair, he was the best around. That knowledge did little to ease her anxiety as he closed the distance between them, his footsteps soft against the tiled floor. She studied his lined face, searching for a clue about what he had to say and finding none.

The noise in the room ceased as Dr. Gardner quietly studied their faces. His gaze finally rested on Catherine's, searching. She clamped her mouth shut and squared her shoulders, preparing to hear the worst. A hand folded around hers and she grasped it tightly, feeling strength flow into her from the touch.

Dr. Gardner raised one bushy brow in her direction as a smile split his lined face. "Now, Catherine, really. Do I look like the specter of death to you?" Her breath hitched and she nearly choked at his words. "Matty is fine. His lungs are clearing, and he should be ready to go home tomorrow."

"Oh, thank God," she murmured in a rush. Catherine swayed and would have fallen if not for Nathan behind her, supporting her. She closed her eyes and leaned into him. "Oh, thank God."

"I expect he may have had something to do with it," Dr. Gardner said with a slight chuckle. He stepped closer and squeezed her shoulder before returning to

Matty's chart. "We'll keep an eye on him for the next few hours, run a few more tests, but likely he'll be home tomorrow, nearly good as new."

"Will there be complications? The cancer..."

"Catherine, his cancer is gone and his immune system is stronger than ever. But to ease your mind, yes, we ran other tests. Except for the pneumonia, he's a strong, healthy boy. He's fine." He reached out and squeezed her shoulder again then stepped away, assessing her. His glance drifted to Nathan before he spoke again. "In the meantime, you need to rest. Go home and get some sleep. Come back later. Doctor's orders."

Catherine mumbled something as the doctor left. Quiet settled over the room, so different from the tense silence that had hovered over them earlier. Brian let out a deep breath and offered a wavering smile.

"I knew it would be good news." His hoarse voice betrayed him and Catherine gave him a look saying she didn't believe him, then stepped away from Nathan to hug Brian.

"Thank you, Brian, but I know better." Brian patted her back awkwardly before she turned to face Nathan. There were so many things she needed to say. She swallowed and offered him a nervous smile, taking a step toward him. The blank expression on his face stopped her; the look of fear in his eyes confused her.

"Nathan?"

"Hmm?" He shook his head as if pulling himself from a daze and stared at her with unfocused watery eyes. She watched several unnamed emotions flash through the amber depths before a forced grin appeared on his face. "I'm glad everything's okay." The pained grin quickly disappeared and he made a show of looking at his watch. "I, um, I need to get going. Tell Matty I'll catch up with him later."

Catherine stared after him as he walked out the door, not understanding his sudden departure. She may have called his name, but she wasn't sure. The only thing she knew for certain was that he was gone. She took a step forward then stopped, feeling a sense of déjà vu as she stared at the closed door. This had happened once before, not so long ago, when she had asked him to leave, when she had denied what was between them.

It had been a mistake then, she knew that now. A mistake on her part, born out of pride and fear. Pride, because she didn't want to admit she needed someone. Fear, because she didn't want to take the chance of being hurt or rejected.

Catherine turned and stared at Matty, sleeping peacefully, breathing easily. Her son, who had been hurt in so many ways but never let it stop him. Her son, who knew the consequences of taking chances but wasn't afraid to take them anyway.

A smile crossed her face as she stepped closer to the bed and smoothed back the hair on his forehead. Tears welled in her eyes as a small smile fluttered on his lips in his sleep, and she leaned forward to place a tender kiss on his cheek.

Catherine faced Brian, who was looking at her in bewilderment. "Will you stay with Matty in case he wakes up?"

"Where are you going?"

"I'm going to do something I should have done a long time ago. I'm going to take a chance."

Nathan yanked open the center storage console and dug through it, searching for his sunglasses. Papers, CDs and assorted junk spilled out, but no sunglasses. He balled a fist and slammed it on the steering wheel.

"Dammit!" He hit the steering wheel again then slumped back in the seat, drained. This had nothing to do with not being able to find his sunglasses and he knew it. He took a deep breath, hoping to calm his racing heart. It didn't work.

He was scared, beyond scared. Seeing Matty upstairs, helpless, the fear that had gripped him before the doctor had said everything was fine. A shudder went through him. At least Matty was going to be okay.

No parent should ever have to go through that kind of fear and pain. Especially alone. But Catherine wasn't alone. She had Brian to lean on, to support her if she needed it.

A tightness gripped him beneath the breastbone and he rubbed at it painfully, trying to ease it, chalking it up to heartburn from that awful coffee. The excuse rang false to his own mind, but the truth sounded so shallow.

He had wanted Catherine to lean on him, to take the support he had offered. He had wanted to share his own fear with her, tell her he understood and was there for her. There had been a minute when they were supporting each other and drawing from each other's strength.

That moment disappeared when she went to Brian. He hadn't heard what she said to him, was still too shaken with relief from the good news to pay attention to much else besides keeping his own emotions in check.

Nathan knew they were friends, that they had been together through so much; there was nothing wrong with friends comforting friends. But the reality that she would never need him, that there was no place in her life for him, disappointed him.

He rubbed at his chest again. Disappointed, hell. Admit it, he thought. You were hurt, still are. And now he was sounding like a jealous fool, for crying out loud. The only thing that mattered was Matty, and the fact that he was fine.

Nathan blinked his eyes against the gritty film that covered them. When that didn't work, he rubbed them with his thumbs, pushing in until white dots flashed across his closed lids. He must be more tired than he thought, if his eyes were watering and itching so much.

So what the hell was he doing, still sitting in the emergency room parking lot? He shook his head and jammed the keys in the ignition, hit the gas pedal too hard. He ran his hands across his face and through his hair then put the truck in Reverse. He needed to go home, get back to reality, to figure out what the hell he was going to do after the season ended.

A shadow to his left caught his attention a split second before he heard a loud rap on the driver's window. The noise startled him more than it should have, enough that if the truck had been a stick shift, it would have stalled. Instead, the truck eased back an inch before he slammed it into Park with a curse. He turned and saw Catherine staring at him through the window, a look of worry on her face. His heart raced even faster as he hit the button and lowered the window.

"What is it? Did something happen to Matty? Is he okay?" He couldn't control the frantic tone in his voice. Catherine's brows drew together then lifted in something that looked like astonishment. One corner of her mouth tilted upward and Nathan got the impression she found something amusing.

"Nothing's wrong with Matty."

"Then what is it? And what the hell is so funny? How can you even laugh after everything..." Nathan stopped midsentence, noticing his voice was too loud. Too close to revealing his own fears from the night before. Her mouth twitched again before she stepped away from the truck and studied it.

"I didn't know you had a Suburban."

"I just bought it." Again Catherine's mouth seemed inclined to lift into a smile before she carefully smoothed her face into a blank expression. Nathan wondered if maybe the stress had been too much for her. "Are you okay? Is there something you wanted?"

"You just bought it? Why?"

Because his car had been too small for more than two people, he thought. But he wasn't about to tell her that, not when it revealed so much. "Catherine, was there something you wanted? Because if there isn't, I need to leave."

"Um, yeah. I, uh…" Her voice drifted off as she stepped closer to the truck, resting her hands on the door and gripping the frame so tightly that her knuckles turned white. Her eyes darted left then right, looking around. Nathan swallowed again, sensing that something wasn't right, that something was about to happen. He turned away from Catherine and stared out the windshield, focusing on the glare reflecting off the hood of the car parked in front of him.

"Listen, thank you for being here last night. I didn't expect, I mean, I thought you might, but I wasn't sure…"

"I told you I cared for Matty. Did you think I was lying?"

"No. But thank you."

"Sure. No problem. Was that it? Because if it was, you could have waited to tell me."

"I know, but I wanted…" Catherine paused and took a deep breath, letting it out in a rush so heavy Nathan could feel its warmth against the bare skin of his arm. He shot a quick glance in her direction then just as quickly looked away. Her face was red and her teeth pulled at her lower lip, sending unwanted thoughts and memories through his mind. "This isn't easy…."

"So then maybe you'd better wait," Nathan suggested, thinking he should probably make himself scarce. Whatever she wanted to say couldn't be good for him if she was this nervous about it.

"No, I can't wait. I've waited too long already." She took another deep breath, then another, stepping away from the truck as she did. Nathan shot her a quick glance, wondering if she was hyperventilating or something. Her brown eyes were teary when they met his and he felt something like a punch under his breastbone again. He clamped his jaw shut, preparing for the final blow.

"I love you, Nathan. I just wanted you to know that."

The words echoed in the stillness around Nathan. He sat in the truck, feeling as if he had just been run over by a freight train, wondering if he had understood what she said.

I love you.

A full thirty seconds went by before he realized he hadn't been hearing things, a full thirty seconds for him to digest her words. The pressure in his chest escalated before the pain exploded, turning into something…warm. Catherine loved him. Now what?

Five seconds passed before he allowed himself to smile, and another five before he finally let himself admit he loved her back. Hell, who was he kidding? He had loved her months ago, he just hadn't been able to put a name on it. She loved him.

So where the hell did she go?

Nathan turned around in the seat just in time to see Catherine walk through the doors leading to the emergency room. He threw the door open, not caring when it slammed into the car next to him and left a dent, not caring that it didn't close all the way when he pushed against it, not caring that the keys were still in the ignition and the motor was still running.

He dashed across the parking lot, nearly colliding with a car that was pulling in. He ignored the blaring horn and kept going, twisting sideways to go through the sliding doors before they opened all the way. People were milling around the waiting room and Nathan had to stop, searching for Catherine. He caught a glimpse of her as she turned a corner and he raced after her.

"Catherine, wait!" He rounded another corner and saw Catherine swiping her badge through a reader. A sign on the door read *Authorized Personnel Only.* "Catherine!"

She finally heard him. Turning around, her damp eyes widened in surprise. Nathan quickened his pace, shortening the distance between them until he could reach out and gently place his hands on her shoulders.

"Catherine, did you say what I thought you said?"

"I, uh..."

"That's what I thought." He took a deep breath and pulled her closer. "I love you, too."

She looked up at him, her wide eyes shimmering with moisture. Her lower lip started to tremble. "Wh-what?"

"I love you." He lowered his head and briefly touched her lips. "I love you, Catherine. I want to be with you. And with Matty. I don't want to lose you."

"Nathan..." Her voice trailed off as a tear rolled down her cheek. He wiped it away and pressed his forehead against hers, smiling as she reached up and wiped his own cheek. "I love you. But I'm scared. I've never taken a chance like this before."

"I think that's what it's all about, taking the chances together. I love you, Catherine." He dropped a kiss on her forehead then pulled back, gripping her hands firmly in his own. "Are you up to taking a chance?"

Catherine stared up at him, her eyes shimmering. "I am if it's with you."

* * * * *

Set in darkness beyond the ordinary world.
Passionate tales of life and death.
With characters' lives ruled by laws the everyday world can't begin to imagine.

nocturne

It's time to discover the Raintree trilogy...

New York Times bestselling author
LINDA HOWARD
brings you the dramatic first book
RAINTREE: INFERNO.

The Ansara Wizards are rising and the Raintree clan must rejoin the battle against their foes, testing their powers, relationships and forcing upon them lives they never could have imagined before...

Turn the page for a sneak preview
of the captivating first book
in the Raintree trilogy,
RAINTREE: INFERNO by LINDA HOWARD.
On sale April 25.

Dante Raintree stood with his arms crossed as he watched the woman on the monitor. The image was in black and white to better show details; color distracted the brain. He focused on her hands, watching every move she made, but what struck him most was how uncommonly *still* she was. She didn't fidget or play with her chips, or look around at the other players. She peeked once at her down card, then didn't touch it again, signaling for another hit by tapping a fingernail on the table. Just because she didn't seem to be paying attention to the other players, though, didn't mean she was as unaware as she seemed.

"What's her name?" Dante asked.

"Lorna Clay," replied his chief of security, Al Rayburn.

"At first I thought she was counting, but she doesn't pay enough attention."

"She's paying attention, all right," Dante murmured. "You just don't see her doing it." A card counter had to remember every card played. Supposedly counting cards was impossible with the number of decks used by the casinos, but there were those rare individuals who could calculate the odds even with multiple decks.

"I thought that, too," said Al. "But look at this piece of tape coming up. Someone she knows comes up to her and speaks, she looks around and starts chatting, completely misses the play of the people to her left—and doesn't look around even when the deal comes back to her, just taps that finger. And damn if she didn't win. Again."

Dante watched the tape, rewound it, watched it again. Then he watched it a third time. There had to be something he was missing, because he couldn't pick out a single giveaway.

"If she's cheating," Al said with something like respect, "she's the best I've ever seen."

"What does your gut say?"

Al scratched the side of his jaw, considering. Finally, he said, "If she isn't cheating, she's the luckiest person walking. She wins. Week in, week out, she wins. Never a huge amount, but I ran the numbers and she's into us for about five grand a week. Hell, boss, on her way out of the casino she'll stop by a slot machine, feed a dollar in and walk away with at least fifty. It's never the same machine, either. I've had her watched, I've had her followed, I've even looked for the same faces in the casino every time she's in here, and I can't find a common denominator."

"Is she here now?"

"She came in about half an hour ago. She's playing blackjack, as usual."

"Bring her to my office," Dante said, making a swift decision. "Don't make a scene."

"Got it," said Al, turning on his heel and leaving the security center.

Dante left, too, going up to his office. His face was calm. Normally he would leave it to Al to deal with a cheater, but he was curious. How was she doing it? There were a lot of bad cheaters, a few good ones, and every so often one would come along who was the stuff of which legends were made: the cheater who didn't get caught, even when people were alert and the camera was on him—or, in this case, her.

It was possible to simply be lucky, as most people understood luck. Chance could turn a habitual loser into a big-time winner. Casinos, in fact, thrived on that hope. But luck itself wasn't habitual, and he knew that what passed for luck was often something else: cheating. And there was the other kind of luck, the kind he himself possessed, but it depended not on chance but on who and what he was. He knew it was an innate power and not Dame Fortune's erratic smile. Since power like his was rare, the odds made it likely the woman he'd been watching was merely a very clever cheat.

Her skill could provide her with a very good living,

he thought, doing some swift calculations in his head. Five grand a week equaled $260,000 a year, and that was just from his casino. She probably hit them all, careful to keep the numbers relatively low so she stayed under the radar.

He wondered how long she'd been taking him, how long she'd been winning a little here, a little there, before Al noticed.

The curtains were open on the wall-to-wall window in his office, giving the impression, when one first opened the door, of stepping out onto a covered balcony. The glazed window faced west, so he could catch the sunsets. The sun was low now, the sky painted in purple and gold. At his home in the mountains, most of the windows faced east, affording him views of the sunrise. Something in him needed both the greeting and the goodbye of the sun. He'd always been drawn to sunlight, maybe because fire was his element to call, to control.

He checked his internal time: four minutes until sundown. Without checking the sunrise tables every day, he knew exactly when the sun would slide behind the mountains. He didn't own an alarm clock. He didn't need one. He was so acutely attuned to the sun's position that he had only to check within himself to know the time. As for waking at a particular time, he was one of those people who could tell himself to wake at a certain time, and he did. That talent had nothing to do with being Raintree, so he didn't have to hide it; a lot of perfectly ordinary people had the same ability.

He had other talents and abilities, however, that did require careful shielding. The long days of summer instilled in him an almost sexual high, when he could feel contained power buzzing just beneath his skin. He had to be doubly careful not to cause candles to leap into flame just by his presence, or to start wildfires with a glance in the dry-as-tinder brush. He loved Reno; he didn't want to burn it down. He just felt so damn *alive* with all the sunshine pouring down that he wanted to let the energy pour through him instead of holding it inside.

This must be how his brother Gideon felt while pulling lightning, all that hot power searing through his muscles, his veins. They had this in common, the connection with raw power. All the members of the far-flung Raintree clan had some power, some heightened ability, but only members of the royal family could channel and control the earth's natural energies.

Dante wasn't just of the royal family, he was the Dranir, the leader of the entire clan. "Dranir" was synonymous with king, but the position he held wasn't ceremonial, it was one of sheer power. He was the oldest son of the previous Dranir, but he would have been passed over for the position if he hadn't also inherited the power to hold it.

Behind him came Al's distinctive knock on the door. The outer office was empty, Dante's secretary having gone home hours before. "Come in," he called, not turning from his view of the sunset.

The door opened, and Al said, "Mr. Raintree, this is Lorna Clay."

Dante turned and looked at the woman, all his senses on alert. The first thing he noticed was the vibrant color of her hair, a rich, dark red that encompassed a multitude of shades from copper to burgundy. The warm amber light danced along the iridescent strands, and he felt a hard tug of sheer lust in his gut. Looking at her hair was almost like looking at fire, and he had the same reaction.

The second thing he noticed was that she was spitting mad.